"*I*—I—" She stopped, and then confessed, "I don't know what I'm doing. Not when it comes to kissing someone like you."

"Like me?" His features softened. "Then let me guide you. Close your eyes."

She did as instructed.

"Now." His deep voice hummed through her body. "Part your lips and breathe deeply."

As she took the breath, his mouth covered hers, and it was magic. His hold around her tightened. She melted against him, breasts to chest, thighs to thighs, the juncture of her legs against the juncture of his. He didn't push. He kept himself still . . . and all was good.

Because she was safe, she realized. She didn't need to guard against Beckett.

No poet, no writer could have prepared Gwendolyn for what the kiss meant. If she hadn't been in love with him before, she would have tumbled into it now . . .

By Cathy Maxwell

A Touch of Steele

A Gambler's Daughters Novel

CATHY MAXWELL

AVON

An Imprint of HarperCollinsPublishers

A TOUCH OF STEELE. Copyright © 2025 by Catherine Maxwell, Inc. All rights reserved. Printed in the United States of America. No part of this book may be used or reproduced in any manner whatsoever without written permission except in the case of brief quotations embodied in critical articles and reviews. For information, address HarperCollins Publishers, 195 Broadway, New York, NY 10007.

First Avon Books mass market printing: May 2025

Print Edition ISBN: 978-0-06-324125-1
Digital Edition ISBN: 978-0-06-324130-5

Cover design by Amy Halperin
Cover illustration by Juliana Kolesova

Avon, Avon & logo, and Avon Books & logo are registered trademarks of HarperCollins Publishers in the United States of America and other countries.

HarperCollins is a registered trademark of HarperCollins Publishers in the United States of America and other countries.

FIRST EDITION

25 26 27 28 29 BVGM 10 9 8 7 6 5 4 3 2 1

For Amy Fisher, Morgan Perry, Beth Douglas Atwater, and all the other imaginative, fun-loving librarians who celebrate and promote the books we love to read ...

A Touch of
Steele

CHAPTER ONE

November 1816

London

He'd asked for the oldest whore in the house.

Beckett Steele knew this wasn't the most out-landish request ever made, not even in a single night of any bawdy house. However, he was not here for the usual reason men patronized London's many brothels.

"Y'aren't here to take off an edge?" The whore settled back against the head of the bed, her wrinkled skirts hiked up to her knees. Her iron-gray hair was a tangled mess. She combed it with her fingers as if suddenly self-conscious. Such was a whore's thinking. If he had walked into the room and plowed into her, she'd not have given her looks a thought. But those hadn't been his actions. He'd told her he hadn't sought her out for a poke.

The room—indeed, the whole house—smelled of tallow candles, unwashed bodies, whisky, and sex. When he finished with this evening, he'd bathe as he had every night for the last three months, trying to rid himself of the sour, heavy scent.

The whore's surprise that he wasn't going to drop his breeches shifted to a tired, shrewd knowing. "Wot are ye then? A watcher? A crier? A talker?"

Crier? That was a twist Beck hadn't heard before. In truth, the woman wasn't a bad-looking sort, considering her age, which was perhaps fifty? He hadn't met many as old as her, and that meant she might know the answers to his questions.

Instead of answering, he took out a stack of coins and set them on the bedside table next to the candle. The money was for her alone. Clients had to pay the whore mistress before they were even allowed to climb the stairs. She'd have to work weeks for what he'd just given her.

She eyed the money. "I don't do the odd nonsense. I don't let cocks do anything that is annoying. And I'll not let you hit me." She pulled a knife from under the bedclothes where she kept it hidden and let him see it before secreting it back in place.

"Quite wise," Beck answered politely. Respect was not something women in this profession received often. A bit of it could go further than money. "I have a few questions, that is all. I won't even come near you."

Her eyes lit up. A smile showing missing incisors spread across her face. "I 'eard about you. Askin' after some whores from what—years ago?"

"At least twenty-five."

"I weren't around that long."

"I asked for the oldest lady in the house," he said. "Perhaps you may have heard stories over your years in the trade?"

"Aye, I'm the oldest." The whore shrugged. "It's yer time and ye've paid for it." Her loose dressing gown dropped away to reveal one naked shoulder as she took the money and tucked it close to the knife. "Ask."

"There was a brothel in London where the walls and all the furnishings were dark green, like a forest. Does that sound familiar? The whore mistress liked being called Madam, and dark green was her favorite color. All her girls had to wear it, too. She said the color matched her eyes. The brothel was known as the Greenhouse. Have you heard of it?"

"Houses change names. And they are all called Madam now," the whore answered. "'Cept for those who call themselves *Madame*." She said the word with an exaggerated French pronunciation. "Their accents are fake, too. Showy bitches."

"She had a bruiser working for her called Dervil. Have you heard of him?"

She searched her brain a moment and then said, "Nah."

"What of the name the Marquess of Middlebury?"

She adjusted her position on the bed. "A marquess, eh? Fan-*ceee*." She drew out the word mockingly. "But I can tell ye, yer wasting your time. Even if we did know, why would we tell the likes of you?" She indicated with a long finger his polished boots, his black, well-cut coat.

He understood. The appearance of wealth carried great weight in such establishments when it came to passing through the door. However, it earned little trust, something only honesty could overcome. "Because I'm one of you. I lived in that brothel. I helped in the kitchen, emptied chamber pots, did whatever."

Her gaze narrowed as she studied him with this new information. "Whatever?" she echoed, a challenge.

Beck didn't take the bait. Some patrons liked young boys. Madam had protected him from their ilk. She'd said he was too young. He had known even back then he had been lucky. "I believe one of the women working there was my mother."

"So yer lookin' for yer ma?" She made a clicking sound against her teeth and shook her head. "Don't, not if she was one of us and didn't keep track of ya. Ye look like yer doin' well. Go on with life. That's wot she would tell you. It's wot I'd tell one of me own bairns if they ever came for me. They won't, though. Too much time has passed."

Beck wasn't here for advice, and there were two other brothels on the street he wanted to investigate before he turned in for the night. Although in truth, he was tired. This was grim work. He reached for the door handle, but she stopped him.

"Wot's 'er name? Yer mam?"

"I don't know."

"Then why are ye searchin' for 'er?"

Because of the dreams, he could say.

They had started after he'd been wounded at the Battle of the Nive. A head wound that had carried him close to death . . . until the dreams of a beautiful woman with his own dark hair, a woman *in danger*, had forced him back to life.

Even though all around her was blurry and unfocused in that way of dreams, her face was clear to him. He could see the woman laughing and hear her singing. He'd recognized her—*his* mother.

The sound of her music filled him with joy and a sense of peace . . . until the dream changed. Her song turned to screams. Screams that haunted him.

He couldn't see the threat, but he always felt her fear. He would startle awake with his heart pounding in his chest and an overwhelming sense that *he* had betrayed her.

The singing woman, his mother—a woman he'd never known—called out to him. He didn't know her name or if she was alive or dead, but he had to learn her story. Nor did the dream leave after he'd healed. He'd wake, sweating and shaken in his camp cot. He knew he'd shouted out in his sleep. He could see it in the faces of those who served beside him. It wasn't unusual for men at war to cry out from night terrors. It was unusual for *him* to show any sign of weakness.

Once Napoleon had been vanquished, Beck had resigned his commission and turned himself over to a new quest. The name Dervil and the color of evergreen were his only two certain memories of where he'd spent the beginning years of his life until he was roughly six years of age. That was when the Marquess of Middlebury's man, Olin Winstead, had appeared one day to take him away.

That was also the day that Madam had slipped and mentioned that Beck was Middlebury's bastard. Otherwise Beck wouldn't have known. For her error, Winstead had backhanded her and warned her to "shut her mouth."

The action had shocked Beck. No one had ever touched Madam or spoken to her so rudely in Beck's presence. Her power was omnipotent. Beck remembered that Dervil had surged forward to protect her but Madam had warned him back. That had seemed even stranger to young Beck. He'd witnessed Madam turning Dervil loose on other men for much smaller offenses.

Winstead had then grabbed Beck by the scruff of the neck and marched him out of the evergreen house. In the waiting coach, he'd told Beck that he was never to speak the marquess's name or ask questions. "Else I'll track you down and cut out your tongue."

Beck had believed the threat. He'd seen the man hit Madam. That meant he was more powerful than she was, and she had ruled Beck's life.

Winstead had also claimed that "Beck" was a humiliating name. Apparently Madam had shared that the ladies called him that name because he was at the beck and call of the house. "You should have a man's name," Winstead had said. He'd thought for a bit and then said, "Beckett. Beckett Steele. Yes, that is it," he'd said, "because you'll need to be as strong as steel to survive what life is going to throw at you."

He'd been right. Life had not been easy.

Winstead had delivered Beck to Faircote, a school for lads as miserable as he was but who had families. Even the bastards, of which there were several, had fathers who gave them their surnames. Beck had no one—until that moment in a field hospital when the singing woman began haunting him.

Now he was desperate to find her.

The whore's gaze narrowed. "Ye aren't goin' to tell me yer reasons, are ye?"

"Thank you for your time." He turned back to the door. Opened it.

"She's probably dead," the whore said.

He knew that.

"Most of us aren't good mothers," she added, another warning. "We can't be."

He walked out the door.

The brothel was busy. He could hear sounds of men having the "edge" taken off of them, as the whore had described it. There were cruder terms, but Beck liked hers.

He had to wait by the entrance as a group of giggling young drunkards charged into the house, stumbling over each other as they hurried in. At last he could step outside and was thankful for the chill in the damp night air and breathing room.

The hour was coming on midnight. Beck debated continuing to the other two brothels. He had to be up early in the morning. He'd fallen into an interesting line of work. There were people looking for their missing loved ones who could use the skills he had developed from his own search.

So far, he'd rescued a rector's daughter who had been kidnapped by a jilted swain, found a beloved elderly parent who, in a befuddled state, had wandered off, and tracked down a young ingrate who had disappeared from his university and his family to live a rake's life in Amsterdam. Tomorrow he was to call upon a wealthy merchant who wished him to discover the name of his much younger wife's lover.

The work wasn't necessarily savory, but it was proving lucrative. So much so that Beck found that instead of payment, he sometimes asked for favors. There was power in having wealthy, well-connected people in his debt. Considering his father, the Marquess of Middlebury, was one of the most important men in Society's hierarchy, he might need that power.

One more, he promised himself. The brothel was close, just down the street. Then he could turn in for the night.

Stifling a yawn, he set his wide-brimmed hat on his head, left the house's lighted step, and started down the dark street. The darkness didn't bother him. He'd become used to it. Besides, he could see the porch light of—what was it called? Mrs. Elderberry's. The name made him smile. It sounded benign for a bawdy house—

A beefy hand came out of a passageway between two buildings and yanked him into the shadows.

Beck lost his balance in the surprise attack.

Strong arms pulled him deeper into a passageway that smelled of rot and urine before throwing him against a brick wall. A heavy body that smelled of chipped wood, sweat, and sour ale slammed into him. The gravelly voice that Beck had never forgotten said, "What did I tell you about asking questions?"

Olin Winstead.

Suddenly Beck's mind reeled, and he was that small child riding in the close confines of a coach with the one man he feared above all others. The one who had threatened to cut out his tongue.

Except Beck was no longer a child. "I'm not making a claim against the marquess," Beck bit out. "I don't care about him. I'm searching for my mother—"

A fist punched him hard in his abdomen. His air left in a whoosh . . . but Beck had anticipated just such a move. He'd braced himself. The blow had hurt, but it hadn't done the damage that had been intended.

Or that could disable him from fighting back.

Winstead was beefy and strong, but he didn't have Beck's youth. Or agility.

Beck ducked as Winstead's fist came at his head for a lethal blow. Instead of hitting his intended target, Winstead smashed his hand into the brick wall. He screamed in rage and pain, grabbing his hand as if crippled. Beck moved quickly. He lowered his shoulder and plowed into the older man as hard as he could.

Winstead lost his balance. He fell back. Beck followed. The passageway's ground was still slick from the day's rain. Both of them fell into the mud.

There was a mad scramble to see who could regain his feet quickest. Winstead won and tried to bring his fists down hard on Beck's back, but he missed his mark. His aim was off enough that Beck was able to grapple him around the middle. Then, using all his strength, he lifted Winstead up and flipped him over his shoulder.

Winstead went down hard, and there was the sickening sound of bone snapping.

Beck whirled, ready for Winstead to attack again. Instead, the man lay where he had landed.

Long minutes passed. Beck did not let down his guard, and yet Winstead did not rise.

At that moment, the clouds covering what little there was of the moon shifted. Its wan light caught and was reflected in Winstead's glassy, unseeing eyes. His head was at an awkward angle. He was dead.

The moonlight also bounced off the long, thin blade of a knife in Winstead's hand. Only then did Beck realize he'd been struck. He put a hand up to his shoulder. His fingers came back wet, but the wound was not serious. He also had a tear in his coat. He was not happy. He liked this jacket.

And then he realized he couldn't let anyone find him with a dead man, especially a man in the employ of the Marquess of Middlebury.

Beck whirled and, keeping his head down, walked out of the passageway. The street was still not busy. He found his hat where it had fallen off his head when Winstead had grabbed him. He picked it up and, with unhurried movements, set it on his head.

He didn't bother visiting the other brothel. The Marquess of Middlebury had sent Winstead after Beck. He wanted to stop Beck. It didn't make sense. The two of them had never met. More than that, until Beck had started his search, he had never once said his father's name. He'd kept his part of the bargain.

His father had not kept his.

He'd also been actively spying on Beck. He'd known of his search—and he'd not wanted Beck to learn the identity of his mother. So much so, he'd sent Winstead on a murderous errand. Beck walked through London toward his quarters down by the docks. His mind was busy as he mulled over this turn of events and realized he'd been searching in the wrong direction. He might not know whom his mother was, but he did know his father. Middlebury was the link. Middlebury had all the knowledge. And Middlebury was willing to kill him.

Once the marquess realized his man was dead, he would attack harder. Beck reasoned he had two choices: he could live continuously on guard, or he could take the battle to the notoriously reclusive Middlebury.

It was said he rarely left his estate, Colemore. People thought it was because he was famously eccentric.

Beck now wondered if there was another reason for his infamous isolation. Why did he want to prevent Beck from searching for his mother? And, if he wished his illegitimate son dead, why hadn't he had Winstead kill him years ago instead of sending him to school? Or paying for his commission? The marquess could have even left Beck in the evergreen brothel instead of searching him out. The streets would have done what Winstead had just attempted and with no effort on the marquess's part.

Nothing made sense.

Except now, Beck was more determined than before to find answers.

CHAPTER TWO

Late August 1817

London

"Morley plans to make an offer," Dara Brogan exclaimed as she burst into the sitting room overlooking the back garden. She'd just returned from a luncheon with some of her new friends who were other wives of Members of Parliament. She hadn't even bothered to remove her hat. She sank down on the settee beside her older sister, Gwendolyn Lanscarr. "That is all anyone could talk about. They say he is besotted with you." Both Lanscarrs spoke with the slightest hint of Ireland to their voices, although their English and their manners were properly genteel—to a point.

Gwendolyn looked up from the book she had been enjoying until her sister's interruption and frowned.

Last spring, the Lanscarr sisters, Gwendolyn, Dara, and the youngest, Elise, had gambled everything for a Season in London. The venture had been Dara's idea. After their father had disappeared and was presumed dead, their cousin Richard had taken over Wiltham, the family estate in County Wicklow, Ireland. He'd not been keen to provide the girls with dowries. However, they were from a good, albeit impoverished, family. They also had looks, intelligence, and youth. Dara claimed they deserved dukes for husbands, and they could certainly snag them. She had been very convincing. After all, the Gunning sisters, who had also been poor Irish beauties, had succeeded fantastically in London during their Season decades ago. They had married some of the most important men of their day.

It was possible it could happen for Lanscarr sisters, or so Dara had argued.

Besides, what choice did they have, other than Gwendolyn sacrificing herself to a marriage with a local squire so they could have a roof over their heads? Richard had made it clear he would happily hand them over to the first men willing to pay to take them off his hands.

The most challenging aspect of their venture had been money. London Seasons were expensive. To understand what they needed, Dara had pored over the papers from London, searching for details and clues. The sisters did have some funds. They had carefully squirreled away a coin or two without Cousin Richard's knowledge. Dara had suggested that they take this small hoard of coins and gamble with it.

This idea was not far-fetched. Their father was a keen gambler. He'd not spent much time with his daughters, but when he was there, he taught them how to play cards. Of the three sisters, Gwendolyn had his talent. She could sense which cards would come up next. Therefore, she was the one, disguised as a widow with a heavy black veil, who had been sent into the Devil's Hand, a Dublin gaming hall. The goal was to win the three hundred odd pounds needed for a Season.

Gwendolyn had been successful, in large part because of a gentleman named Beckett Steele. He had helped her win the money when the unscrupulous faro dealer had tried to trick her.

Consequently, the sisters had come to London and conquered Society, just as Dara had hoped.

Dara had married first. Michael Brogan might not be a duke, but he was an important Member of Parliament representing Ireland. The couple was very much in love.

To everyone's surprise and delight, Elise married the duke. The wedding had only been two weeks ago, and now Elise and her Winderton were visiting Ireland. He'd wanted to see where his love had once lived.

That left Gwendolyn, who, as the unmarried sister, resided under Michael and Dara's roof, as one must.

"I'm not ready to marry, Dara," Gwendolyn said.

The corner of Dara's mouth tightened. "But you are five years *older* than I am."

Gwendolyn shrugged. "True. So?" She silently dared her sister to say something about the dangers of Gwendolyn being declared a spinster.

Dara was wiser than that. "Morley is very handsome and well-liked. You would be a viscountess."

Except the truth was, Viscount Morley had already asked Gwendolyn for her hand in marriage. He'd done it while the two of them were strolling in Hyde Park the week before.

He had not first spoken to Michael because he'd wisely surmised that Gwendolyn would not appreciate him doing so. He had been right. She would never understand why her male relatives were allowed by Society to make decisions for her. As Dara had pointed out, she was six and twenty. She could speak for herself.

And Morley had been grateful he hadn't approached Michael when Gwendolyn had—tactfully, she thought—refused his offer.

Of course, she hadn't shared this information with Dara because she didn't want the argument. Or to be reminded she was six and twenty. Gwendolyn might be the oldest, but Dara was the force in the family.

Gwendolyn and Elise had learned long ago to dodge topics that would churn up Dara's meddlesome ways. Refusing an offer from a viscount was one of those topics.

She rose, closing the book. "I'm to Hatchard's." Gwendolyn referred to the circulating library.

"Again? You were there earlier this week."

"I've finished my book."

"Just this moment?"

"Yes. I need another." *And to escape Dara and her matchmaking talk.* Reading was an excellent escape.

"Don't forget to take Molly with you," Dara said, as she *always* said. Molly was the maid. Being chaperoned everywhere was another trial for

Gwendolyn. She missed the days when she could walk Wiltham's green moors and hills without a maid's shadow.

Before Dara could offer more advice that Gwendolyn didn't need, she was out of the room and calling for Molly to come down with her bonnet and gloves. A few minutes later, Gwendolyn and the maid were out the door.

Hatchard's was not far, and Gwendolyn enjoyed a good stretch of the legs. She smiled, enjoying a little taste of freedom. The air carried the stirrings of summer's end and autumn's beginning.

She also knew that Dara would bring up Morley again. Eventually, Gwendolyn would have to confess she had refused him. Her sister would just shift her focus and begin the search for someone else for Gwendolyn to marry.

Gwendolyn would resist that suitor as well . . . because the truth was, she was already in love with someone—Beckett Steele.

She'd fallen for him the night he had helped her win the money she and her sisters had needed. He'd almost kissed her then. Gwendolyn had wanted him to. Looking back, she wished she had grabbed him by the ears and planted her lips on his mouth.

Instead, she'd been somewhat overwhelmed. It had been a wild night. However, before Mr. Steele's lips could meet hers, her sisters had interfered. One of them—Dara or Elise, she never learned which— had clubbed him over the head with a hefty piece of wood. He had dropped like a bag of sand, and they had been proud of themselves. They believed they had rescued Gwendolyn.

After the clubbing, there was nothing to do but run. Few men were happy being bashed over the head. Furthermore, Gwendolyn had also been concerned about what Mr. Steele *had* asked for in payment for his help—a favor. At the time, she'd believed it a rather inappropriate price. She had even attempted to return the money he had loaned her out of her winnings. He'd refused. He had insisted he preferred a favor.

However, since their arrival in London, Gwendolyn had crossed paths with Mr. Steele several times, and the more she saw him, the more she realized exactly how attracted she was to him.

He was more than handsome and worldly. He was a mystery. He wove in and out of Society at will, and his name was spoken in a hushed whisper by both upper and lower classes. She'd come to believe there wasn't anything he couldn't do.

She no longer minded owing him that favor. Someday he would ask her for it and expect her to comply. Gwendolyn couldn't wait.

And if he ever tried to kiss her again, he'd not escape her a second time.

But he'd better act soon. She couldn't put Dara off forever. Especially if Elise returned to London and joined forces with her. They might sway Gwendolyn. An unmarried woman's life was a boring one. Other than Hatchard's and shopping, there was little Gwendolyn could do with just a maid for an escort. The truth was, Gwendolyn wasn't eager to marry. Her heart longed for adventure and challenges like the characters in her favorite novels. She didn't want the life of a gentlewoman where the biggest thrill was marriage, followed by children, old age, and death. Her sisters might find this path suitable; Gwendolyn did not.

Most of all, along with adventure, Gwendolyn wanted Mr. Steele. It was that simple. No other man would do. She admired the way he determined his own destiny. She envied his freedom to do as he pleased. Gwendolyn was perfectly at peace being alone, but if she was to share her life, then she wanted someone *exciting*.

And if Dara knew what her oldest sister was thinking, she would lock Gwendolyn up in a trunk and ship her back to Ireland.

Therefore, if ever there was a woman needing a good book to hold the problems of life at bay, it was Gwendolyn. She prayed Hatchard's had that Maria Edgeworth novel that had been sent to a subscriber in the country several months ago. She had been impatiently waiting for its return. She couldn't understand why they hadn't just purchased another copy for their patrons. If the Edgeworth wasn't there, she might seek out something on mythology. She adored the stories of the gods.

She left Molly outside on a bench by the front door. Gwendolyn delighted in the feel of paper and the smell of glue and bindings and could spend hours asking the clerks to take books down for her to consider. She did not want Molly's sighs of boredom to interfere with her pleasure.

"Hello, Mr. Peters," she sang out as she entered the shop. There were several clerks busy with customers and fussing with books behind the counters. However, Mr. Peters always rushed to see to her needs, and she liked the extra attention.

"Miss Lanscarr, what a pleasure." Mr. Peters was around her age. He had prominent ears that turned bright pink whenever she addressed him. Sometimes, to his great embarrassment, his voice would crack. "I was just thinking of sending you a note."

"Really? Why?"

"We have a book here with your name on it." He pointed to a ledger where a record of requests was kept.

"Has the Edgeworth finally come in?" She moved expectantly to the counter. "I seem to have been waiting for it forever."

"It is a popular novel and, unfortunately, it has *not* been returned yet. Never fear, I'm watching for it for you. However, here is the other one you requested." He turned and took a slim volume off a shelf.

"I've made no other requests," Gwendolyn said, confused.

"It has your name on it. Of course, if there is a mistake, I can put it back—"

"No, no, let me see it," Gwendolyn said, holding out her hand. "Perhaps I asked for something and forgot. That is possible."

He smiled as if he didn't believe she could ever make a mistake, and as he did so, he noticed the title of the book. "*Oh*—" He paused. "I—I just noticed the name of this book. Someone else set it aside for you. I don't believe this is proper reading for a gently reared woman."

Proper reading? A chill of outrage went down her spine. No one supervised her reading, especially not the milk-and-water Mr. Peters. "Whatever do you mean?" she asked, too sweetly.

He turned the book around for her to read the title. "It's Dante's *Inferno*."

"Is it in the original Italian?" she queried haughtily.

Mr. Peters appeared confused. He shook his head. "It is the Boyd."

"I have not read that one."

"Have you read the Italian?"

Gwendolyn could not read Italian. "Of course." She waved her flat hand impatiently, showing she expected the book.

His brow furrowed in concern as if she had fallen a notch in his estimation. She could live with that.

He handed the book over and then, his own back stiff, he busied himself behind the counter.

Gwendolyn didn't give a care. There were other clerks who could check the book out for her. Instead, she moved toward the center of the room. She knew she hadn't requested it.

She opened the book. A calling card had been placed between its pages. It fluttered to the floor. She quickly picked it up. On one side was the engraved word *Steele*.

On the other was a handwritten message addressed to no one.

You will receive an invitation. Accept it.

Gwendolyn slammed the book shut, the card safely in its pages.

Several of the other patrons gave a start as if the sound had startled them. She smiled, pretended all was normal, and yet her heart was racing.

He was ready to claim the favor she owed him. She was certain of it.

Gwendolyn checked out the book and left the circulating library, the bell on the door jangling merrily with her departure.

Her maid, Molly, was slumped over as if having a little nap. Gwendolyn tapped her shoulder. Molly jumped and looked up wildly. "You are done, Miss Gwendolyn? That didn't take long. You are usually in there much longer."

"Come along, Molly, hurry. We must be home as soon as possible." She set off down the street.

"Is there something the matter, Miss Gwendolyn?" the maid said in confusion and then skipped a step or two to catch up. "Is there a reason to hurry?"

"Yes," Gwendolyn assured her without bothering to turn around or slow her step. *The very best sort of reason*, she told herself. She was going to see Mr. Steele again.

And soon.

That thought alone was enough to put Mercury's wings to her feet.

JEM WAGNER MADE a low whistle of appreciation. "She's a lovely one," he said, turning to look up at Beck, who leaned against the building behind him.

They stood at the corner of Sackville Street, where they could watch Hatchard's front door. Beck grunted a response to Wagner's comment. He wasn't so much interested in Gwendolyn's looks as her reaction to his message. She held the book, and there was a haste in her step. Good.

He wondered what she thought of his choice of book. He'd been surprised to learn of Gwendolyn's eclectic taste in reading. She enjoyed all of the usual fare gentlewomen favored, but also philosophy, religious treatises, histories, and, what seemed to be her favorite, travelers' journals. It was as if she dreamed of faraway places.

When Beck didn't answer immediately, Wagner said with the easy familiarity of comrades who had fought together, "Ah, come now, Major. Don't tell me you haven't noticed her looks. I won't believe you if you do."

Beck didn't reply. Instead, he turned and began walking down the street. His plan was now in motion.

"You don't feel something? Lovely lass like that one? Not even a tingle in the dingle?" Wagner fell into step behind him. He was shorter than Beck's six feet and three inches and a bit bandy-legged. His eyes perpetually squinted whether it was the dark of night or the light of day. He also had a hooked nose that could smell a Frenchman or trouble. In short, he was a good man to have by one's side.

"Dingle?" Beck sneered at the word.

"Dangle?" Wagner suggested helpfully. "Call

it whatever you wish, but you can't tell me you aren't interested. You were watching her more intently than you ever watched Soult's calvary approach."

"I'm beginning to regret asking for your help," Beck muttered, side-stepping a sweating clerk carrying a heavy wooden box, who wasn't paying attention to where he was going.

Wagner had left the military when Beck had, after Waterloo. He'd claimed he wished to enjoy the remaining years of his life with his wife, Lucy, and their four children on a yeoman's share in Sussex. However, when Beck had reached out to him for help with his plan, Wagner had not hesitated to join him.

That didn't mean he wasn't going to annoy Beck in that way good friends could.

"I don't know why you aren't interested in her looks," Wagner continued conversationally. "If I didn't have Lucy, I'd be right on that."

Beck didn't respond but concentrated on crossing the street's heavy traffic.

"Do you know what your problem is?" Wagner asked.

"I suppose you will tell me," Beck grumbled.

"I will. It is that general's daughter. What was her name?" Wagner pretended to search his memory. "It is the name of a flower."

Violet Danvers, Beck thought just as Wagner said happily, "I have it—Pansy. Wasn't that it? General Danvers's daughter? *Pan*-seee." He chuckled over his own pronunciation. "That part I'll never forget."

Beck did not correct him. It would just encourage him.

"You are the bravest officer I ever served under, sir, but you are afraid of women."

Beck flipped around so fast, Wagner almost walked into him. Ignoring the pedestrians who had to flow around them, he said, "I am *not* afraid of women."

Wagner widened his squinty eyes and feigned surprise. "Then what is it, sir? I mean, they practically crawl into your bed, and still you run."

"I'm not going to listen to this." Beck began walking again.

Wagner was at his heels. "Just having my say."

"You've said enough."

"Not nearly."

Beck didn't answer. Wagner always had to have the last word, and an exchange like this could go on for hours. However, there was one way to change the subject with Wagner. "Fancy a pint?"

"Always."

They ducked into a corner tavern. The place was busy with the hum of male voices dominating the air. They wove their way through the crowd and found a table in the corner by a window. Leaving Wagner at the table, Beck went up to call for two ales. He carried back the tankards and set one down in front of the sergeant.

"When do you start working?" he asked Wagner.

"I travel to Colemore tomorrow. I was hired on as a stable hand." Colemore was the Marquess of Middlebury's country estate.

Beck had decided that since Middlebury did not come to London, he would have to take himself to the reclusive lord . . . however, in consideration of Winstead's murderous attack, he wasn't about to announce his presence. No, he had spent months preparing a ruse that had come together because of both luck and determination. Gwendolyn Lanscarr was part of his good luck. In fact, without her, or a crusty old lady named Lady Ellen Orpington, he wouldn't be able to execute it.

However, he was no fool. In case all went wrong, he wanted Wagner close at hand. For that reason, he'd asked his friend to find work at Colemore.

"I hear the horses are some of the finest in England," Wagner said.

"When one has that much money, one has the best of everything."

"What is this gambit about?" Wagner asked.

"Meeting the Marquess of Middlebury," Beck said.

"What of the woman at the bookshop?"

"She is the means to an end. The marquess and marchioness host a house party where whist is a serious game. I was hired by Lady Orpington, one of their usual guests, to find a whist player of uncommon talent to be her partner. That player is Miss Lanscarr."

"Oh," Jem said, and pulled on his nose. "She doesn't look like a card sharp."

"She is. An excellent one. And if Lady Orpington approves of her, she will include me as a member of her party when she goes to Colemore."

Wagner raised his brows. "I don't see how all of this will play out, Major, but I'm with you. As to the lady, I don't think you are as blind to her as you'd have me believe. Otherwise I wouldn't have teased you." With that he toasted the air with his drink and drained the tankard dry.

Beck didn't touch his drink. Bringing Gwendolyn into this plan had been a necessity, but Wagner was right—she did threaten Beck's peace of mind. Gwendolyn Lanscarr was forbidden fruit. She made him yearn for what a man like him could not have, just as Violet had once done.

Gwendolyn had been reared for the life of a gentlewoman. Titled and moneyed men lined up outside her door to woo her. Men more suitable to her than Beck. He knew because he'd been watching. He couldn't help himself.

So, Wagner was right. Beck was not blind. If he could have found another woman with Gwendolyn's intelligence, grace, and skill, he would have stayed away from her. She was the line he'd dared not cross.

And he would not let himself forget that fact . . .

CHAPTER THREE

$\mathcal{G}$wendolyn strode through the door of the house almost before their butler, Herald, could open it. He was a tall, stately man with a head of white hair. He had accompanied them from Wiltham.

"Thank you, Herald," she said politely before launching into, "Has anyone sent an invitation to me?" The question came out in a rush of words.

"I—ah, um, no, Miss Gwendolyn," he managed to stammer out in surprise. She wasn't usually this forward. Dara was the inquisitor of the family. "There have not been any cards received."

She huffed her frustration and then instructed, "Expect one."

"Expect what?" Dara asked, catching a bit of the conversation. She came from the direction of the back sitting room. She held a sock she was darning in one hand. "I'm surprised you are home so quickly. Usually you are hours at Hatchard's. Has something happened? And look at you, Molly. Why are you so red in the face?"

The maid had come in several steps behind Gwendolyn. She held her hand to her side as if she suffered a stitch. "Miss Gwendolyn ran me home, Mrs. Brogan."

"I did not," Gwendolyn shot back at the maid as she handed her bonnet to Herald. She still held the slim book in her hand and set it on a table beside the door to remove her gloves. "I just set a quick pace."

"Miss Gwendolyn, your legs are much longer than mine," Molly didn't hesitate to complain.

"And mine," Dara noted dryly.

Gwendolyn frowned and pulled off her second glove before putting it into the bonnet Herald held. Then, taking both items from him, she handed them to Molly. "Please, carry these upstairs?"

Molly puffed air out of her cheeks in annoyance before mumbling, "Yes, miss." She marched toward the stairs, her back as stiff as a governess's.

"Excuse me," Herald murmured and went down the hall to see to some other task. He filled several roles in the household.

"What is this about an invitation?" Dara said.

"You hear everything," Gwendolyn accused her, but without heat. She picked up the book and walked into the front sitting room. It was more formal than the other rooms in the house. *And*, there was a window that overlooked the street. She sat on the settee, positioning herself so she could watch the traffic and be the first to notice the arrival of a messenger. She flipped open the book so she could pretend to read. She wasn't about to share Mr. Steele's message with her sister—

"What is this?" Dara asked. She bent to pick up something on the floor. *Mr. Steele's card.* It must have fallen from the book.

Gwendolyn set the book aside on the settee and came to her feet. "That is *mine*." She started for her sister, but Dara was already frowning at the handwritten message. She turned over the card.

Just as Gwendolyn reached her, Dara whispered, "Steele?" Her blue eyes met her older sister's brown ones. "*He* was at Hatchard's? He gave *this* to you?"

"No." That was actually true. Mr. Peters had given it to her.

"Then how did you come by this?" Dara waved the card. "An invitation to what?"

"I don't know." Gwendolyn decided not to dissemble. She held her hand out for the card. "I'm waiting to find out. Please, hand that to me."

But Dara did not obey.

Instead, she walked right by Gwendolyn and into the sitting room. "This is not good, Gwendolyn. Not good at all."

"I see nothing wrong with it. He is just advising me to expect an invitation. "

"For something he has *obviously* orchestrated. And any invitation he could send you would *not* be to your benefit."

"I disagree. He has been a good friend to us. Dara, he is the one who saw that we received invitations to our first ball when every door was shut to us. You would not be married to Michael or Elise to Winderton if not for him. I find that admirable."

"He did those things because he wants something from us. No, not us, *you*."

"We owe him a favor. That is the payment for his help, and he has helped us greatly."

"But at what cost?" Dara shook her head. "He is not accepted in Society. Not truly."

"Unless they find him useful," Gwendolyn felt honor bound to point out. "But sooner or later, we need to pay him back. It is the right thing to do. He is asking me to accept an invitation." She shrugged. "I see no problem. Let us discover what the invite is, and then we can argue."

"The problem is that you find him attractive."

"He's an attractive man." Gwendolyn shrugged as if to pretend Mr. Steele's looks meant nothing to her, when in truth, she adored his dark wildness.

"You can do better," Dara said. "The whole reason we made this trip to London was to find husbands of *our* social class. You could have married a squire or a pig famer back in Ireland."

An edge came to Gwendolyn's tone. "Mr. Steele is not a pig farmer. Far from it."

"He's handsome," Dara murmured with a shake of her head. "But he is no viscount."

"I turned down Viscount Morley," Gwendolyn was pleased to say.

Dara's reaction was as Gwendolyn had anticipated. She collapsed onto the settee in shock. "Refused him? I thought you liked him."

"He is a nice man, but I don't wish to marry him."

"You could be a viscountess."

"That is an interesting point, Dara. *You* don't have a title. However, I didn't quibble over your choice, because you were marrying a man who I believed you loved."

"I do love him." Dara's features softened. "He is the most admirable man I've ever met. However, all that being said, he *is* a Member of Parliament. He has a good reputation."

"Mr. Steele has a good reputation."

"For doing shadowy things."

"And he excels at them."

Dara looked wildly around the room as if she could not believe what she was hearing, and Gwendolyn took pity on her. She sat on the settee next to her sister, moving the book she had tossed aside earlier. "Dara, I like Mr. Steele."

"You more than like Mr. Steele," her sister muttered.

"True. And I appreciate that you would prefer for me to be viscountess."

"I'm not trying to be pompous. I just want to save you from a horse thief."

"Mr. Steele is not a horse thief."

"We don't know what all he does," Dara reminded her.

True. It was also true that if he was a horse thief, Gwendolyn would still be madly attracted to him.

She also believed she had enough sense of his character to vouch for him. "He is not a horse thief or a highwayman or a pickpocket or a smuggler—" She stopped. He *could* be a smuggler. He could always be found at a tavern down by the docks that was rumored to be the haven of smugglers. So she ended her disavowals right there.

Instead, she took Dara's hand and said as kindly as she could, "I'm not like you and Elise. Your mother was a noblewoman. Your family has been Irish nobility for generations. I'm your half-sister. I don't have those bloodlines."

"Our father was knighted," Dara declared. "That gives you some weight in this world."

"Not much," Gwendolyn countered. "And Father may have been knighted; however, knowing what we do of him, we, his own daughters, don't understand *why* or *how*. Nor was he 'Sir John' when he married my mother, who was just the daughter of a British civil servant. My mother and my grandfather were wonderful people, Dara, but I have no pretense to nobility—"

"You are *my* sister."

"I am your *half*-sister."

Dara made an impatient sound. "Half? Whole? Who cares? Those are just words, and they don't matter, Gwendolyn. You are the most caring person I know. After Mother died, you watched over and guided Elise and me—and we were so afraid, Gwennie." She used the pet name that her sisters had called her when "Gwendolyn" was too much of a mouthful for them. "You let us cling to you because you understood what it was like to lose a mother. Then, after Gram's death and Richard taking over our home, you would have sacrificed your own happiness for us. Again, to keep us safe. Well, now, Elise and I are in a position to help you. We want you happy."

"Mr. Steele makes me happy."

Dara rocked back at the simple statement. She searched Gwendolyn's face as if testing its veracity. Finally, "I fear he will break your heart. Or worse, you find yourself married to a scoundrel like our father."

There it was—the truth. Dara had finally admitted it.

"We once adored our father," Gwendolyn reminded her.

"Yes, before we knew who he truly was."

Captain Sir John Lanscarr had been proud to be a gambler. When he could have stayed at Wiltham with his motherless daughters, he'd left, always to search for the next game.

The Lanscarr sisters had spent most of their young lives waiting in anxious anticipation for the moment he paid a visit. What would then follow were days when they'd done all in their power to please him so he wouldn't leave again.

He'd always left.

Dara shook her head. "We were misled," she said. Another truth.

"Mr. Steele is not Papa," Gwendolyn said.

"Or so you hope."

A third truth.

"I will be careful," Gwendolyn promised.

In response, Dara threw her arms around her and gave her a fierce hug as if offering a cloak of protection. "Elise and I will always be here for you."

"I do know that."

"And Tweedie, too." She referred to her great-aunt who had traveled with them to London and had served as the Lanscarr sisters' chaperone.

"Of course."

They bowed their heads together as they'd done as children. Sisterly love circled them. Yes, Gwendolyn wished Dara was less managing. Just as, she was certain, Dara wished Gwendolyn was more malleable.

A knock on the house's front door interrupted them.

Gwendolyn sat up, all senses alert. She rose and moved a few steps so that she could see out the window, even as Herald, pulling his black jacket over his shirtsleeves and waistcoat, hurried forward to open the door.

Dara came to her feet, as well. The door between the front sitting room and hall was half-open as they had left it. She glanced at Gwendolyn, who was frustrated she could not see the front step. "Do you see anyone?" she whispered.

Gwendolyn shook her head. She tried to breathe naturally . . . but she was too aware that something momentous was about to happen.

You will receive an invitation. Accept it.

They heard someone speak to Herald. It was a young male voice, not Mr. Steele's. "This is from Lady Orpington. I am to wait for an answer."

Lady Orpington? Gwendolyn had never heard of her. She moved now toward the sitting room door so she could discreetly catch a look at the servant on the step. He wore an expensive-looking wig and was dressed in plum-colored livery.

Dara came up beside her and clamped a hand on her arm, gripping it tightly as if in alarm—or excitement? Her expression was hard to read.

Herald told the messenger that he should wait on the step. He shut the door. Michael and Dara's house was a fine one but small. There was no room for messengers to cool their heels and allow the family privacy, so he'd left him outside.

With great ceremony, Herald walked the few steps it took to enter the sitting room and said, "An invitation from Lady Orpington. She requests an immediate answer."

Gwendolyn took the letter, her name written with great flourish on the outside. She cracked the wax seal and read what was written before looking to Dara. "She requests I call upon her tomorrow morning. She will send a coach. Do we know Lady Orpington?"

Her question was Dara's cue to rip the letter from Gwendolyn's hands as if she needed to read the message herself. "*Yes*, we know of her. Gwendolyn, she is one of the grand dames of Society. The highest of the high. The Top One Hundred Families of England . . . and she wishes *you* to call on her in the morning? How does she know you?"

"Mr. Steele," she reminded her sister. "He told me to expect an invitation. I am to go."

Dara shook her head in disbelief, offering the letter back. "How does he find entrée to half the places in Society we have found him?"

"Society adores a rogue," Gwendolyn observed.

"More like Lady Orpington owes him a favor."

"I'll find out on the morrow." She said to the waiting Herald, "Please tell the messenger I will be ready at the appointed hour."

"Yes, Miss Gwendolyn." He turned with proud formality to relay her answer.

After the door was shut and Herald had retreated from the hall, Dara said with a hint of worry, "I believe I need to accompany you."

"She asked that I come alone."

"I don't know if that is wise."

"And yet it is what is requested."

Dara looked up at Gwendolyn. "By Lady Orpington? Or Mr. Steele?"

It didn't matter to Gwendolyn who had invited her. She was going. She kissed her worried sister's cheek. "I'll be safe. I'll be in Lady Orpington's private coach." She picked up the Dante book and started for her room.

She was going to see Mr. Steele on the morrow.

And she was going to look stunning.

CHAPTER FOUR

You're Irish." Lady Orpington's pronouncement upon receiving Gwendolyn startled both her and the brown-and-white, overweight, and obviously very spoiled King Charles spaniel sleeping in the folds of her ladyship's purple dress. It looked up and growled as if agreeing with its master's outraged declaration.

Her ladyship was not an attractive woman. She appeared to be barely five feet tall with watery brown eyes, a too prominent nose, and a mouth sporting the deep lines of a permanent scowl. In short, she and her dog shared a strong resemblance, and neither was happy.

Gwendolyn didn't quite know how to respond.

All of London knew the Lanscarr sisters were Irish. Gwendolyn knew for a fact there had been many conversations behind closed doors in Society about the *Irish* Upstarts, a well-worn pet name for her and her sisters. The comments stemmed from jealousy and silliness. However, no one had ever curled their lip in Gwendolyn's face.

She could have explained that, actually, no, she wasn't Irish. It was her half-sisters who had the proud Irish heritage. But she did have a lilt to her speech, a soft one.

However, she wouldn't give her rude hostess the satisfaction. If anything, an Irish accent was going to be in every word she said to Lady Orpington from this moment on if the woman didn't change her manner.

And where was Mr. Steele?

He had not been in the coach that had been sent for her. He was also not in this room.

"Dear, dear cousin," a woman sitting in a chair beside Lady Orpington's chaise lounge said in a softly chiding voice, "you are being a trifle disrespectful to Miss Lanscarr?" She was perhaps sixty years of age, the same as Lady Orpington—but she was taller and less well-dressed.

Her ladyship was a vision in purple half mourning and what seemed like a hundred onyx stones around her neck, pinned to her turban, and on her fingers. Even the dog collar had onyx.

In comparison, the other woman's clothing was drab. She wore a brown dress with a gray pelisse, two colors that Gwendolyn would not have put together. Her hair, which might have once been red, was now the faded color of a mouse pelt. She held knitting needles and appeared to be working on a blanket. A brown blanket.

"I'm Mrs. Newsome," she said, introducing herself. Her voice was quiet, but Gwendolyn sensed she wasn't completely subservient. "I'm Lady Orpington's cousin and companion."

"*Distant* cousin," Lady Orpington clarified as if wishing to distinguish the difference between herself and this dowdy woman.

"It is a pleasure to meet you, Mrs. Newsome."

Mrs. Newsome smiled a response, then suggested with proper timidity, "Could Miss Lanscarr be invited to sit?"

"This will not work," Lady Orpington replied, shaking her head. "Absolutely not. Nothing good comes out of Ireland." The dog in her lap grumbled an agreement.

"My dear," Mrs. Newsome said with a hint of forceful patience, "perhaps you are being hasty? You have been looking for the right partner for a very long time."

"I have."

"Time is running out," came another gentle reminder.

"It is." Lady Orpington's gaze narrowed on Gwendolyn as if she was still not certain. "She appears presentable. And she doesn't sound coarse or annoying." She gave a sniff, a sound echoed by the pup. And then, reaching a decision, she waved a purple gloved hand at Gwendolyn. "Sit in a chair, Miss Lanscarr."

In truth, Gwendolyn would have happily walked out the door at the "nothing good comes out of Ireland" comment. However, her purpose here was to see what Mr. Steele wished of her. She did believe he would make an appearance—

sooner or later. Therefore, she would persevere. And she *would* be polite. But Lady Orpington had best be careful.

She started for the comfortable-looking chair next to Mrs. Newsome. Lady Orpington redirected her. "Not that one. The one directly across from me." She pointed at a severe-looking high-backed wooden chair that stood out plainly against the cream-and-gold furnishings of the room. "Prepare everything, Vera." She directed this comment to Mrs. Newsome.

"Leonard?" Mrs. Newsome said in her fluttery voice to the butler who waited by the door. "Please have the table set up for whist."

Whist?

Two bewigged footmen in plum livery came forward to carry a gaming table from the wall and set it between Gwendolyn and Lady Orpington.

"Here, take Magpie." Her ladyship held up the dog to one of the footmen. Magpie, who had been grumbly but docile, came alive. With a growl, she snapped her unhappiness at the footman, who pulled his gloved hand back just in time. "*Go on.* Take her," Lady Orpington said. "She needs to wee."

As if on command, Magpie did exactly that, in the direction of the footman's chest. To Gwendolyn's amazement, he calmly took the dog, still weeing, and carried it from the room. The other footmen followed, leaving the women alone.

Lady Orpington acted oblivious to her pet's actions. Or the urine that was on the plush India carpet covering the floor, not to mention the footman's livery. Instead, she reached for a small inlaid chest and set it on the table. She took out a deck of cards, squared them up, and then looked to Gwendolyn. "Shuffle."

"Because?" Gwendolyn said pointedly. It was high time someone explained what was going on.

Lady Orpington frowned as if confused that Gwendolyn wasn't jumping to her command. She glanced at Mrs. Newsome, who had set aside her knitting. She gave her cousin a small shrug as if to say she didn't understand Gwendolyn's question either.

"Because we are going to play whist," Lady Orpington snapped out.

Gwendolyn decided directness was best. "Lady Orpington, why am I truly here?"

"Didn't he tell you?"

"*Who* tell me?" Gwendolyn wanted to hear her say Mr. Steele's name.

Lady Orpington did not comply. "I am looking for a whist partner. I now wish to know if you are any good. He claims you are. However, by the looks of you, I doubt it. Too pretty. And you are Irish."

"Then, obviously, there has been a mistake," Gwendolyn said coolly, rising to her feet. She was done with this woman's manner. "Please, if you will have your coach carry me home, I shall remove my Irish self from your presence."

She would have turned and walked out, but Lady Orpington barked, "*You will stay right here.*" She looked over to Mrs. Newsome. "Since we have her, we should see what she can do."

"What if I don't wish to do anything?" Gwendolyn countered, vastly annoyed with this woman who didn't speak to her directly except to bark orders.

"Then that will be a disappointment," Lady Orpington said. "I was assured that you were the partner I needed to defeat Lady Middlebury. Time is running out. Her house party is next week."

"The Middlebury house party?" The Marquess and Marchioness of Middlebury owned Colemore, rumored to be the finest estate in all of Britain. Their house party was one of the most coveted invitations of the year. Even Gwendolyn knew the significance of it.

"Yes, I need a partner," Lady Orpington said with the dismissive air of someone who believes a matter to be solved. She began taking off her purple gloves, preparing to play. "Now, shuffle."

Gwendolyn would not be spoken to as if she was a servant who had to let her ladyship's dog pee on her. "Tell Mr. Steele that if he wishes to speak to me, he may pay a call." She turned to go—

"*I said you will play.*" Lady Orpington's voice echoed through the room. "If I wish you to play, you will play."

"*Please*, Miss Lanscarr," Mrs. Newsome said as if she hastened to tack on a touch of gratitude to her cousin's edict. "This game is very important to Lady Orpington. We need to find a partner before next week."

"Why?" Gwendolyn pushed again, insisting they explain themselves to her.

Lady Orpington blinked several times as if Gwendolyn had splashed water in her face. Apparently no one ever challenged her rudeness. She was surrounded with money, luxury, and servants. Everyone jumped to her command . . . but not this *Irish* Upstart.

Abruptly, Lady Orpington's manner changed. She gave a snort of laughter. "He told me she wasn't one to be cowed, and he was right, wasn't he, Vera? Very well. *Please*, play, Miss Lanscarr. Let us test your skill on the card table to see if it matches your pride."

"I am not a dancing bear, my lady," Gwendolyn replied, unwilling to cave just yet. "Besides, I'm Irish. How good càn I possibly be?"

"It is only the Irish comment that has upset you?" Lady Orpington reached for the deck of cards and shuffled them herself, cackling as she did so. "Very well. Hooray for the Irish. Long may they live. Happy now?" She didn't wait for an answer. "Vera will be your partner, Miss Lanscarr, while I shall play two hands of cards."

"That puts you at an advantage," Gwendolyn pointed out.

"I know," Lady Orpington said happily. "Now sit."

Gwendolyn hesitated. She didn't know how she felt about all of this.

"Please, Miss Lanscarr," Mrs. Newsome said again. "It will make my cousin happy."

And then Gwendolyn remembered that when she'd first met Mr. Steele, she had been playing cards. He had complimented her play . . . for a purpose, she now realized.

She would dearly enjoy teaching Lady Orpington a little *true* respect for the Irish. But first—

"Why is finding a whist partner important to you, my lady?" Gwendolyn asked.

"I told you. The Middlebury house party is next week. Whist is the game we play."

"Lady Middlebury is devoted to whist," Mrs. Newsome offered helpfully. "As is my cousin."

"Do you gamble on it?" Gwendolyn asked.

"Of course." Lady Orpington shook her head as if that had been a silly question. "However, the money is of no consequence."

"What is *of* consequence?" Gwendolyn asked.

"Winning." Lady Orpington said this as if it should be obvious. "Proving who is the best player. Who can amass the highest points. But what does it matter to you? You play. That is all that is being asked."

"Except I wish to know who I am playing with and why winning matters." Gwendolyn knew people went to Mr. Steele for many reasons. Some to find missing loved ones like she and Dara had for Elise. Others because they had special requests that only they understood. "Why do you wish to win so badly you are willing to play with a stranger? Or go to whatever lengths?" Mr. Steele's services always came with a cost.

Lady Orpington set the stack of cards in the middle of the game table, her expression bullishly solemn.

Mrs. Newsome prodded. "Tell her, Ellen."

At the soft words, tears suddenly welled in Lady Orpington's eyes. She blinked them back. "You do it."

Mrs. Newsome looked as if she would have patted her cousin's hand but stayed herself as if knowing such a kind gesture would be unwelcome. "Lady Middlebury is a devoted player," she said to Gwendolyn. "She hosts a whist tournament at her house party. It is well-known."

Not to Gwendolyn, but that was unsurprising.

"Lady Orpington's partner—winning partner, I should add—was her late husband. They were a very good team. They always won. Lady Middlebury had long wished to defeat them."

"Her desire to best us was about more than the cards," Lady Orpington said. "My husband and I were a love story. She was jealous of us."

Mrs. Newsome nodded agreement. "Lord Orpington did adore you. He was also a brilliant player. A great mind."

"Charles and I knew each other's thoughts without speaking," Lady Orpington declared. "That is how close we were."

"Unfortunately," Mrs. Newsome continued, "during last year's party, he began to fail."

"His mind . . . it went away," Lady Orpington whispered. "It came about so suddenly. It didn't make sense." She squeezed her eyes shut as if hating the memory.

"Yes, it was sad. And quick. Nothing was wrong until they started playing, and then he somehow became lost in the game," Mrs. Newsome said. "He made the wrong bids."

Lady Orpington took over the story, doubling her fists and placing them against her chest as if her heart hurt. "I saw it happen immediately. There was a change in his eyes. They became unfocused. I asked Franny—" She paused, looked at Gwendolyn with hard eyes and said, "Franny, Lady Middlebury, who was my childhood friend, whom I have bolstered and guided and cared for all of the years since we were very young girls—I asked her to put the play on hold. Stop the tournament for that year. The matter had to be handled delicately. Men do not accept they are not all they wish to be."

"What happened?" Gwendolyn asked.

"She refused. She said honor was at stake. They always had the tournament. The games had started. She couldn't, or wouldn't, cancel. Nor would she let us withdraw. She was very hard about it."

"Lady Middlebury takes her whist seriously, and these games at her house party are important to her," Mrs. Newsome said. "Her husband is very private. He does not come to Town."

"So I have heard," Gwendolyn murmured.

"He keeps her locked away on that estate with him," Mrs. Newsome said.

"Therefore, we go to her," Lady Orpington said. "Once a year, he allows her to entertain, and her whist tournament is infamous. However, I thought friendship was more important." She placed her palms on the table. "Charles realized he wasn't playing well. He was conscious of it, except his pride wouldn't let him cry quarter. I told him that no matter the consequences, we should drop out and return to London, that the tournament wasn't important. And then Franny taunted him. She made a pouty face and claimed that leaving would be poor sportsmanship after so many years of being the reigning winners. That touched on Charles's sense of honor. He always was one to finish what he had started." The tears that threatened earlier now rolled silently down her cheeks. "We lost. Of course we did. He was ill. It didn't help that he felt as if he had failed me. I told him I didn't care about the tournament, but Franny, who was once my great friend, mocked my husband for losing. She couldn't stop crowing about it."

"This is so," Mrs. Newsome said.

"We returned to London immediately, but our physician said it was too late. His mind just grew worse. He died lying in our bed beside me." Lady Orpington wiped her eyes with her hands until Mrs. Newsome offered a kerchief. She buried her face in the small piece of linen.

The room was silent as Lady Orpington composed herself. She lifted her gaze to Gwendolyn. All sadness left her eyes. In its place was a burning desire for revenge. "Lady Middlebury had the audacity to refer to herself as the new Queen of Whist in a letter to a mutual friend."

"It was unsettling," Mrs. Newsome agreed. "I had always rather admired Lady Middlebury, until that moment."

"Franny has always had a streak of meanness in her, especially after our first Season," Lady Orpington said. "She wanted Orpington, but Charles chose me. We were a love match." Her chin lifted. "Can you believe it? At a time when marriages amongst important families with fortunes were arranged, I found the only man I could ever love. She was jealous of us and our money."

"And yet she caught a marquess," Gwendolyn pointed out. "A very wealthy one."

"Oh, no," Lady Orpington said. "Back then, Middlebury was a second son. His brother was the marquess. What a fine gentleman he was, far more appealing and enchanting than Walter." She drew out the syllables of his name with disdain. "Secretly, I think Franny wanted the older brother. However, everyone claimed he was a confirmed bachelor. Then, to the world's amazement, when he was almost forty, he married a Spanish beauty. She was the daughter of a diplomat. Everyone adored her, except Franny. Especially after she gave him a son."

She leaned toward Gwendolyn as if imparting a secret. "You see, Franny had discovered a purpose to her marriage. She'd given her husband a son, and she'd reasoned that her son would inherit the title. Over the years, she's given him another son *and* a daughter. She never fails to point out that I'm barren. It didn't matter. Charles *loved* me."

The pride in her voice coupled with the sense of loss brought home the depth of the woman's feelings for her husband, more so than the wearing of half mourning over a year later. Gwendolyn found herself sympathetic. "But then something happened," Gwendolyn noted.

"As it does," Lady Orpington agreed. "Not

long after the birth of his son, the oldest brother collapsed while at his club. They say he was dead before he hit the ground. *It was a sad day.* Everyone was shocked. He had been an energetic man. Orpington had admired him very much. Not long after, the Spanish wife and the son died. It was quite tragic. A whole family wiped from this earth. The upshot is that Franny became the marchioness. Her son is the heir, just as she wished."

Lady Orpington shook her head with disgust. "But she lacks the grace of her title. And she demonstrated her true nature when she put my husband in such a state—" She paused, swallowed, continued, "She disgraced him. She showed no kindness, no gentleness. She and the marquess didn't even attend his funeral."

"Because they do not leave Colemore," Mrs. Newsome reminded her.

"And what silliness is that?" Lady Orpington demanded. "Orpington deserved that last respect." She looked to Gwendolyn. "Franny thinks that my husband and I won because of his skill, but I was always his equal. Whist is a game of partners. Unfortunately, I have not found a partner to match my husband's skill and I can't win alone, not for this level of play. Part of the problem is who the players are. Colemore has a reputation. It is difficult to be around so much wealth. It unsettles people. However, *you* don't intimidate easy, Miss Lanscarr."

"The Irish rarely do."

Her lips curved into a conspirator's smile. "You won't let me live that down, will you?"

"Should I?" Gwendolyn removed her gloves and reached for the cards. She wasn't certain what she thought of Lady Orpington. Then again, the world was full of people who believed they were more special than others.

Besides, she was here for Mr. Steele.

She began handling the cards, using a special shuffle that her father had taught her. He'd said that it warned players at the table they were in the presence of someone who understood their game. Her fingers moved with a will of their own, slipping the cards under, over, flipping them back and forth.

Lady Orpington and Mrs. Newsome watched the cards' movement as if she was performing magic.

"You are good," Lady Orpington said with a note of delicious anticipation.

Gwendolyn placed the card deck in front of her. "Anyone can perform a simple card trick."

"Understood," her ladyship answered. Then she smiled. "Charles would have said the same."

Gwendolyn's attitude toward Lady Orpington had changed. She wanted to help this woman because she understood loss—her mother, her stepmother, Gram—and she also understood the desire for respect.

"Please deal, my lady," Gwendolyn told her.

Whist had been one of the first games Gwendolyn's father had taught her. It was a simple game of collecting cards of a kind or "tricks." When the cards were finished, the winner wasn't just the team with the most tricks, but the one with the highest card values. Hence, it made it a good game for gamblers.

The challenge was to understand what cards your partner held and how to use them, and yours, to the greatest advantage. Skill was involved, but more important was paying attention to the cards as they were played.

Gwendolyn had been born with an almost uncanny ability to remember cards, numbers, people, and ideas. It was her gift.

She now used it. She quickly assessed that Mrs. Newsome was not a skilled or even interested player. She had no intention of besting her cousin in cards.

On the other hand, Lady Orpington was an enthusiastic player. She also liked to win, and she had the knowledge of two card hands since she was playing her own partner.

However, her eagerness to win was her downfall.

In contrast, Gwendolyn noted the cards being played. She knew her ladyship was not playing anything that she believed would give her opponents an advantage in the points.

That was fine. After allowing Lady Orpington to take two tricks, Gwendolyn believed she'd gained a good idea of what cards were still left to be played among all four hands. She and Mrs. Newsome began taking tricks.

They won the game with higher points. Mrs. Newsome behaved as if she'd never bested her cousin before.

"Again," Lady Orpington said. "Only this time, I shall play with Vera."

So Gwendolyn had two hands of cards.

She won handily.

Lady Orpington kept them playing, sharing Mrs. Newsome as a partner back and forth between them. Her ladyship won a few games. The wins gave Gwendolyn insight into how her mind worked. Lady Orpington did have a good understanding of strategy.

Nor had Mr. Steele been wrong in his assessment. She and Lady Orpington were excellent whist partners.

Her ladyship said as much at the end of the eighth game. "We can do this," she said to Gwendolyn. "You and I can defeat Franny and whomever she brings against us." She looked down at the neatly laid out tricks on the table. "You might even be a better player than Charles was."

"Thank you, my lady." Gwendolyn now understood what high praise that was from his widow.

Lady Orpington stood and rang a bell. The butler opened the door. "Have this cleared up. Bring in Magpie, and I would like to see Mr. Curran."

The man bowed and left the room. A beat later, footmen entered and removed the gaming table, but not the cards. Gwendolyn noticed that Lady Orpington returned them herself to their inlaid box.

Once the table was cleared, Gwendolyn heard the complaining whines of an upset dog in the hall. The door opened, and Magpie came padding in, her little head high as if she had suffered a grave insult.

And right behind her came, not a Mr. Curran, but Mr. Steele.

Time stopped at the sight of him.

He appeared different than she had ever seen him. He appeared the very image of a Corinthian, handsome, broad-shouldered, commanding. Instead of his usual black, a bottle-green jacket was pulled snug across his broad shoulders. Buff leather riding breeches clung to the thighs of a horseman, while his boots, sporting a single spur in manly fashion, shone with the gloss of a champagne blacking that only the most expert valet could achieve.

He'd even cut his hair. It no longer brushed his collar. Instead, his dark curls with the light smattering of gray gave him the air of a poet, and yet there was still that sense he was untamed. Every dandy on the street would have eagerly aped his manner of casual, very masculine elegance.

Thankfully Gwendolyn was sitting, or else she would have been tempted to run up to him like an infatuated girl fresh from the schoolroom. She squeezed her trembling hands into fists. Yearning tightened inside her the way it did whenever he was near.

She prayed she did not give herself away . . . and yet she could not stop smiling.

Lady Orpington lifted Magpie beside her on the lounge. "Nicholas, you are right about Miss Lanscarr. She is exactly who I need." She spoke to Mr. Steele.

"I did not think she would disappoint," he responded with lazy good humor. His voice rolled through Gwendolyn like thick honey. His faint praise was just as sweet.

"Miss Lanscarr, this is my nephew, Nicholas Curran."

He bowed politely on cue . . . just as someone she did not know would behave. "Miss Lanscarr."

Gwendolyn tried to gather her scattered wits. *Nicholas?* And the surname was Curran, no?

But this *was* Mr. Steele. A well-shaved version, but Mr. Steele all the same. The erratic beat of her pulse proved it.

However, what game was being played? And what was her role? Was it possible Lady Orpington did not know his true identity?

Of course she knew. She'd introduced him as her nephew. She had to know that was not true.

Dara would really not be pleased with this at all.

But Gwendolyn was almost giddy with excitement. Something was afoot. And whatever was about to happen, Mr. Steele was including her.

Lady Orpington spoke. "Miss Lanscarr, you will come with us to Colemore next week. I shall pick you up on Wednesday midmorning. I expect you to be ready on time. Prepare to spend two weeks."

"Of course," Gwendolyn murmured, pleased she sounded poised and unruffled. "I shall look forward to the adventure." She began pulling on her gloves, needing to have something to do with her shaking hands.

"Adventure? Ha!" Lady Orpington said. "There will be good food, boring company, and, hopefully, excellent cards. One can't ask for more, can one?" She looked to Mr. Steele. "Nicholas, will you please escort Miss Lanscarr home?"

"Happily," his deep voice answered. He stretched a hand toward the door, an invitation for Gwendolyn to leave with him.

CHAPTER FIVE

*B*eck watched with admiration as Gwendolyn hid her obvious confusion behind a graceful curtsy. "Lady Orpington, Mrs. Newsome. It was a pleasure to meet you," she said.

"I look forward to playing with you," the old dragon replied, her words dripping with a sweetness Beck had not associated with Lady Orpington.

She had been a handful ever since they had made their agreement; he would find a whist partner for her, and she would give him entrée to Colemore. From the moment he'd spied Gwendolyn in Dublin, he'd known she would meet Lady Orpington's needs—well, save for the Irish aspect. Lady Orpington, like so many of her class, thought of herself as socially superior to everyone outside their close circle of acquaintances. So Beck had delayed this meeting until he knew Lady Orpington couldn't afford to be arbitrary.

Gwendolyn walked through the door he held open, her head high, her back straight. However, once out in the hall, she started to turn to him. He could feel her excitement and knew she was bubbling with questions. "Not yet," he warned under his breath.

With a quick nod that she understood, she continued moving.

Beck was surprised by the number of footmen who all of a sudden appeared stationed along the hallway and her path. They hadn't been there when he'd arrived.

And he didn't like the way their gazes followed Gwendolyn's tall, refined figure as she passed them. He was certain they noticed the way her hips moved with a gentle sway and imagined exactly how long her legs were.

For her part, she seemed oblivious to the hearts she was conquering. At one point, she smiled in the direction of a footman. The man's faced flushed red.

Beck understood. Gwendolyn had that effect on every male of her acquaintance . . . including himself. There were times when she shot him a look of complete hero worship. She romanticized him, and if he wasn't careful, he would see himself through her eyes. He would forget exactly who he was. He was a loner. He didn't need entanglements. He liked his life the way it was. Besides, he brutally reminded himself, Gwendolyn could do much better than him. She *deserved* better. His job was to see that no ill befell her. She was doing him a great favor, and he was determined to keep her safe. Middlebury hadn't sent his man Winstead to coddle Beck but to kill him.

That was why the conversation he was about to have with her was critical.

And he didn't anticipate her being happy about it.

Downstairs, a footman held her bonnet. Gwendolyn took the hat and tied the crisp ribbons under her chin at a fetching angle. The ribbons matched the blue in her dress and made her golden-brown eyes stand out even more.

For his disguise, Beck had given up his preferred wide-brimmed hat for a curled-brimmed beaver that all the gentlemen wore. He tipped it low over his eyes and offered Gwendolyn his arm. She rested her gloved hand lightly on his sleeve, and they went out the front door. Lady Orpington's coach waited for them.

A footman jumped down from the rumble, the seat at the rear of the coach, to place a small step by the coach door. She held Beck's hand as she climbed in, and there was something about her grace, her presence, that made him feel ridiculously gallant.

"Drive until I tell you differently," he instructed the coachman. He removed his hat and climbed into the coach. He took the seat opposite hers, his back to the driver, and set the hat beside him.

The footman closed the door.

Beck pulled down the shades to protect them from prying eyes. Gwendolyn watched his every movement, her hands folded in her lap. He sat back against his seat, and that's when he noticed how close the space was.

Or did it feel close because he was with her? He couldn't name the scent she wore, but it reminded him of summer, of wildflowers and sparkling streams.

She wasn't fair-haired and blue-eyed like her sisters. However, he liked Gwendolyn's dark looks, her heavy, glossy hair that was as black as a raven's wing and her startling golden eyes that seemed to look right into the heart of him.

The tightening in his loins, that damnable need that roiled a man's blood, assured him that the sooner he set her against him, the better.

Beck knocked on the roof, a signal for the driver to leave. The coachman shouted "Ha," and they began to move.

"What is going—" Gwendolyn started as if she could contain herself no longer, but Beck held up a gloved hand. She must still wait.

Gwendolyn sat back, a small line furrowing her brow, her pressed lips a sign of impatience— and then she wet them. The sight of the tip of her tongue caught and held him.

Dear God, she had no idea of her impact upon men, and it made her all the more enticing—

"I am not who you believe I am," he said abruptly, the opening to his planned speech warning her not to expect anything from him, especially if it involved her heart.

Before he could launch into his planned admonishments, she interrupted him with mock dismay. "Oh, are you telling me you *aren't* Mr. Curran?"

"Miss Lanscarr," he said in warning.

"Mr. Steele," she replied in the same formidable tone.

"I'm attempting a serious discussion."

"As am I. You wish to be Mr. Curran. Very well. Yes, Mr. Curran? What do you need to tell me? Oh, you aren't the man I believe you to be? Well, that makes sense, because I know you as Mr. Steele. Does Lady Orpington know?"

"Of course she does," he snapped. "She hired me to find you. And she knows I'm not her nephew."

"And in return for you finding her a whist partner she likes, she owes you a favor. You asked that she pretend you are her nephew. I'm correct, aren't I? I'm assuming you are doing this to go to Colemore. Why? What is your game?"

His intention had been to inform her that he was *not* someone she should focus her hopes on. He was *not* heroic. He didn't deserve her longing looks or wetting her lips in that innocently seductive way of hers. He was not a man like Jem who wanted a wife, a hearth, and a cluster of children.

Unfortunately, Gwendolyn had seized control of the conversation. She was also justified in asking questions. He would do the same in her position. At his silence, Gwendolyn waved a hand as if to wake him up. "What is the ploy? The scheme? What are we about to do?"

"You act as if I want you to help rob the Post—"

"Do you?" she asked, her eyes lighting up as if she would be game, God help him.

With great deliberateness, he said, "Miss Lanscarr, curb your imagination. *You* will be a guest at Colemore. You will be Lady Orpington's whist partner. You play cards and nothing else."

"Do you want me to win?"

"Lady Orpington does."

She considered that a moment and then pressed, "But what do you want me to do?"

To let me kiss you. To fall into my arms and let me make love to you.

He could have smacked himself in the head for his errant thoughts. They had just popped up without encouragement . . . Well, the tilt of her head as she'd looked up at him under dark lashes had encouraged them, and her asking him what he wanted her to do. Such an innocent question . . . that every male part of him had come to life upon hearing it.

"Is something the matter, Mr. Steele? You seem unsettled. How may I help?"

Another question, with a lewd undertone—except to her. She was looking at him as if she was a green recruit and this was the first day of training. And that made him feel even more awkward. He hid behind sternness.

"By playing cards," he responded. "That is *all* I ask of you." He said the last as a reminder to himself. Especially since the rolling of the coach over London's cobbled streets brought her knee repeatedly in contact with his knee. It was not intentional, but then, it apparently didn't need to be for him to hear the double entendre in her replies.

She sat forward, the peak of her bonnet almost brushing the roof of the coach. "Then ask more of me," she said.

And there was another one. Did she realize what she was saying? The very male part of Beck roared to life with desire. Instead, he shifted his weight, moving his knee as far as he could from bumping hers, and masked his reaction.

Gwendolyn frowned as if she thought him behaving strangely, and that only added insult to all of it. She, apparently, was not affected by his presence, while he hadn't been so rattled since he'd first discovered there was a difference between men and women. His intended lecture about not expecting anything other than a working relationship now seemed egotistical on his part. *He* was the one having the problem. Gwendolyn Lanscarr seemed unbothered by his close proximity. To the devil with all of this. He started to reach up and tap on the roof, a signal to the driver to take Gwendolyn home—but she grabbed his arm, pulling it down.

Her boldness and the contact surprised him. Even through the layers of his jacket sleeve and shirt, sparks shot through him.

"You cannot return me home yet," she informed him. "I will not partner with Lady Orpington until I know what is happening. There is more to this than a whist game."

The sparks died. Few challenged Beck. He did not like it. His equilibrium returned. "You owe me a favor, Miss Lanscarr."

Her chin came up at the finality in his voice. "I am willing to pay it . . . but I would be a fool to involve myself in something I didn't understand. Why can't you go to Colemore as yourself? What is the scheme?"

"The less you know, the better."

Of course, that didn't appease Gwendolyn Lanscarr. "I doubt that, Mr. Steele. And if you wish me to keep your true identity hidden from the Marquess and Marchioness of Middlebury, I believe I'm owed an explanation."

"You wouldn't betray me."

"Is that a chance you wish to take?"

"I shall find another cardplayer," he said.

"By next week?" She shook her head. "That isn't possible, not now that someone as stubborn as Lady Orpington has given me her approval. Besides," she continued as if her hand was being forced, "I can send a letter to Colemore. Let them know you are planning some sort of subterfuge—"

Beck's temper ignited. "Don't test me, Miss Lanscarr." Why was he always attracted to the wrong woman?

"Then you must explain yourself. I have a right to know why you are impersonating someone else." She spoke reasonably, and that made her words all the more infuriating.

And it didn't help that he actually did need her. Desire was one thing. Being in a position where he had no other recourse was another.

In truth, he'd brought in several partners for Lady Orpington. They had been mostly men and with minor titles, the sort Lady Orpington had thought she wanted. But Beck had known Gwendolyn would be the one. She had the talent for cards and the aristocratic bearing to fit in with the Middlebury set. She would make Lady Orpington look good. More important, she would deflect attention from himself and his purpose at Colemore.

"I'm attempting to protect you," he said tightly.

"So you keep telling me."

Very well, he would give her the truth. *All* of it. He would make her retreat in distaste, and then he'd never have to worry about her being infatuated with him.

"I am the bastard son of the Marquess of Middlebury. My mother is some nameless whore." He paused, giving her a moment to react, expecting her to recoil in delicate horror. But he'd misjudged her—once again.

Instead, she plunged into questions. "Does the marquess know you are his son? Is that why you are pretending to be someone else?"

"He knows of me, but he doesn't know me. *We* have never met."

"This seems a strange way to introduce yourself."

"I'm not introducing myself. I don't want him to know my true identity." She didn't need to know about Olin Winstead's attack, a sign that someone at Colemore would go to great lengths to stop him. As for her safety, he would protect her.

She changed the subject. "You speak well for a whore's son," she observed as if it was important to their conversation.

"I'm not uneducated."

"How did you become educated?"

He made an impatient sound. "Middlebury paid for my schooling and purchased my commission."

"All that money and he doesn't know who you are."

"He doesn't wish to. There, curiosity satisfied?"

"Not completely. You were in the military? Of course. That explains much about you. No wonder you do not enjoy being challenged."

"Does any man?"

"Does any person?"

His frustration overcame his command of the situation. "Gwendolyn, you try my patience."

"I find you somewhat challenging as well," she replied without heat, and then there was a quick smile. "I also like the way you say my given name. You linger on the first syllable."

Only then did he realize he'd taken the liberty of her name, the name he used when he thought of her. "Not on purpose," he answered, "but because you can be exasperating, Miss Lanscarr. I should not have forgotten myself. Please forgive me."

Her lips formed a pout. "We are back to formalities. I give you permission to use my name, if you wish."

"I do *not* wish. I was improper. I beg your pardon."

"No pardon needed," she assured him.

What he had anticipated to be a three-minute conversation of him telling her not to form an attachment to him had turned into her talking circles around him. "Miss Lanscarr, do *not* allow me liberties—"

"I—" she started, and he rolled right over her, cutting off whatever she was about to say. She needed to see sense.

"I spent my childhood in a brothel. I *lived* among *whores*."

There, he'd said it. He wasn't just the son of a whore. He'd lived that life. It was his shame, his secret. Not even Wagner knew about his mother or any of the circumstances of Beck's parentage. Fortunately, it wasn't a conversation that came up among men at war.

Except there were those who knew, or so he suspected. The murkiness of his past had been one of the reasons he believed General Danvers had frowned upon his suit for Violet's hand. There was something unsettling about a boy raised without family or ties. Any caring father would be wary of him.

Except, Gwendolyn didn't shudder with horror. Instead, she interrogated him. "You lived in the brothel until—what? You said you went to school."

Beck threw himself into the corner of the coach and crossed his arms against his chest. He no longer cared that his leg brushed hers or that she smelled of clover and daisies. No, right now, she was maddening, and he knew she had bested him. She'd not rest until she was satisfied. "You want the whole story?"

"I expect it."

"So be it," he ground out. "When I was around five or six, maybe seven—"

"You don't know your age?"

"No."

"Didn't your mother tell you?"

"I don't know my mother." That was a terrible thing to confess. Except Gwendolyn nodded as if it made sense. "I don't know when I was born," he reiterated as if she didn't completely understand. "Whores don't keep careful records."

"I suppose *some* do."

Beck scowled. "*Mine* didn't. I don't even know who she was. I never knew her."

"How did you survive? You were very young to be on your own."

"By doing what I was told and staying out of harm's way." Something she would be wise to emulate. "I worked in the scullery, I emptied chamber pots, I cleaned out ashes, the jobs a child could do."

"But you have no inkling of how you came to be there?"

He paused, considering, and realizing that he'd never truly thought deeply about how he had ended up at Madam's. "I was young. I can't recall."

"But you did know whom your father was?"

"Not until Middlebury's man came to see Madam. She was the bawd who owned the house. The next thing I knew, I was yanked out of the only home I'd known and sent to Faircote, a school up north."

"I've heard of it."

"Wonders never cease," he said. "An answer you accept without another question."

A hint of a smile came to her eyes as if she enjoyed his sarcasm and even this conversation between them. He realized he didn't mind it all that much himself. He preferred keeping his affairs private . . . but he knew Gwendolyn would push until she knew all. Besides, she hadn't flinched over learning his parentage, and he had to admit he was impressed . . . and a bit grateful.

Therefore, he continued. "I wasn't even to know I was Middlebury's until Madam made a comment about it. She gave up the secret, and she shouldn't have. Middlebury's man struck her so hard she fell to the floor. Up until then, she was the most powerful person in my life," he explained, wanting Gwendolyn to understand how shocking this was. "She had a bodyguard named Dervil who could snap the arm of anyone who created trouble at the house. Everyone was afraid of Madam. She was afraid of Winstead."

"That is Middlebury's man?"

Beck nodded. "When he left me at Faircote, he said that if he ever heard Middlebury's name pass my lips, he would cut my tongue out. I believed him."

"But you have said his name freely just now."

"Because he is dead. I have no fear of him."

"How did he die?"

Beck wasn't about to confess he'd killed him. He kept silent.

Gwendolyn waited, watching him as if she could stare him into answering.

She couldn't.

Finally, she gave a small huff of annoyance before asking, "You never met your father?"

This he could answer, although he secretly enjoyed his small victory. "Never. I lived at the school, stayed at the school, and then went off into the military." He shrugged. "I didn't have a desire to meet him either."

"Because of what this Winstead said?"

"I'm not fond of people who want to cut out my tongue."

She seemed to actually consider this, and then admitted, "I wouldn't be either."

"I'm not surprised," he murmured.

Her grin was quick. Beck liked watching her eyes sparkle with humor.

Then she sobered. "Why do you wish to confront the marquess now after all of these years?"

"My desire is *not* to confront him."

"Then why infiltrate his home? I mean, you are going under a different name."

"I believe it safest."

"And your purpose?"

"I suffered a head injury at the Battle of the Nive." He didn't mention he was cited for valor, that his actions had helped to stave off Soult's men until the Peninsula army could regroup. "The injury led to—" He paused, then said, "Dreams." Actually, it felt like madness. "Dreams" was a kind way of describing them.

Her expression has softened as if she understood what he had not said. "Go on," she prompted. "We will not speak of any of this beyond the confines of this coach. Tell me of the dreams."

Beck shifted his weight. How to explain? "They *may* be memories," he said. "I'm not certain. The dream always starts with a beautiful woman, a singing woman. Her song makes me happy." He looked to Gwendolyn for understanding. "I feel as if I belong with her."

She nodded.

"But then things change," he said. "The song turns to screams. I try to reach her. I want to help her, but I can't, and I'm afraid. Petrified with fear, actually. I keep calling for help, but no one hears me. And someplace in there is Middlebury . . . or at least a man. I don't know if it is him."

"Do you still have these dreams?"

"Not as often once I made up my mind to confront the marquess. It is as if the dream was prodding me on the path I should take." The dream had also pushed him further into being alone.

Gwendolyn spoke. "I understand the desire to know one's parent and one's history. I was about the same age you were when I was sent from the only home I'd known in Barbados to my father in Ireland. My mother had been dead a year or so, and I had dreams, too. I still do. I hardly remember her, but sometimes, I dream that she watches over me. As for families, they are rarely what we expect them to be if we could do the choosing."

"I'm not looking for a family."

"Aren't you? Do you not think the woman in the dream could be your mother? What if she needs you? What if her screams are a warning?"

"What if it is foolishness caused by almost having my head shot off?"

He spoke harshly, but she did not take offense. Instead, she smiled. "You believe it is a memory. You referred to it as that."

"But I don't know."

"Still, you wish to find out. You know there is a truth waiting for you, Mr. Steele. Truth matters."

It did.

Beck leaned toward her. "After I left the military, I started searching every brothel in London trying to find Madam's house or anyone who could give me information. I wanted to know who the woman in the dream is."

"Did you have any luck?"

"After twenty-five years or so? No. That world is always changing."

"So you are going to Colemore to poke around, to see what you can learn."

"Yes."

"And perhaps meet your father?"

"My father is unimportant."

"But is he?" she challenged. "Aren't you at least a bit curious?"

"No."

She shot him a look as if she knew better. "This is a good plan. You really have no other choice. Your other avenues for learning who you are have been closed off. Do you believe the woman in your dreams is still in danger? Is it possible this is a premonition, and *that* is the reason you feel an urgency to find her?"

Beck hadn't considered that. "I don't know. I'm not one to believe in a spirit world. The dream woman might not even exist."

"Oh, she exists. This is important to you."

It was.

"I'm glad I am going," Gwendolyn said. "I can help you search for this woman—"

"You will do no such thing."

"I must. This is a mystery. I adore a mystery."

"Miss Lanscarr, you are there to play cards—"

"And to help you," she said confidently. "I can be very resourceful."

"No."

"I can be a great help."

"You help me by doing as I say."

She had the audacity to smile at him.

It was a heart-melting smile. It declared louder than words that she would do anything for him. He remembered his true purpose in talking to her privately. He needed to be direct.

"You must stop this infatuation with me," he said. "It is not returned." He spoke firmly. "Do you understand? I despise being brutally honest, but I don't want you to feel misled."

Her brows gathered like miniature storm clouds. "Don't claim you don't feel the attraction between us. It is too strong to belong to myself alone."

"There is nothing there," he lied. "You are a lovely woman, but there are many lovely women." Although few as vibrant and intelligent as Gwendolyn.

"Why are you trying to put me off you? Is it your past? Is that why you wished me to know you believe your mother is a whore?"

"We come from different worlds, Gwen—" He caught himself in time. "Miss Lanscarr," he finished.

"Please, you don't believe in that silliness about different class stations in life. I'm not special, Mr. Steele. You have more titled blood in your veins than I have—"

"It is none of that. Gwendolyn. I don't have"—he paused, as if testing the next word—"feelings for you."

"You are lying." Her expression turned defiant. "Anytime I have needed you, you've been there."

"You were a client who owes me a favor, which I am calling in. That is all that is between us."

"That night in Dublin, you wanted to kiss me," she reminded him.

"And my head was bashed in for my efforts. That being said, don't read too much into a kiss."

Her head gave a little jerk, and her eyes widened as if he'd struck her. She folded her hands in her lap in that ladylike way of hers. She looked away as if she could see through the window shade. He waited, hoping for a tear or something that said she accepted his rude rejection.

And it felt mean. Too mean.

"I'm a loner, Miss Lanscarr. I like my life the way it is. I do not want any entanglements."

"No one wishes to be alone. Not truly," she answered.

"I do," he assured her. "Especially for my work."

"Skulking around." She gave a dismissive sniff.

That offended Beck. "I do more than skulk."

"And you could do it without staying in the shadows. Don't you want more from life, Mr. Steele? Don't you wish for more?"

"No."

Her shoulders tightened. She looked away, her lips pressing together.

"Don't think you can change me," he said, his voice quiet and not unkind. "I don't want to be changed."

There was a long silence. He wondered what she was thinking. He reminded himself that this was for the best. Better to have it clear between them now, because the wound to her pride would be deeper if she misunderstood what was truly between them and he rejected her later.

And then, with a small shrug, she said, "Very well."

"I do not wish to hurt you or offend you."

"Understood. We are merely partners—"

"We are *not* partners." This was what he feared. "You are to play cards. You do what I say. There is no partnership here." He moved his hands back and forth to show that she had her work, and he had his.

"But if I learn something of importance—"

"*You* are to play cards."

"Even if . . . ?"

"*Cards only.* Can you not understand?"

She gave him no answer. Instead, she seemed to study some point behind him. He knew then she was never going to agree.

Ultimately, it didn't matter, he decided. Once they were at Colemore, Lady Orpington would keep her busy. Supposedly, the card playing began early in the morning and went into the night. There would be no time for her to pry.

And if he was lucky, he'd quickly find the answer to questions he didn't know to ask. Sometimes life worked that way. A man had no choice but to take action and hope for the best.

He knocked on the roof, the sign to take Gwendolyn home.

They were quiet the rest of the way. She acted lost in thought. He believed the best way to reinforce his message was to let her be.

He reminded himself that the Lanscarr sisters were not afraid to defy convention. That had been the secret to their success. Well, that and tremendous luck.

They were like beautiful pirates who had set sail to conquer the *ton*, and conquer they had.

But this battle was his. He was the captain of this ship.

The coach rolled to a halt, and he peeked out of the shades to see they were in front of the Brogan residence. Beck reached for his hat so that he could help Gwendolyn down from the coach.

She stopped him with a hand on his arm. "You mustn't. I am certain my sister is watching for me. She will be upset if she believes I have been riding alone with you."

Well, at least she had that good sense.

The coach's footman opened the door and put down the stool. Gwendolyn started from the vehicle, but then stopped. She looked back at Beck.

"I shall behave," she whispered, "because this means a great deal to you. However, you are wrong about the two of us. You can't fight what already exists any more than you can stop dreams of your mother from haunting you."

"Gwendolyn—" he started to correct her, frustrated by her stubbornness. But she was already out the door. Her manservant stood in the open portal of the house. She disappeared inside.

The footman picked up the stool. "Is all good, sir?"

"Fine," Beck answered absently . . . but he knew that wasn't true, because Gwendolyn was right.

What was between them already existed.

CHAPTER SIX

Of course Dara had questions for Gwendolyn when she walked in the door, the most immediate one being, "Did Mr. Steele make an appearance?"

Gwendolyn took her time removing her bonnet and gloves. She handed them to Molly, who waited to carry them upstairs, because apparently she was interested in the answer as well. Even Herald lingered. Carefully Gwendolyn said, "I met Lady Orpington's nephew. Mr. Curran."

"Oh," Dara said brightening. "That is interesting. I didn't know she had a nephew. However, was Mr. Steele there?"

"Mr. Curran was the only man in the room." Gwendolyn didn't like her little fib, except she was tired of Dara dictating what she should and shouldn't do.

In truth, Gwendolyn often deferred to Dara. She kept the peace by going along . . . but not on this matter. She would not let Dara interfere when her heart was involved, a heart that Mr. Steele wished to reject.

Fortunately, Dara didn't press the matter. Instead, her active mind leaped to, "What did Lady Orpington want?"

"To invite me to Colemore for their house party next week."

If an earthquake had shaken the very foundations of the house, Dara could not have acted more astounded. *"Colemore?"*

Gwendolyn nodded.

Her sister danced a jig. "Gwendolyn, this is spectacular. The people you will meet! The opportunities. I am so happy for you. The Marquess and Marchioness of Middlebury are the very cream of the cream. They are even more important than Lady Orpington. Did you know that a member of the Chaytor family rode with William the Conqueror? They say that he was the Conqueror's right hand, and many of the laws and rites we accept today were designed by him. They say he even helped lay out London's streets. No one outranks them, not even the House of Hanover."

"They are more important than the king?" Gwendolyn said, not believing it.

"Oh, yes. Their bloodlines are pure."

Gwendolyn made a dismissive noise. "I find it disturbing, Dara, when you talk about people as if they are broodmares." She started for the back sitting room. Of course her sister followed.

"In many ways we are," Dara opined.

Gwendolyn hummed an answer. Herald had followed them and asked, "Tea? Sherry?"

"Definitely sherry," Gwendolyn said. She went into the room and sat in a rocker chair. She closed her eyes. Her knee had brushed Mr. Steele's thigh repeatedly during their journey. Except for the almost kiss in Dublin, she had never been so close to him. His shaving soap had a hint of spice. The scent of it would be what she dreamed about.

"Just to be certain I understand," Dara said, interrupting Gwendolyn's thoughts, "*you* have been invited to the Colemore house party?" She was perched on the settee adjacent to the rocker.

"Yes. Lady Orpington will pick me up on Wednesday."

"I don't mean to sound as if I'm doubting you are worthy. You know that. But why? Out of the goodness of her heart?"

"She wants me to be her whist partner." Gwendolyn told her sister of her ladyship's desire to best Lady Middlebury while Herald brought in sherry and poured a glass for each. He withdrew from the room. Great-Aunt Tweedie had gotten the sisters in the habit of an afternoon sherry now that, because of Michael, they had the money to enjoy it.

"She could not have found a better partner," Dara said. "How did she know of you?"

"Mr. Steele."

Dara scowled as if this was what she feared. "Mr. Steele?"

"Yes, the invitation to the house party is the one he told me to expect."

Dara sat still a moment. "I thought," she said carefully, "that Lady Orpington's invitation was the one to which he referred?"

"It was," Gwendolyn answered breezily. "But then she invited me to Colemore as her partner."

There was another heavy silence. Then—"And he was *not* at Lady Orpington's?"

Gwendolyn did not hesitate this time in saying, "He was not."

Her sister studied her. Gwendolyn ignored the accusing stare by focusing on her glass of sherry. She might need a second one if Dara kept this up.

Dara broke the silence. "So, what is this Mr. Curran like? Do you think he has possibilities? If so, I can see what I can learn about him." Dara was very good at research. She devoured the social columns for tidbits on the illustrious people. That was how she knew every detail of Viscount Morley's prospects.

"None whatsoever," Gwendolyn replied, because it was the best answer. She set her empty sherry glass on a side table and stood. "I believe I shall go read." It seemed the only sensible thing to do after such a frustrating conversation with Mr. Steele.

"Read? Oh, no, we have work to do. We must plot out what you shall be wearing. For one, you will need a habit," Dara said, proving to Gwendolyn that there were times when her younger sister did know best. "You have been saying you wish you could ride. I imagine the Colemore stables have excellent horseflesh, and you will want to look your best. Have you heard of Lord Ellisfield?"

"I have not."

"He is the Middlebury heir and, I believe, around five and thirty."

"Have we met him around London?"

"He doesn't attend balls or take part in the Season," Dara said. "However, he is one of the most eligible bachelors in the kingdom. They say he is very handsome. I have never met him, but when so many gossips make that claim, it is probably true."

"Dara—"

"I know. You are not interested. But there may be someone at Colemore who will spark your interest, and you will wish to look your best."

Gwendolyn thought of Mr. Steele, and she smiled. "Where do you suggest we start?"

"You need a new day dress and, of course, several for country dinners. Of course, a new shawl or two can liven a dress." Dara reached for their small collection of *The Lady's Magazine* stacked on a side table. It had fashion plates of the latest styles. The sisters used them as a pattern for their dresses in spite of them being a year or two out of date. However, they lived in London. They noted what was all the rage and gave it a bit of their own individual flair. For example, Gwendolyn preferred white and light pastel colors. She kept her designs simple, and it worked for her.

A few hours later, Tweedie found them with their heads together, sketching out a riding habit with gold-covered buttons and braiding that would have made any officer envious.

In two days' time, Michael returned home from his trip to Ireland to see that the riding habit was almost finished.

He was impressed with the news that Gwendolyn would be off to Colemore. "If you have the chance," he said, "encourage Lord Middlebury to see to his duties in the Lords. His presence is much missed. Occasionally he sends Ellisfield, but not often enough."

Dara lit up at the mention of Lord Ellisfield. "Making Michael's request will give you the opportunity to catch Lord Ellisfield's attention. He'll definitely notice you then."

"Do you think either he or his father will listen to me?" Gwendolyn wondered.

"He hasn't listened to any of our entreaties," Michael answered. "You may have more sway. Especially in that blue habit."

"*Marine* blue," she corrected him, but she knew he was right. She wore the habit well. Dara had even insisted they purchase a hunting hat that was a feminized version of the one men wore. Gwendolyn had spent a morning sewing a gold ribbon band and pheasant feathers to it. She adored the outfit's sporting look.

Through all their preparations, Lady Orpington sent daily invites for Gwendolyn to play cards. This meant that Dara cut and sewed the dresses practically herself. She didn't complain. For all of Dara's managing ways, she was truly quite generous and wanted what was best for Gwendolyn.

And so it was that by Wednesday, Gwendolyn had a wardrobe that would do her proud. She couldn't wait for Mr. Steele to see her in the riding habit.

For travel, she chose a day dress of green-and-lavender sprigs on a light amber background that brought a glow to her skin. She wore an emerald pelisse over it.

Her ladyship sent a coach for Gwendolyn's luggage and Molly early that morning. Her ladyship's personal coach arrived at ten o'clock sharp.

Gwendolyn took a moment to introduce Lady Orpington and Mrs. Newsome and even Magpie to Dara and Tweedie, and then, with much waving and Dara's calls for them to enjoy safe travels, they were off.

They were barely to the end of the street before Gwendolyn asked, "Where is Mr. Curran? I thought he would be traveling with us."

She had not seen Mr. Steele since their coach ride together.

"Nicholas?" Lady Orpington made a dismissive sound. She was busy directing Mrs. Newsome on how to set up the traveling card table while holding Magpie up and out of the way. Apparently they would play whist all the way to Colemore. "He'll be along. You know how gentlemen are. They like to ride ahead." The table up, she plunked Magpie into Mrs. Newsome's lap, right on her knitting. "You shall play the two hands against Vera and me."

"But he *will* be joining us?" The thought had struck Gwendolyn the night before that Mr. Steele might change his plans. She didn't want that to happen. Not until he'd seen her in the riding habit. Her purpose might be to play cards, but her goal was to bring the man to his knees, if at all possible.

"I suppose he will be joining us," Lady Orpington answered. "Now, shall we play cards?"

Gwendolyn sighed and agreed.

They would be on the road for a good six hours. Colemore was in Kent. It wasn't that far, but Magpie required numerous stops. Gwendolyn began to wonder if there was something very wrong with the dog. "No, she just likes to wee," a slightly flustered Mrs. Newsome assured her. "Since Charles's death, the world revolves around this dog, and Magpie takes full advantage. I'm surprised she doesn't expect to be spoon-fed. My cousin would do so."

They stopped by a winding brook for a lunch set up by the footmen. There were a table, chairs, white linens, and an excellent repast of cold chicken, fruit, cheese, and bread. It was all washed down with a sweet cider.

On the road after such a repast, Lady Orpington opened a book, and both she and Magpie promptly fell asleep over it. Mrs. Newsome had returned to her knitting, although she didn't seem to be much further along on the brown blanket than she had been last week. She stopped often to pick out stray Magpie hairs.

Gwendolyn's intention was to stay alert for Mr. Steele . . . although she had not been sleeping well. The card playing, the dressmaking, the adventure of her trip, coupled with the mystery that was Mr. Steele kept her awake at night. Even if she'd been tired when she'd turned to her bed, all the what-ifs had kept her awake.

Until now.

It must have been the movement of the coach. She didn't even remember dropping off into a deep sleep. It had just happened. One moment she was watching Mrs. Newsome's fingers work her knitting needles, and in the next . . . *she was riding a horse alongside a coach rolling through the woods. She was wearing the new habit, but her main concern was, where was Mr. Steele? She'd expected him to be in the coach, but no one was there. And then she heard his low, rumbling voice, and she tried to turn toward him—*

Gwendolyn came awake with a small gasp for air that sounded suspiciously like a snort. A ladylike snort, but a snort all the same.

She was scrunched in the corner of the coach. Her head had been bent at an awkward angle, and she feared that her mouth had been gaping open.

Glancing around, she groggily realized that the coach wasn't moving, and her two companions weren't with her.

Gwendolyn sat up and then heard Lady Orpington say, "You may ride inside with us."

"I'm fine on my horse." The speaker was Mr. Steele.

The sound of his voice had not been a dream. He was here, and Gwendolyn's immediate fear was that he had looked in the coach and seen her sleeping as if she was some fishmonger's wife dozing in the sun.

She attempted to check her appearance. Her first action was to be certain she no longer had drool on the corner of her mouth. Some pins had come loose in her hair. She began pushing them in—

"Miss Lanscarr, you are awake." Mrs. Newsome had poked her head in the coach. "Mr. Curran is here. Come join us. We were just taking a moment to stretch our legs and to give Magpie another break before we set off again."

"Yes, of course." Gwendolyn still sounded somewhat dazed. She reached for her bonnet from a hook on the wall and put a foot out on the step beside the coach.

Lady Orpington was already walking down the road away from the coach with Mr. Steele at her side. His back was to her. A footman followed with Magpie on a leash. The dog was not being obedient. Lady Orpington was oblivious.

Mr. Steele did not glance Gwendolyn's way.

"Would you care to walk a bit with me?" Mrs. Newsome asked.

Her question made Gwendolyn realize she was staring at Mr. Steele's retreating figure and probably with an anxious expression on her face. Embarrassed to be so discombobulated, she nodded to the kind older lady and tied the ribbons of her bonnet under her chin.

Mrs. Newsome didn't wait but began walking in the opposite direction Lady Orpington had taken. Gwendolyn hurried to catch her.

Mr. Steele was here. He'd finally arrived . . . and he was ignoring her. Gwendolyn knew that as clearly as she knew her own name. Even though Lady Orpington had given her a nod, Mr. Steele hadn't glanced in her direction, not even to say hello. Assuredly Lady Orpington's nephew Mr. Curran would have done so. It was only the polite thing to do.

In fact, his rudeness incensed Gwendolyn. Yes, he'd said that there was nothing between them, but that was *not true.* She'd caught the way he looked at her when he didn't think she was watching. Granted, they hadn't been around each other often—

"You can do much better," Mrs. Newsome said in her perpetually pleasant voice.

"Much better than what?" Gwendolyn grumbled, knowing what she meant.

Apparently Mrs. Newsome understood that as well, because she didn't explain. Instead she said, "We shall be at Colemore in an hour or so. You will make a good impression. You are a lovely young woman but also a self-possessed one. Very few people can hold their own around my cousin. She is quite imperial."

"That is true."

"However, you don't bow to her. At the same time, you treat her with respect. She thinks highly of you. I do, too."

Gwendolyn murmured a thank-you. The Lanscarr sisters had been bred to be well-behaved.

And then Mrs. Newsome said, "If you want Nicholas, you need to push him away."

"That seems counterproductive."

"Most men are counter-everything. Or at least, that has been my experience. Miss Lanscarr, it is not my place to offer advice, but I feel I must. You wear your heart on your sleeve, and that is not where it belongs. First, Nicholas is—" She paused as if searching for a word, then said, "Well, he might be a good man, but he seems rather feral."

The description startled Gwendolyn. "What does that mean?"

"It means he believes he doesn't need anyone. That happens sometimes when people are forced to rely on their own instincts. It is not an uncommon trait amongst men. They become either jaded or too confident in their own opinions. Sometimes both."

"But feral?"

"Born in the wild. Left to his own devices. Same difference, wouldn't you agree?" She didn't wait for an answer but said, "You and Nicholas met before he entered into this arrangement with my cousin. You are not strangers to each other."

"Why do you say that?"

"The way his expression softened when he saw you sleeping in the coach. If it is any consolation, he'd been looking for you."

The information was comforting and panic-inducing at the same time. "I was not at my best."

Mrs. Newsome laughed. "You looked charming."

"My mouth was open. I was sleeping with my mouth open."

"Yes, it is very human." She paused before saying, "But don't make the mistake of thinking he is the only man for you. Because he has a purpose in mind. Until he gets what he wants, there is no room for anyone in his life."

Her words echoed Mr. Steele's warning.

Coming from her, they also made sense. She was telling Gwendolyn to be wise.

And yet every fiber of Gwendolyn's being rejected them.

"Be careful, Miss Lanscarr. I see our Nicholas's attraction. He's handsome and, yes, a touch dangerous. That is an allure, is it not? But he lives on the fringes of Society for a reason. If you pursue him, you might catch him, and you may regret doing so."

Gwendolyn studied the ground, noticing the clover growing along the road among the grass. The toe of her walking shoe kicked a gray pebble. She looked over to Mrs. Newsome. "Why are you telling me this?"

"Because my cousin and I are growing fond of you. You have given her hope to reclaim her husband's honor. I have not seen her this animated since before his death. I, too, want you to defeat Lady Middlebury."

"Because?"

It was Mrs. Newsome's turn to look away, her expression pensive as if she debated something. Then she said, "You will understand when you meet Lady Middlebury. My cousin makes excuses for her old friend, but the truth is, she is unkind. She isn't a comfortable woman."

Gwendolyn frowned, uncertain of what she meant, but then Lady Orpington called out, "Come, Vera. We must be leaving."

Turning, Gwendolyn saw that Mr. Steele was already mounted. The horse was a bay without a touch of white. Mr. Steele was dressed in a black riding jacket and black breeches with black boots. This was the man she knew. One who liked to blend into the shadows.

And yet he appeared the perfect picture of a Corinthian and his beast. The horse pranced as if anxious to go. Mr. Steele held his seat, as relaxed as if the horse was standing still.

Of course he would be an excellent rider.

One more thing to admire about him.

At her shoulder, Mrs. Newsome said quietly, almost urgently, "Also, I, too, once loved a man who wouldn't promise to commit to me. At the time, I believed I loved him enough for both of us. I knew he cared about me as much as he could any other person."

"Did it work?"

"Well, he married me."

"And?"

"I loved him. Although I don't believe he was ever happy or content. Too many demons surrounded him."

"Where did that leave you?"

"Here, doing my cousin's bidding. He left me because I wasn't enough." Mrs. Newsome took Gwendolyn's arm, and they started back to the coach.

When they were still not in earshot of the coach, Mrs. Newsome leaned close to Gwendolyn and whispered, "I always wished he'd been fully mine. I regret I did not choose more wisely. Commitment is important, Miss Lanscarr. Commitment is all. Remember that."

$\mathcal{B}$eck watched as the footman helped Mrs. Newsome and Gwendolyn into the coach to join Lady Orpington. Gwendolyn didn't look at him, not even to nod hello.

That was what he had wanted, he reminded himself. He'd told her to keep her distance, and she was. He'd even chosen to see his own way to Colemore instead of riding with the ladies.

Yes, this was what he wanted . . . except he discovered he didn't like it. He'd had a taste of Gwendolyn's bright, inquisitive mind, and he found he wanted more. He'd spent the last week thinking about their conversation and replaying it in his mind.

The coach started forward. Beck's intention was to ride ahead. Instead, he rode beside it. He could claim to be a guard, but they didn't need one. Not with this many footmen, and not in Kent.

No, he rode beside the coach because Gwendolyn was there . . . and also because he couldn't make himself charge forward. The reason for that was complicated.

Beck had known of Colemore since his school days. The Faircote headmaster was aware of his connection to the marquess. After all, the school payments had come from him. The headmaster had once mentioned the estate. Here was a connection to his unseen father, and Beck had become determined to learn all he could about it.

That had not been a difficult task. Colemore had an almost mythical status among the English. It was said to be the finest property in all Britain. Perhaps even the world.

These pronouncements had fed Beck's young imagination. He'd tried to picture what his father's home looked like. He'd found a book titled *A Tour of Colemore and Its Gardens*, a collection of essays written about the estate in the early 1700s by the rector of St. Albion's church. Beck had even seen drawings of the church, knew it was of Norman origins and within four miles of Colemore.

However, now that the moment was at hand when he would see this great estate for himself, Beck felt conflicted.

What was it Gwendolyn had suggested? That she understood *having a desire for family*?

He had given deep thought to that statement. Families were a mystery to him. Perhaps that was one of the reasons he found Gwendolyn and her sisters' very strong bonds a curiosity. He couldn't imagine them abandoning each other. Or one of them abandoning their child.

In the dream, he felt as if he had to reach the woman to save her. He always woke before he knew why she was frightened. And he wondered if that fear was what had held her from him.

Now he was about to meet the father who had kept him at a distance. Gwendolyn had suggested meeting the marquess was Beck's sole reason for going to Colemore. Her suggestion troubled him . . . because it might be true.

Beck decided he was being ridiculous. All of this thinking—about the dream, his father, Gwendolyn—was making him morose. He kicked his horse forward and yet fell back to ride alongside the coach again.

The vehicle began to slow. They turned down a country lane. Beck had no choice but to move forward or else ride in the coach's dust. They traveled for a mile and then came another turn. A stone post marked the road. Carved into it was the word *Colemore*.

They had arrived.

A sense of apprehension settled on his shoulders. He didn't understand it. He was arriving at Colemore disguised by another name. No one here knew him or had even laid eyes on him as far as he knew.

The bay took an anxious step as if picking up on Beck's uncertainty. He sat deeper in his seat and told himself there was nothing to fear. He was a man of war. Whatever lay ahead, he could manage it.

And he would protect the women in the coach. He'd even watch out for that ridiculous dog.

All was safe.

He kicked the gelding forward.

The road was as rutted as the country lane and meandered through a surprisingly heavy forest. Lady Orpington had leaned out of the coach window to shout to Beck that it was going to be at least an hour more of travel.

"Are we on Colemore property?" he asked.

"Oh, yes. Middlebury owns this all the way to the river," she answered, and then sat back in her seat as overhanging branches threatened to whop her in the face. Beck ducked them and pushed his horse to pick a way along the road using the woods.

He heard Gwendolyn say in that crisp manner of hers, "I've heard talk of the magnificence of this estate. It seems more like an untamed wood."

"Parts of it is," Lady Orpington answered. "But just wait."

The window shades were up, and from inside the coach, Gwendolyn looked over to Beck. Then she almost made him laugh when she rolled her eyes heavenward. He understood. The rich were eccentric.

They went around a bend, and the road smoothed out into a well-graded drive, one wide enough to accommodate two coaches. It was better than any post road.

Fifteen minutes later, they came upon a manicured lawn. Green grass stretched out around them to its forest border.

The change was so abrupt that Beck made a sound of surprise, and Lady Orpington chuckled. "More to your liking, eh? The marquess has some queer notions about privacy. He feels that having an overgrown entrance will keep the common folk at bay. I'll warn you, he is odd. And his little forest ruse doesn't fool anyone. Everyone knows that a mile down the way is the true beginning of the estate."

"He must have a battalion of gardeners," Beck said.

"Two battalions," Lady Orpington answered. "The man is as wealthy as Croesus."

"Is he as vain?" Beck asked. Hubris had been what had destroyed Croesus.

"I shall let you answer that for yourself, Nicholas," she replied.

Gwendolyn sat forward. "Look," she said with delight and pointed to a sculpture out on the lawn. A graceful bronze stag was frozen in flight as it leaped into the air. Its hooves shone with gold. "That is lovely."

"Look close," Lady Orpington said. "Do you see the dogs?"

Beck trotted ahead so he could see over the coach team. He studied the lawn and the distant line of trees.

Gwendolyn was doing the same, because she called out, "I see them. There, off to the left as if approaching the deer."

He saw them then, a pack of bronze hounds running as if they could capture their quarry. Several had tongues hanging out, and their ears were flying. Their paws barely touched the ground. They were more of a marvel than the stag.

"The fourth Marquess of Middlebury had them made, the brother of this one. He appreci-

ated art, as did his father, the third marquess,"
Lady Orpington explained. "They say the third
was inordinately proud of his deer. Then one day,
he came riding out, and there was the dog pack.
His son, the fourth," she said helpfully so that
they could follow her story, "had them made to
tease his father. I've heard it said that the fourth
had a playful sense of humor, and it must be true.
Every time I see those dogs chasing the deer, I
smile. Those who knew the fourth admired him
greatly. He was very successful at promoting the
Whig agenda. So unlike his brother, who doesn't
step a foot into Parliament or anywhere beyond
Colemore."

Beck had fallen into line beside them, interested in the gossip about this family he did
not know. Now that he was on their land, their
presence, their personalities, took on a stronger
meaning.

"Was the older brother much older?" Gwendolyn asked.

"No, just a few years."

"Then this marquess is the fifth, correct?" Gwendolyn asked.

"Do not forget the fourth, and his marchioness
had a son. He hadn't been born more than a month
when his father died. He was the fifth marquess.
The current one is the sixth." She lifted Magpie to
clutch against her as if needing the solace of her
pet. Magpie growled a response. She lowered the
dog to her lap.

Gwendolyn remembered. "The mother *and* the
son died, correct? How did it happen?"

"I can't remember the details. Franny does

not like to talk about it." Lady Orpington ran a gloved hand along Magpie's thick fur. "She and Middlebury used to be quite social before the tragedies. Afterward they were in mourning for several years. And then they started their house party," she finished on a brighter note.

Beck wondered if grief could be a reason his father kept his distance from London. Could grief have caused him to disavow Beck instead of shame, as he'd believed?

"The family's tragedies are all quite sobering," Lady Orpington said. She slipped her fingers under Magpie's onyx-covered collar and gave her a scratch. "None of us knows how many hours we have on this earth. I never expected Charles to die, and yet he did." Tears filled her eyes. Gwendolyn leaned forward to touch her hand, her features softening.

Beck frowned. Much more of this and he'd have a coach of weepy women. Well, save for Mrs. Newsome. She was dry-eyed.

And then Lady Orpington brightened. "Although matters did work out well for Franny," she said. "She'd married a second son, but now her husband is the sixth marquess. Her rank is well above mine and almost everyone else we knew back in those days. She also has *two* sons, and so the inheritance in her line is ensured."

Gwendolyn spoke up. "Lord Ellisfield. He is the heir."

"Have you met him?" Mrs. Newsome asked. Beck wanted to know the answer, too.

"No, I have not," Gwendolyn answered. "However, my sister claims, as she does for several gentlemen, that he is the most eligible bachelor in London."

"Just like his late uncle," Lady Orpington agreed.

"Although he didn't make an appearance over the Season at any of the affairs my sisters and I attended," Gwendolyn said. "At least, I was never introduced to him."

"And you may not meet him here. He often doesn't attend." Lady Orpington scratched Magpie's ear while the dog opened his mouth for a yawn and then a sneeze. "Oh goodness," her ladyship said in a squealy voice as if the dog had done something brilliant.

Beck liked dogs. He wasn't certain he liked Magpie. The dog had tried to chew on his boot when he'd visited with Lady Orpington the other day, and she'd used the same squealy voice to chastise him. It hadn't deterred Magpie's behavior. Instead, Beck had waited until her ladyship was looking away and given the dog a good shake of his boot. Magpie had retreated.

Lady Orpington smiled out the window up at Beck. "We are coming to the crook in the drive. It won't be long now—oh, wait, *what*?" She was looking beyond him.

Immediately Beck turned in that direction to see what had upset her. A group of riders had burst from the woods and were riding at a tear directly for the coach. They showed no signs of reining in even as they closed in on Lady Orpington's team. Instead they seemed to charge harder.

The coach horses immediately sensed a threat.

They tried to turn to confront the other horses. When they couldn't, when the driver stood to hold them, one began bucking in his traces.

Beck expected the riders to come to a halt. They didn't. When he realized what was about to happen, he jumped from his saddle, dropping his reins, and ran to the lead horses just as an oncoming rider sent his horse, a powerful chestnut, up in the air to jump over the team.

The other riders had pulled up. They now cheered as the chestnut seemed to fly through the air, man and beast as one.

Of course, the action sent Lady Orpington's team into a panic.

Beck had grabbed the lead horses' cheek straps and, using the weight of his body and the command of his presence, pulled their heads down to prevent them from shying or bolting.

The jumper landed heavily on the other side of the road. His friends began shouting and clapping.

And Beck vowed that once he had this team under control, he would pull the heads off of every fool who had thought this was a great idea.

Lady Orpington's team wanted to bolt. They didn't because Beck and the driver wouldn't let them. One stamped on Beck's foot, but he kept his hold.

And then it was quiet.

"Good horses," Beck said in a low voice as the footman in the driver's box leaped down to help him. Together, along with the driver, they managed to settle the team.

Gwendolyn opened the coach door and hopped out. She ran to the back of the vehicle. Concerned for the women, Beck gave over the handling of the team to the servants and went after her.

She was bent over a footman who had fallen off the coach. The moaning man held his arm. She looked up at Beck. "I think it is broken."

"You are right," he agreed, his disgust now complete. There was no broken skin, but the man was in too much pain for there to not be a break. He helped him up.

Lady Orpington leaned out of the coach window. "Have Evers come here," she said, referring to the footman. "You shall ride with us until we can find help."

"Thank you, my lady," the servant said, and Gwendolyn helped him to the door.

"Now I can set the step for you," she told him. She turned to fetch the small stool from its place on the coach.

"No cause, Miss Lanscarr. I can step in." And he did even though Magpie growled her disdain.

Beck shifted his focus to the riders. They had joined their champion on the other side of the road. Beck began walking toward the chestnut's rider, who had lost his hat during the jump. He was a blond-headed man with laughing blue eyes. He apparently had thought that this was all just good fun. He began riding toward Beck, a huge smile on his face.

His friends, a group of three men, followed. They were in good humor, and Beck realized why once he was close enough to catch the whiff of brandy fumes all around them. So it didn't bother him to reach up for the blond rider and jerk him off his horse with one hand.

The rider tumbled to the dirt.

"*That is Ellisfield,*" one of the trio shouted in outrage.

Beck didn't care if it was the King of England. "Beg my pardon," he responded and grabbed Ellisfield by his jacket to yank the befuddled man up to his feet.

Behind him, Lady Orpington leaned out of the open coach door. "*Nicholas.* That is the son of our host. Stop it."

Beck did not acknowledge her words. His plan was to put his fist in Ellisfield's face. See if the man would like to jump after that.

The trio of riders just stared dumbfounded without lifting a finger to stop Beck.

And yet someone tugged on the arm he had pulled back. It was Gwendolyn. "I think you have made your point, Mr. Curran."

He frowned. "I'm only beginning."

"I see that," she said, looking up at him. "But you are very direct, and perhaps we should let the matter stand since everyone is somewhat all right?"

The wisdom of her calm words broke the tension inside him. Sanity returned.

He looked at Ellisfield. He still had his hand clamped around the lapel of the man's riding jacket—but his lordship wasn't looking at Beck. No, he was staring at Gwendolyn as if he had never seen a more beautiful woman.

She wasn't wearing a bonnet because she hadn't bothered with niceties when she'd left the coach to help the footman. Her cheeks were flushed, while several dark strands of her thick hair had come loose from their pins and curled around her shoulders. As disheveled as she was, she looked delectable. Enough so that Ellisfield and his companions had gone speechless.

Now Beck truly did want to give the man a thrashing so he'd keep his eyes to himself. Except, as Lady Orpington had pointed out, Middlebury might not appreciate Beck teaching his son manners. He released his hold. "I'm done," he said to Gwendolyn.

"Thank you," she said with a radiant smile that made him feel ridiculously pleased with himself, until he realized that Ellisfield and his friends were all as enchanted as he was.

"Please return to the coach," Beck said.

Gwendolyn looked at him, then at the others, and shook her head. "Very well." He watched her retreat to the vehicle.

The trio of friends began to make angry noises at Beck, but Ellisfield held up a hand as if warning them to be quiet.

He turned to Beck, his expression remarkably sober, even though it was obvious he had been drinking a great deal. However, he appeared to realize just how foolish he'd been. "Accept my apology?"

Beck wasn't going to let this be easy. "For what? For being reckless and dangerously stupid? And it was Miss Lanscarr's life, along with Lady Orpington's and her companion's, that you endangered. Not to mention breaking a foot-man's arm. They are the ones due an apology."

Too late, Beck realized exactly how poorly he was handling this.

But Ellisfield didn't take offense. He was al-most as tall as Beck and perhaps a few years older. He had the golden, blue-eyed, masculine looks women seemed to admire. He gave a bark of laughter. "You are right." He now trotted his handsome self after Gwendolyn, who had not yet reached the coach. He caught up with her, moved in front of her, blocking her path. He bowed. "Please accept my apology for being 'reckless and dangerously stupid.'"

Beck suspected he'd quoted him as a jibe. However, before Gwendolyn could respond, Lady Orpington, who had climbed out of the coach and walked over to them with Magpie in her arms, trilled happily, "My lord, this is my card partner, Miss Lanscarr."

The dog growled at Ellisfield as he growled at everyone, but Beck felt it was fitting in this circumstance. He hoped Magpie chewed on El-lisfield's boot as well.

"My dear godmother," Ellisfield replied, bow-ing respectfully. "Please forgive me. I'm bored and, perhaps, have been imbibing too much."

"Perhaps?" Lady Orpington queried. "The fumes are all around you. Come, I have a footman who has been injured by your sporting fun. We need to find him help."

"I will be happy to accompany you," his lord-ship said. "And Miss Lanscarr, the pleasure is mine to meet you. I have heard of the Lanscarr sisters. They did not exaggerate when they acclaimed your beauty."

Beck cringed at the flowery words that tripped off Ellisfield's tongue. They sounded false to his ear and too ingratiating.

However, to his horror, Gwendolyn made a small curtsy, lowering her lashes down over her eyes so they brushed her cheeks. "You are most flattering, my lord."

Ellisfield was smitten.

Beck could feel it in the air. Gwendolyn had effortlessly conquered him.

He should have busted his lordship in the nose when he'd had a chance. That would have changed his looks.

"Come, let me accompany you to the house, Godmother, so that we can see to your man." Ellisfield helped Lady Orpington and Gwendolyn into the coach. He threw over his shoulder, "Come, lads." His friends moved their horses forward as if they were cavaliers accompanying the King of France. Ellisfield squeezed himself into the overpacked coach—right next to Gwendolyn.

Lady Orpington suddenly leaned out the window. "Ellisfield, I almost forgot. I want to introduce you to my nephew, Nicholas Curran."

From inside the coach, his lordship's voice called out. "Pleasure is mine, Curran. See to my horse, will you? Ride him to the house, and a stable lad will take care of him." Lady Orpington trilled a laugh as if Ellisfield was clever and gallant . . . in giving Beck orders. She ducked back inside the vehicle.

Beck watched the coach roll away in disbelief.

His bay had been tied to the rear of the coach, and even he went happily along with Lord Ellisfield.

And he was stuck with the chestnut.

Raking his fingers through his hair, Beck wondered where the devil the hat he'd paid a small fortune for had disappeared. He walked back to Ellisfield's horse and took the reins. The animal was sweaty, its head low as if exhausted. Beck took the reins. He found his hat beside the road. A horse had stepped on it.

He slapped the hat back into shape, put it on his head, and mounted the chestnut. After a few steps, he dismounted. The animal was limping slightly as if it had come down wrong after taking that jump. With a heavy sigh, Beck began leading the horse to the house. The chestnut bumped him with his nose as if in gratitude. "I'd be thankful not to have that arse on my back, too," Beck muttered in agreement.

The road took them up a knoll, and at the height of it, Beck came to a halt.

Colemore was spread out before him. His father's home.

A palace would be smaller. However, it wasn't the size of the manse that made him think of royalty. It was the whole scene—sunlight bouncing off a pair of stone gates leading to a stately yellow brick home with sizeable wings off the main building. A row of white columns framed the facade. The front drive was busy with guests, servants, and dogs. A bevy of footmen came running to meet Lady Orpington's coach. Beyond the house were gardens, trees, and a pond in the distance.

And this could have been his home, if he'd been born on the right side of the covers.

He stood, wondering if he should be feeling jealousy or anger. Or even a sense of homecoming. Would they not be understandable emotions considering history and his station in life?

No. All he experienced was a rather detached interest, the sort of feeling any traveler would have upon reaching his destination. The house was grand and admirable for what it was. However, Colemore didn't call to him. There was no filial yearning deep in his soul or sense that, at long last, he was where he was destined to be.

Instead, Beck watched as Lord Ellisfield helped first his godmother, then Mrs. Newsome, and finally Gwendolyn out of the coach. The man hovered around her as he walked her toward the door, his step apace with hers. He placed a gloved hand on her elbow as if claiming her. That sparked an emotion in Beck.

"Bastard," he muttered.

The chestnut gave him another agreeing nudge.

Beck made his way down the knoll and through the stone gates of Colemore. A young stable lad ran up to him to claim the horse. "His lordship said you were coming," the boy said. Beck handed over the reins and began walking toward a massive wooden door beneath the house's center columns.

A woman stood in the doorway, greeting guests and directing servants. She was elegant, stately, and completely in her element. The sun that lit the planes of the house caught the fading strands of gold mixed in through the white of her hair, and yet there were few lines on her face. She had light blue eyes, much like Ellisfield's. Beck knew just by her sense of command that this must be the Marchioness of Middlebury.

And his immediate reaction to her was intensely visceral, to the point he took a step back.

He did not like her. He didn't know her, but he would not trust her.

Almost as if she sensed his presence, she slowly turned. Their gazes met, and her smile widened . . . but it did not meet her eyes. There was no greeting for him in them. If anything, she had the calculating look of a French general deciding where to set the bayonet line.

"Welcome to Colemore, Mr. Curran," she said as if she'd been expecting him. Her tone was cultured. She enunciated carefully.

Then she waved someone forward who was apparently standing close to the doorway. The woman came at her hostess's bidding. "Please, sir," Lady Middlebury said, "you remember Lady Rabron? She and her husband are new to our party this year as well, and I believe she is an old friend?"

Beck swung his attention to the other guest and froze. Lady Rabron was Violet Danvers, the woman who had rejected his love because he hadn't been good enough for her family. He had not bothered to learn her married name or the title she had sold herself for.

Violet was older now, but still lovely in that fawnlike way of hers. Her eyes widened in mutual recognition. She started to say something, but before she could, Lady Middlebury cut in, "Lady Rabron, this is Mr. Nicholas Curran, Lady Orpington's *long-lost* nephew who has made a sudden appearance. Fortunate for her, isn't it?"

She smiled as she spoke, and Beck was certain she knew exactly who he was. He had no idea how she had come by the information. He'd been very careful.

However, for whatever reason, she was apparently not going to call him out.

At least, not yet.

He met Violet's confused gaze, silently pleading with her to pretend, to not call him out.

There was a tense moment, and then Violet said, "It is a pleasure to meet you, Mr. Curran."

$\mathcal{G}$wendolyn wished Lord Ellisfield would leave her alone.

They stood in a crowded reception room where guests gathered to enjoy light refreshments and become acquainted while waiting to be taken to their rooms. There had to be close to fifty people milling around. Lady Orpington had turned her over to his lordship while, with an annoyed Magpie tucked under her arm, she flitted around clasping hands and kissing the cheeks of her acquaintances. Mrs. Newsome had disappeared down a hall to a room where the other companions gathered.

However, the décor of the reception room was spectacular. Angels cavorted across the ceilings and around star-shaped lamps that Lord Ellisfield said a great uncle had brought back from the Ottoman Empire. Four wall-sized tapestries depicting different stories from the Bible hung over cream walls. "Those are from when the family was more pious," Lord Ellisfield confided. He also pointed to the parquet floor. "The family crest is

inlaid in the center along with the family motto."
He said this as if she should be impressed.

She was. The flooring was lovely. A far cry from
the cold stone floors of her beloved Wiltham. She
couldn't imagine how much parquet cost to keep.
"What is the motto?" she asked politely.

"We reign forever," he said proudly, and she
smiled, because it wasn't a very interesting motto
as far as those things went.

She had to admit that Lord Ellisfield was a remarkably handsome man with his square jaw,
fair hair, and even features. Considering the few
portraits she had noticed upon entering Colemore
through its baronial entrance hall, he was one of
a long line of attractive people. She could almost
hear Dara's enthusiasm at the attention he was
paying her. He also acted sincere, if one discounted
the waft of drink and horses on his person.

Or that he had endangered everyone in the
coach by doing something infantile. Gwendolyn
was not a fan of immaturity.

She also tried not to keep looking at the door,
hoping Mr. Steele would join them soon. She
feared she was in need of rescuing.

Maybe because of the drink, Lord Ellisfield
didn't notice her distracted air. Instead, he enthu-
siastically wished her to befriend his three riding
companions, who seemed to follow him around
like Magpie trailed after Lady Orpington. "This
is Mr. Penrose Mason—"

A somewhat pudgy man, with thin hair that
he wore swept forward, bowed over her hand.
"Mr. Mason," she said in acknowledgment.

He blushed furiously. However, he responded

in a bored, affected drawl that annoyed her. "Misss Lannnsssscarr."

"And this is Captain Royce McGrath—" Lord Ellisfield continued.

The sandy-haired captain wore a uniform jacket of what seemed to be his own design since Gwendolyn had not seen anything like it before on a soldier around London. It had a collar so high, he could barely move his head. She wondered how he'd managed to ride comfortably being so propped.

"—and the Honorable Franklin," Lord Ellisfield finished.

Gwendolyn had heard of Mr. Randell. He was a Member of Parliament. Her smile was genuine as she said, "My sister is married to Michael Brogan. Perhaps you know him?"

Mr. Randell's eyebrows rose to his hairline in disdain. "The *Irish*man?"

"Yes, the well-known, highly respected, up-and-coming Irishman who is one of the leading Members of Parliament," she agreed cheerfully, adding the lilt of Ireland to her words, and Lord Ellisfield laughed.

"You take no prisoners, do you, Miss Lanscarr?" he said in admiration.

"I see no purpose to it," she replied. "Nor do I appreciate having my heritage disparaged."

"My thoughts exactly," he answered, and then smiled to himself.

"Is something amusing, my lord?" Gwendolyn asked.

"Mother said I might find myself intrigued with the house party this year. It is why she insisted I come." He waited a beat and then said, "I believe she is right."

"Miss Lanscarr intrigues you, eh?" Lady Orpington said, coming upon them. She signaled for one of the Middlebury footmen in their deep-purple-and-silver livery.

The man approached as if wary of what she wanted. "Magpie needs a walk." She shoved the dog into the man's arms. Magpie snapped her thoughts on the matter; however, the servant was quick, or prepared. He held Magpie at arm's length and made his way through the guests.

"Don't let Magpie close to one of those male hounds," Lady Orpington shouted to the man as if remembering a sudden concern. "You remember what almost happened last year."

The footman kept walking.

Gwendolyn wasn't going to ask what had almost happened last year. She was conscious of several of the guests hiding chuckles, whether at Lady Orpington's imperial manner or because they knew what had transpired.

Oblivious to anything other than her own wishes, Lady Orpington turned to them, and Gwendolyn realized that Lord Ellisfield looked upon his godmother with true affection. The expression humanized him, and perhaps he wasn't as arrogant as Gwendolyn had labeled him.

"Who intrigues whom?" a feminine, cultured voice echoed. Lady Middlebury joined their group. Lord Ellisfield's three friends quickly stepped back.

"You just wish to hear me say you are right, Mother," Lord Ellisfield answered.

"About Miss Purley?" she asked. "I came over here to let you know she and her friends have come down from upstairs." She looked to Lady Orpington and Gwendolyn. "I'm certain you have made Miss Purley's acquaintance in London. Her father is Archibald Purley."

Gwendolyn did indeed know Miss Purley.

Archibald Purley was a wealthy banker held in high esteem by Society. His daughter had been one of those who had done her best to spread malicious gossip about the Lanscarr sisters. Gwendolyn looked around the room and caught sight of not only Miss Purley but also her friends Lady Julia and Lady Beth. They followed her around the way Lord Ellisfield's friends trotted after him.

Without thinking, Gwendolyn let go a sigh of annoyance, and immediately regretted it.

"Is something the matter, Miss Lanscarr?" Lady Middlebury asked.

"The travel," Gwendolyn improvised with a small wave of her hand. "I'm certain you understand, my lady."

"Mrs. Nally, the housekeeper, will be over soon to lead you to your rooms."

"That will be excellent," Lady Orpington said. "After all, we want to be fresh for the cards this evening."

"Ah, yes, Miss Lanscarr was to be your partner," Lady Middlebury said before her expression turned carefully regretful. "Unfortunately, dear, *dear* Ellen, we aren't playing cards this year."

Lady Orpington's head snapped back as if she had been bopped on the nose. "*Why not?* We play cards *every* year. It is what we do."

"But there is nothing that says we must," the marchioness answered serenely. She might have tried to move away to see to other guests, except for Lady Orpington sliding a step into her path.

"Franny, it is what we do. We come here and play cards. I brought Miss Lanscarr with me to play cards."

The corner of their hostess's mouth tightened. "We are not this year. Excuse me. I need to see to my guests." She walked away.

Lady Orpington appeared ready to swoon from the outrage. She looked to Lord Ellisfield. "I can't believe . . . ? *No*, this can't be true."

"I know nothing about this," he replied gently.

Her ladyship righted herself. Her eyes were still puzzled and angry, but she seemed to gather herself. "Well . . ." She paused as if ready to say something else, but then repeated, "Well."

"I'll talk to her," Lord Ellisfield offered.

Lady Orpington nodded. At that moment, Lady Middlebury called her son over. "My son, I need you here for a moment." She was standing with Miss Purley, her friends, and her father.

Now it was Lord Ellisfield's turn to sigh heavily. "You will excuse me, but don't move," he said as an aside to Gwendolyn. "I will be back."

He went to join his mother, his three friends marching behind him.

As he approached his mother, Miss Purley's gaze swung to welcome him, and then widened as she caught sight of Gwendolyn. She acted surprised and then alarmed to see a Lanscarr here.

It gave Gwendolyn great pleasure to smile and give a small finger wave. Miss Purley refused to be baited. She turned her attention to Lord El-lisfield.

"She doesn't wish me to defeat her, to reestablish myself as the best player," Lady Orpington said for Gwendolyn's ears alone. "She is afraid. She knows how determined I am."

For a second, Gwendolyn thought she referred to Miss Purley, but then realized she was talking about Lady Middlebury.

"She might have other activities in mind for her guests," Gwendolyn felt she should suggest.

"*Pfffft*," was the rude reply. "She is doing this to spite me. Magpie. I need Magpie. Where is my Magpie? What did that servant do with him?" She charged off to track down her dog.

And Gwendolyn found herself alone. Fortunately, Mr. Steele entered the room. She was relieved to see him and would have smiled, until she realized he wasn't by himself. A lovely, very curvy and petite redhead walked beside him. She gazed up at him with nothing short of adoration.

To his credit, Mr. Steele appeared uncomfortable. However, the woman seemed to glow, and Gwendolyn had a sense, in that way women seemed to know things, that they were not strangers to each other.

She'd always heard that jealousy was an ugly emotion. It wasn't until this moment that Gwendolyn understood what people meant. She had never been jealous in her life, but now a mixture of anger, inadequacy, and alarm took hold of her.

She watched as the couple stopped in front of an arrogant-looking man with a beak of a nose. He was almost as tall as Mr. Steele. The three of them spoke. It appeared the woman was introducing Mr. Steele to the other man.

There was a stiffness in Mr. Steele's movements, as if he was forcing himself to be *affable*? It was a strange word to attach to him. Perhaps that is how he believed his new persona Nicholas Curran would behave . . . except instinctively she knew this was more than just discomfort. She wondered why.

She tried to catch his eye. Should she rescue him? Did he need her help?

When she couldn't make Mr. Steele notice her efforts, she did something that she wouldn't have done in other circumstances—she began walking toward the trio, intent on discovering what was going on.

Mr. Steele seemed to sense her approach since his back was to her. He half turned and motioned her forward.

"Lord and Lady Rabron," he said, "may I introduce you to Miss Lanscarr. She is Lady Orpington's whist partner."

Lord and lady. The redhead was married. Gwendolyn could have collapsed with relief.

"How interesting," Lord Rabron said, without sounding interested. His gaze barely touched her. Instead, he seemed to search the room for something that was "interesting." Or someone more worthy of his time.

Lady Rabron was not so haughty. She gave Gwendolyn a warm smile. "You must be very good at whist. I've heard tales of Lady Orpington's play." Her lashes might have been blond, but they were the longest Gwendolyn had ever seen on a woman and made her cornflower-blue eyes stand out all the more in her pale face. The effect gave her a feminine, otherworldly air that most certainly would draw men to her. Well, that and the ample bosom she proudly displayed.

"Do you play, my lady?" Gwendolyn asked politely.

Lady Rabron started to shake her head, but her husband deigned to join their conversation and answer for her. "She has no head for strategy. She wouldn't survive. I can't even teach her chess."

An urge to stomp on his arrogant foot almost overtook Gwendolyn. Lady Rabron merely smiled and gave a helpless shrug of perfect shoulders, her blue eyes searching out Mr. Steele as if she needed him to defend her.

Gwendolyn's jealousy came roaring back because she couldn't have acted defenseless if her life had depended upon it. She also had little patience for women who became fluttery and silly in the face of rude men. Especially those to whom they were married. It seemed to her that marriage should give a woman some agency over telling her husband when he was disrespectful. Or behaving like an ass.

"Are you enjoying your first visit to Colemore?" Lady Rabron asked Gwendolyn, who decided to take the high road and spare the woman's husband the sharp side of her tongue.

"I'm overwhelmed," she confided. "How many guests will be with us?"

"I'm not certain," Lady Rabron said. "This is our first year as well. Reginald is looking forward to the hunt—"

"Do you hunt, Curran?" Lord Rabron asked Mr. Steele, interrupting his wife.

He deserved to have *both* arrogant feet stomped on.

"Not if I can help it," was Mr. Steele's reply.

"Pity."

Gwendolyn edged herself between Lady Rabron and her husband, wanting to give him a taste of what it meant to be cut off. It was a kinder action than the foot stomping. "You were saying?"

Lady Rabron almost gasped. She knew what Gwendolyn was doing. Or perhaps she was surprised someone wished to hear her out. With a nervous smile, she said, "I was saying there are thirty-five bedrooms, and I am told they are all full. But then the table only sits sixty in the main hall, so I imagine Lady Middlebury must limit the number somehow."

"Are you suggesting some guests will not be allowed to eat? Worried about your own meal, my dear?" Her husband chuckled as if he was very clever. He had moved closer to Mr. Steele so that it was men on one side, women on the other.

Forget stomping on his foot. Gwendolyn wanted to elbow him so hard he would double over in pain. Then she would push him into the potted plant located right behind him. She was also frustrated that she was torn between jealousy over the hungry looks Lady Rabron kept sneaking at Mr. Steele and the desire to champion the clueless woman. What woman with any common sense would marry someone like Rabron?

Fortunately for his lordship, at that moment, Lady Middlebury decided to address their guests. "Welcome, everyone. Welcome. My husband and I are pleased you could join us. You will see him at dinner," she assured them as if someone had asked. "Remember, we keep early hours at Colemore. Dinner will be served in an hour and a half. Cook has designed a menu that will certainly please you, Lord Kirkham."

"Beefsteak?" the gray-haired lord barked out.

"And plenty of it," she confirmed. "But first, we have some new faces in our company. Let me introduce Admiral Abbott—" She waved a graceful hand in the direction of a stern-looking man who had heavy jowls as if he'd spent his time at sea scowling.

Guests murmured greetings.

"—Miss Gwendolyn Lanscarr."

Heads turned in Gwendolyn's direction. She lowered her head demurely. She knew her role.

"Lord and Lady Rabron—"

Lord Rabron appeared pleased with the attention.

"—and my dear, *dear* friend Lady Orpington— who brought us Miss Lanscarr—has also given us her nephew, Mr. Nicholas Curran."

Mr. Steele stood as stoic as any Corinthian would if he was worth his salt—tall, confident, and radiating masculinity. Female hearts from every corner of the room fluttered in response.

Of course, Gwendolyn understood why women were attracted to him. Yes, Mr. Steele was handsome in a dark and wild sort of way.

But there was also an energy about him, a sense of purpose, especially when compared with the other young men in the room.

They were an indolent group. Mr. Randell was in government, but she didn't sense he had any true passion for the position the way her brother-in-law Michael did. She suspected that Captain McGrath spent more time deciding on the buttons for the military jackets he wished designed than in actually serving king and country. And Mr. Mason was just a lost cause, a man trailing behind other men so that he could fit in.

As for Lord Ellisfield . . . ? She sensed he had some worth. Granted, he was heir to a vast fortune, but she preferred men who forged their own lives.

It must be the gambler in her, she decided. Her father had always advised his daughters to seek opportunity. And if Gwendolyn was going to put money on the value of someone, it would be on Mr. Steele over *any* other man in this room.

A question directed to the marchioness caught her attention. "What is this I hear, my lady, that there will be no whist tournament this year?" The speaker was Lord Kirkham, a man of middling years. Lady Orpington had introduced Gwendolyn to him earlier. Her ladyship stood not far from him, Magpie in her arms. She'd been stirring the pot.

Lady Middlebury was unperturbed. "We are doing new things this year, my lord," she answered.

"And what new things are those?"

She gave him an expansive smile to include the room and answered, "Whatever *I* decide."

Her declaration was met with a polite ripple of laughter. No one would join in criticizing her decision because she was the hostess to a party so exclusive it bestowed upon each guest a bit of importance in Society. In fact, Gwendolyn believed that if Lady Orpington was wise, she would end her whist campaign now and accept defeat.

Knowing few would question the whist decision further, a triumphant Lady Middlebury stepped back toward the door. "My lord husband and I shall see you at dinner. We will gather in here beforehand." She walked out into the entrance hall.

"What else is there if we don't have the tournament?" Lady Orpington said, proving that she was not crying quarter.

Lord Kirkham grumbled, "I'm not up for hunting. Too much fresh air."

"It would be good for you," someone called out jovially, and the conversations resumed, although many were being escorted to their rooms by maids in the Middlebury livery. Among the first to be led away were, to Gwendolyn's happy relief, Lord and Lady Rabron.

Gwendolyn turned to Mr. Steele. She wanted his thoughts on this sudden change of plans about the card game. However, an older woman stepped between her and Mr. Steele. She elbowed Gwendolyn out of the way with a breezy and insincere "I beg your pardon" before smiling up at him.

"I'm Dame Agnes. No, we haven't been introduced, not formally," she said before Mr. Steele could ask. "However, we are in the country. Some liberties may be taken. Especially since I am of advanced years. But I so wished for you to meet these young gentlewomen." She angled him toward Miss Purley and her friends and began introducing Mr. Curran to them. The young women were all smiles and gleaming, hungry eyes.

Mr. Steele did not seem to mind their open admiration . . . or notice that Gwendolyn had been rudely cut out of their conversation. She found herself standing awkwardly alone.

At that moment, Mrs. Nally, a jovial-looking woman with apple-red cheeks, approached her. "Betsy will take you to your room, Miss Lanscarr," she said, referring to the maid by her side.

Gwendolyn had no choice but to leave Mr. Steele to Miss Purley and her friends and follow. As she left, she noticed Lord Ellisfield and his companions had commandeered a decanter of whisky.

And not far from the door, Lady Orpington continued whipping up her insurrection against the whist ban. Few seemed to share her outrage.

However, Gwendolyn's strangest observation was that, as the maid led her to the double staircase in the entry hall, they passed Lady Middlebury. She had gone out the door and yet had not traveled far.

Instead, she lingered in the hall, just out of

sight of the reception room entrance. She appeared focused on someone in the other room to the point she seemed to barely register anyone around her.

Gwendolyn stole a look in that direction, and realized Lady Middlebury had her sights on Mr. Steele. By the harsh set of her features, she did not like what she saw.

The hard knot of Gwendolyn's jealousy vanished. *He needed her.* He might not want her help in his search for answers, he might even be overly distracted by Miss Purley, but Lady Middlebury either suspected or knew who he was. She was going to keep an eye on him. He'd not be allowed to poke around freely.

Gwendolyn could. She had no secret identity. She could do what he could not . . . and make herself useful to him.

Abruptly the marchioness took off down the main hall.

Gwendolyn pondered her hostess's behavior. Did Lady Middlebury know her husband had a love child? Did she suspect that child was Mr. Steele? Or Mr. Curran, as he was being called?

Illegitimate children were not unusual among the *ton* where most marriages, especially of the very wealthy, were arranged. Many men openly acknowledged their bastards. That Lord Middlebury did not suggested that he had kept a secret from his wife.

Lady Middlebury's suspicions might explain her imperious canceling of the whist tournament. She knew Lady Orpington hoped to restore her honor. Denying her the opportunity was a punishment, quite possibly because Lady Middlebury felt betrayed by her old friend.

The maid took Gwendolyn up another set of stairs, and then another. The two wings of the house had not been later additions but seemed to have been part of the original build.

One curved staircase off the entry hall led to what they called the East Wing; a second staircase was closest to the West Wing. On each floor, the staircases met at a landing. Guests could choose to go left or right, whichever their preference.

The maid took Gwendolyn to the third floor, which she referred to as the "guest hall." She turned to the right. This was the East Wing. The walls were decorated with landscapes of Colemore and Kent over the years with paintings of horses and livestock for balance. A porter was stationed at the landing between the wings to see to guests' needs.

The maid took Gwendolyn to one of the many paneled doors lining both sides of the hall, opened the door, and stepped back for Gwendolyn to enter. Gwendolyn was impressed.

The bedroom was spacious with a window overlooking the front drive. The furnishings were somewhat severe but balanced by the buttery color of the walls and the blue draperies and linens. Molly had already unpacked Gwendolyn's luggage and had a dress for dinner laid out on the bed. It was one of the white muslin gowns that had become Gwendolyn's trademark around London. White went well with her coloring, and she liked the air of serenity such a simple frock gave her. This one had a soft white stripe sewn in the material, and the low-cut bodice was edged with just a hint of lace.

"The water is fresh in the basin, miss," the maid said. "Your abigail should be in to see you shortly. This room doesn't have a maid's cupboard, so her bed will be in the servants' quarters with the others. They should all actually be eating their evening meal around this time."

"Thank you," Gwendolyn murmured, impressed that Colemore saw not only to her comfort but also that of the servants.

"Will there be anything else, miss?" the maid asked.

"Thank you, I'm fine."

The maid withdrew, shutting the door behind her. Gwendolyn moved to the window. All was quiet on the front drive, a sign that the majority of the guests had arrived. Most would be in their rooms like she was, preparing for dinner.

It was the perfect time for a bit of prying. She could always claim she was giving herself a tour of the house.

Gwendolyn quickly changed for dinner without waiting for Molly. She kept her hairstyle simple, splashed on a bit of her favorite toilette water because it reminded her of Ireland's green meadows, and then cracked open the door. She checked to see if anyone was out in the hall. Not even the porter was at his station. Someone must have sent him off on an errand.

She quietly slipped out of her room.

CHAPTER NINE

*G*wendolyn walked to the end of the East Wing, taking time to study the paintings, especially those of the property, while also straining her ears for sounds or bits of conversation from the other side of the doors. She couldn't hear much.

Colemore, she decided, was lavish and elegant, but there was a coldness about the house she didn't understand. Everything seemed a bit too perfect as if no one lived here. Or at least no one who barreled through life with laughter and good humor in the way she and her sisters had lived in Wiltham. There were no marks on the wall, no signs of wear of any sort. There didn't even appear to be a speck of dust on the floor.

She wondered which room was Mr. Steele's, and then decided it was best she didn't know. Besides, he was probably still downstairs basking in Miss Purley's adoration. Gwendolyn was the one doing the work—but exactly what was she searching for? As she walked back along the corridor, she cataloged what she did know.

Mr. Steele's dreams were of a singing woman who confronted an unknown, mysterious terror. The woman might or might not be his mother.

So, what was it Mr. Steele expected to discover at Colemore?

The identity of his mother, of course—whether she was the woman in his dream or not. The answer seemed obvious to Gwendolyn. Having lost a mother at a very young age herself, she understood the void such a death left. Of course, she was certain he would not agree with her. Men didn't grasp the importance of relationships the way women did, except what else could Mr. Steele be looking for?

And then a new possibility struck her. He might wish to meet his father. The whole journey could be built around a need for him to have that connection. In any case, he was right when he'd pointed out that his father was the only one who had known his mother—

A door opened. A couple left their room. Gwendolyn has seen them downstairs, but they had not yet been introduced. The gentleman had gray at his temples. His lady companion seemed older in that way some self-satisfied women had. He helped her drape a lovely paisley shawl over her shoulders.

Gwendolyn turned, pretending to inspect a portrait of a sow and her tan-colored piglets with black patches. They nodded to her as they passed. The gentleman noted her interest in the painting. "You can see the descendants of that sow in the estate's north quarter," he said to Gwendolyn.

"North quarter?"

"Yes, not far from the river. Middlebury likes to keep his pigs as far from him as possible. They say he has a sensitive nose."

"Oh," Gwendolyn replied, feigning interest. One didn't need a sensitive nose to appreciate the marquess's decision. She wasn't fond of the sour, earthy smell of pigs either.

"A short ride. Worth it. We always enjoy a stroll by the river, don't we, dear?"

His lady gave a wan smile as if truly not interested in being friendly.

"We are going to take a turn in the gardens, if you wish to join us?" the gentleman offered.

"That is very kind, sir, but I'm waiting for Lady Orpington."

"Oh, well, you are on the wrong floor. She stays in the family's set of rooms when she visits. They are one floor down."

"Thank you," Gwendolyn said.

His wife gave a tug on his sleeve, and the couple continued on their way. They went down the stairs without looking back.

Gwendolyn watched them disappear down the steps. She stood, thoughtful for a moment—a terror-filled dream of a singing woman, an unknown mother who had probably been a prostitute, an uncaring father who had also paid all of his illegitimate son's bills, and Lady Middlebury, who was definitely not pleased Mr. Steele was here.

There was an answer in all of this. She'd wager Mr. Steele was right and Lord Middlebury alone might understand how they fit together. It was also possible that the dream was just a recurring nightmare of the sort she'd had when she was a child.

Funny, but she hadn't even thought of her childhood bad dreams until this moment, and yet there had been a time when they had ruled her imagination. She'd started having them when she'd first arrived at Wiltham. They had been so vivid, Gram would hear her crying out in her sleep and gently shake her awake. Eventually they had stopped. Perhaps because Gram and her sisters' love had made her feel secure? Gwendolyn didn't know.

However, there was a difference between her dreams and Mr. Steele's. She'd experienced hers during that dark confusing time when she'd been shipped off to a father and family she did not know. His had started after a head wound when he was an adult. It was as if the dream had lain dormant inside him, only to be shaken loose by being shot. One traumatic event revealing another?

She shook her head at her fancifulness . . . and yet she did believe in omens. What was a dream if not an omen?

Gwendolyn decided to take her investigation downstairs to the ground floor. It seemed a good place to start. As for her search, she would be alert for anything that had to do with the elements of Mr. Steele's dream or secret relationships, and she was rather excited about it all. She felt as if she was stepping into a novel, one of her own making.

Gwendolyn was at the top of the staircase when she caught a glimpse through the ajar door of the first room on the West Wing side of the house.

Books. Shelves of them.

She could not resist having a peek. Books were her weakness. She must see what there was to read. Like a bee to a flower, she moved toward a charming, intimate library and slipped through the half-open door.

The room was the size of her bedroom, but two walls, from floor to ceiling, were shelves painted a dark green to match the room's walls, and every shelf was tightly packed with books. They were even organized by topic, height, and size.

Someone had thoughtfully placed a chaise by the room's single window. There was also a small writing desk and chair close at hand.

The room's window overlooked the kitchen garden instead of the formal ones that covered a good portion of the land surrounding the house, and it made her smile. Flowers were lovely, but she enjoyed herbs and colorful vegetables almost as much.

Hanging over the desk were several landscapes and a few small portraits. She noticed one of the landscapes was of Colemore shortly after the current gardens had been designed. They seemed sparse compared to their lush, late summer glory of today.

However, it was the books that drew her. Gwendolyn walked over to the shelves and started perusing the titles, running her fingers over the bindings as if by touch she could tell what the books held. Many of the tomes were old, their spines stiff and carrying a scent that reminded her of dust and vanilla. They cracked with age when she carefully opened them. And she had to open them. She might need something to read this evening, and this was better than being at Hatchard's because she could feel the weight of them in her hands without an intermediary.

Some of the books appeared to be recent purchases. Poetry took up one full row, and then Gwendolyn's favorites—treatises on travel—took up another. If she had her desire, she would travel. She envied men who had the chance at a Grand Tour. She longed to see the sights, the art, and the lands she, as a woman, could only read about. She pulled a book down titled *Life in Gaul*. She also enjoyed history, especially about older civilizations. She skimmed the first paragraphs and decided the author was too prosaic to read during a house party. She put the book back and then discovered tucked among the botany books all three volumes of Maria Edgeworth's *Belinda*. These were more valuable than gold bars to Gwendolyn.

Almost giddy with happiness, she pulled the slim books from the shelf. She'd take them back to her room for later—and then her eye landed on five black leather binders on a lower shelf. They were oversized, so they stuck out.

Curious, and thinking they could hold maps—an exciting prospect—Gwendolyn knelt to examine them. She set the Edgeworth books on the floor, pulled out one of the binders, and opened it.

Sheet music, she saw to her disappointment. Most had lyrics in English or Latin or French, and there were handwritten notes on the pages, including the sorts of musical signs a musician would use to make notes to himself.

Or *herself.* The handwriting was graceful and precise. And some comments were in Spanish. Possibly Italian. The two languages confused Gwendolyn sometimes—

There was a sound at the door. She closed the binder just as the door swung open wider. Lord Ellisfield leaned against the doorframe as if he had been watching her.

He didn't leer, but his gaze did flick to the swells of her breasts above her bodice. She shifted the binder, wrapping her arms around it to block his view. He gave her a rueful look that was part repentance over being so ungentlemanly and part annoyance over being caught. He invited himself in. He'd changed for dinner. Since they were in the country, he wore boots, but his clothes were finely tailored all the same. His claret jacket over buff-colored breeches seemed molded to his shoulders and complemented his fair hair. His shaving soap boasted a hint of pine. The scent made her nose twitch. She ducked her head to hide her discomfort by pretending to give him a small curtsy of respect.

"I'd heard you were a bookworm, Miss Lanscarr," he said lazily.

Gwendolyn reached down and picked up the Edgeworth books, but she kept the binder for protection. "Guilty. What you heard is true."

He walked toward her with the slow, deliberate steps men used when they wished to impress upon women their interest. Gwendolyn tried not to laugh. Men saw themselves as stalking tigers. But she and her sisters referred to this particular saunter as the "pouncing kitten." She hoped the man was sober.

Lord Ellisfield came to a stop in front of her. "I like you."

She caught a whiff of drink fumes on his breath but not the overpowering scent of earlier. Apparently he had not dived into the whisky she'd seen him holding. "Thank you, my lord," she replied dutifully. She gave him an equally dutiful smile, one that didn't discourage, but also didn't encourage. "Excuse me. I need to take these to my room." She attempted to slip by him, but his arm came out to block her path. They stood so close, she could see the shadow of his beard. Her demureness left. She faced him. A gentleman would step back.

He did not, and it made her angry. Even in his cups, he should not foist himself upon her.

She was about to say as much when he asked, "Who is the man with you and Lady Orpington?"

"Do you mean her nephew, Mr. Curran?"

"My godmother has no nephew. Other than Vera Newsome, she has no relatives."

Gwendolyn did not panic. In fact, the confrontation was a touch thrilling to her. She was in the thick of it, whether Mr. Steele wished her to be or not.

"Obviously, she does," she replied. "Mr. Curran."

Lord Ellisfield studied her intently and then shifted his weight, the arm blocking her path coming down. "I was warned you are a bold one. I now believe it."

"Bold, my lord? Who should I thank for the compliment?" she asked brightly.

He gave a soft laugh. "Lady Orpington."

"And *she* told you that Mr. Curran isn't her nephew?" Gwendolyn pressed, deciding to feign ignorance.

"No, Mother did. Lady Orpington only sings your praise, which means you know how to play whist."

"She is very partial to the game."

"Exceedingly so." He made a self-deprecating sound. "I have no interest in it, which she counts against me."

Gwendolyn laughed because she was certain it was true, and he smiled back. To her relief, he also took a step away, giving her a bit of breathing room.

"Your mother plays as well," she reminded him.

He nodded. "She excels at the game." He tapped the top edge of the binder she held. "What did you find?"

"Oh, maps. I enjoy reading them."

"Beauty *and* intelligence," he murmured admiringly. Gwendolyn simpered a bit, the way women were expected to, while praying he didn't ask to see exactly what was in the binder.

He might be attracted to her, but no man liked to be lied to.

So she confessed, "I also have a book by Mrs. Edgeworth. I'll open it first."

He scrunched his nose as if he could not understand her enthusiasm. "I'm not much of a reader."

Gwendolyn was not surprised. No wonder he acted bored with life. It would explain doing foolhardy things like jumping a harnessed team of horses or drinking the day away. Someone who enjoyed books, whether they be tales or memoir or journals, could never be bored.

And while he was this mellow and pliable, she said, "If your mother enjoys whist—"

"She *lives* for this house party so she can play," he assured her. "The rest of the year she has to content herself with playing the neighbors. The only one who challenges her is the vicar."

"Then why did she cancel the tournament?"

He shrugged and then grinned, the expression actually quite charming, as he said, "Probably to annoy Lady Orpington. My mother can be quite contrary. So can Lady Orpington. They claim to be friends, but sometimes I am convinced they detest each other."

True. "Why do you think that is?"

"Because they are women?"

Gwendolyn didn't hide her annoyance. "You can offer a more thoughtful observation than such a rote dismissal."

He blinked as if startled she hadn't thought him clever. "Are you my governess?" he mock-complained.

"Because I'm pushing you to be a bit more insightful?" Gwendolyn suggested, tagging on silently to herself, *and informative.* After all, he should have some idea for Lady Middlebury's abrupt change of heart about the whist tournament.

"Perhaps." He looked away and then shot her a hint of a smile as if needing her to know he had only been jesting.

She wanted to like him. Although she didn't trust him. She was certain he'd been a handsome boy, one who had grown into a rather distracted and aimless man who could and should do better.

As if reading her thoughts, he turned serious. "Mother and Lady Orpington have always been at it. They are competitive, and I'm assured they were so even in girlhood. But ultimately, in the only game that matters—life—Mother has won. She has the greater title, the more money, the husband who is still alive, and now the reputation as the better whist player, whether it is well-earned or not. She is not the sort to open the door for someone to take anything from her if she can just laze about on her laurels."

Like mother, like son. "Is she truly that covetous?"

"She is," he answered. "If a door is opened, she isn't afraid to walk through it."

"That is an odd statement, my lord."

"But a true one." He walked over to the desk and reached to straighten one of the portraits on the wall. "I am the son of a younger son. I wasn't to inherit." He frowned as if still not liking the way the picture hung, but then turned to her. "Then my uncle died, and his son . . ." His voice had trailed off as if something bothered him.

"His son?" she prompted.

"Yes, his son," he answered. "My uncle had a male child. Robbie inherited when my uncle died, even though he was a newborn. The hierarchy and all of that."

"What happened?"

Lord Ellisfield faced her, leaning back against the desk. "What shouldn't have." His expression was somber. "He drowned, and his mother died trying to save him."

"That's horrible," Gwendolyn murmured.

"Yes." Lord Ellisfield nodded to the portrait he'd just straightened. "That is a painting of my late aunt."

She took a step forward to look at the portrait. A young woman with a heart-shaped face and wearing what had to be her bridal finery smiled out into the world with eyes sparkling with joy. A circlet of white-and-yellow flowers, mostly daisies, rested on her powdered curls piled high on her head. She was posed at a pianoforte. "She was lovely."

He nodded. "Their deaths still bother me. It was the first time I realized we were all going to die. I was six, soon to turn seven. I recall being shocked to learn that people just disappeared from your life. Not adults like my uncle who had seemed very old to my childhood mind, but Robbie. Someone like myself. *And*," he continued, a note of irony in his tone, "that it would be considered a good thing. That people would celebrate. When Robbie died, Mother tried to mourn, but she was pleased with the turn of events. She told me that now, someday, I would inherit Colemore. I was happy because she was happy. But the truth is"—his voice hardened—"the reason my father is the marquess, that he owns all of this, is because of a small child's death. I liked Robbie. He and I were close. My sister, Jane, had been born, but who wants to play with their sister when there is another lad around?" He frowned. "In those days, it seemed death was everywhere. First my uncle, and then my aunt Catalina and Robbie. The household mourned for years."

He straightened and waved his hand in the air as if to clear it. "We are being too serious. Someone's tragedy is another person's windfall. The vagaries of life, no? When I die, someone will secretly be pleased." He flexed his shoulders as if he needed to release tension. "I haven't thought about all of that in a long time. Isn't this the stuff poets write about?"

"The ones who aren't waxing on about love."

Her comment surprised a laugh out of him. "You are quite extraordinary, Miss Lanscarr."

She felt herself blush. "I believe drink has impaired your judgment, Lord Ellisfield."

"It did this afternoon, didn't it? I fear I did not impress you."

"Perhaps because I was in the coach you were jumping?" she pointed out lightly.

He winced as if the memory hurt. "I don't know what I was trying to prove. Ah, yes," he said as if remembering. "I wanted McGrath to know I had the better trained horse." He took her hand. She did not yank it back. That would be too provoking, but she braced herself for the move she knew he was about to make.

He murmured, "I fear all I have proved is that I can be a fool." He leaned in to kiss her.

Gwendolyn knew this game. She turned her

head so that his lips met her cheek. He pulled up with a low, frustrated groan. "Miss Lanscarr."

She made a soft moue back at him. "This is not a good idea. And *I* am not an easy mark, my lord." She kept her tone gentle but firm.

He heard what she didn't say. "I mean no insult."

"Then do not insult me."

Her admonishment seemed to hang between them a moment, and then he released her hand. "I merely wanted a taste. Just one taste of the intriguing Miss Lanscarr." His laughter, dark and moody, punctuated his request. "Is that such a bad wish?"

"Obviously *yes*," Mr. Steele's cold voice said from the doorway.

They both whirled toward him. Gwendolyn was surprised that Mr. Steele had come so close to her and she hadn't felt that tingly sense of his presence that she often did.

Lord Ellisfield squinted. "Oh, it is the mysterious Mr. Curran."

Gwendolyn used the moment to move away from him so that when his lordship turned back around, she was a good three feet away.

He gave her a hangdog expression. "He ruined it for us, didn't he?"

She shook her head, not trusting herself to speak without insulting him.

"Well, then." Lord Ellisfield clapped his hands, and he faced Mr. Steele. "I shall go down for dinner, because I can tell that the Mysterious Mr. Curran wishes to throw me out the window.

Don't worry, Mysterious Mr. Curran. I will leave her alone." He shot Gwendolyn a puckish, hopeful grin and added, "Unless she wishes for my attention."

The problem was that Mr. Steele blocked his exit. Lord Ellisfield walked right up to him. Mr. Steele was taller, but not by much. "If you wish me to leave, Mysterious Mr. Curran, you need to scoot out of the way." He waved his hands as if to shoo Mr. Steele from his path.

With a look that should have cleaved Lord Ellisfield in half if it had been a sword, Mr. Steele stepped aside.

His lordship left the library, but not without a backward grin at Gwendolyn.

She waited until the man was gone before saying, "I'm grateful for your intervention."

Mr. Steele ignored her statement. "We should go downstairs."

"Not yet." She spoke in a hushed tone. "Come here. And shut the door."

Mr. Steele did not comply. "They are gathering for dinner. We are expected."

"I have something of import to tell you."

He didn't move closer to her. "What is it?"

Gwendolyn bit back a huff of annoyance. She took three steps in his direction so she could say in a low voice, "Lady Middlebury does not think you are Lady Orpington's nephew. You came upon Lord Ellisfield asking me who you were."

"*That* was what he was doing? It didn't look like it to me."

At first, Gwendolyn thought he referred to Lord Ellisfield's mocking "Mysterious Mr. Curran" comments, but then realized he meant the kiss. She held up a hand. "Stop. Nothing happened."

"Not because he didn't want it."

"Exactly, and it is what *I* want that counts," she informed him. "However, on a matter of more importance, I believe his mother sent him to ask me what I knew about you."

"You told him I am Mr. Curran, correct?"

"Of course . . ." She wished he had closed the door. She thought about doing it herself, but his mood was strange, and she didn't risk countermanding him—yet. "But Lady Middlebury knows that Lady Orpington doesn't have many living relations. I also fear that Lady Orpington is going to annoy the marchioness with her clanging on about playing whist."

"She is definitely going to do that. However, that won't be a worry."

"Because?"

"Because I believe this was a bad idea. I should not have come here. I regret I dragged you into it."

"I don't regret it, and I believe you are being hasty. I've been thinking about this investigation—"

"*It isn't yours to think about.*" His voice was quiet, but he might as well have roared the words, considering the intensity with which he spoke.

He glanced toward the hallway as if to see if there was a danger of his being overheard and then moved the few steps toward her. "I don't want you involved any deeper than playing cards. Did I not make myself clear?"

"Yes, you did. However, I have some thoughts, some ideas about how we can approach this—"

"There is no *we*. And now you've given me another reason to end this right now. We will return to London." He made as if to turn in the direction of the door.

Gwendolyn shifted her books and the binder to one arm and reached for his sleeve. "Why? What is the matter?"

His gaze dropped to her hand. She did not move it. She had a right to understand his thinking. Slowly, sharp, troubled blue eyes met hers. There was a beat of silence. "I don't like this place. I don't wish you to be involved."

"If Lady Middlebury has sent her son after me to ferret out information, then I am involved. I *want* to be involved."

"Gwendolyn, I can't—"

She stopped him by putting her fingers across his lips. His breath was warm. He smelled much better than Lord Ellisfield. The spice of his soap against the warmth of his skin drew her to him. Best of all, he had used her first name again. It sounded like music on his lips, even though he was about to tell her what he wasn't going to let her do.

But it was too late. She was already doing it.

And then he stepped back, turned away . . . and she wanted to grab him and make him face her. How could he continually pretend there was nothing between them?

She straightened her shoulders. "I *am* helping," she informed him. "You need me, as a sounding board, if nothing else. Something has been stewing inside of you since you first walked into this house. Share it with me. I can be trusted."

He responded to her words with a nod as if conceding that she was right. He shifted toward her, a bleakness to his expression. "I'm not certain why I'm uneasy," he answered, and then, "I don't like Lady Middlebury." He paused. "That sounds petty."

"She is not fond of you either." She told him about catching the marchioness watching him. "Women may tolerate their husbands' affairs, but not many will like it. She must know or sense your connection to Lord Middlebury."

He shook his head. "It is more than that. I feel surrounded by something I don't understand. There is a heaviness here. A weight. Like in my dreams." He shook his head. "This whole plan is a fool's errand. My instincts were wrong. I don't belong here."

"Mr. Steele—"

He pounced on her words. "*Curran*," he bit out in a whisper, his jaw tight. "I can't afford that sort of mistake."

Heat flushed her face at her error. But she didn't want to return to London. She didn't want to part company with him. Not yet. "You mustn't give up so easily," she whispered back furiously. "We only just arrived . . ." Her voice trailed off as she realized he was no longer listening to her.

Instead, he stared at a point over her shoulder, his expression thunderstruck.

She turned. He stared at the wall behind the desk, at the landscapes and portraits. "What is it?"

"That picture." He nodded to the one of the young bride. "*She* is the singing woman from my dreams."

Gwendolyn looked over to him. "She is Lord Ellisfield's aunt. The late marchioness."

$\mathcal{B}$eck walked to the picture. He placed a hand on the canvas. Beneath the light touch of his fingers, the wigged beauty in the portrait laughed up at him. She sat at a pianoforte beneath a blue sky and surrounded by the dark green of the forest. A chill went through him. Why would the woman in the portrait be in his dreams? He had never been to Colemore. He'd definitely never met this woman with her stubborn chin that spoke of strong character.

"Ellisfield said this was the last marchioness?" he asked, his gaze not leaving the picture.

Gwendolyn set her books on the desk and stood beside him. "He referred to the portrait as his aunt. She drowned trying to save her son. Have you heard the story?" She didn't wait for his answer. "Her son was very young, and they believe he fell into the river close by. The thought is that she drowned attempting to rescue him. They both died, and the current marquess inherited."

The story disturbed him, but in a way he

couldn't explain. He looked away from the picture, taking in the quiet of the small library. The back of his neck tightened. There was danger here. He had a flash of memory, of the glint of the knife Olin Winstead had used to attack him, of the man's dead body in the passageway between the brothels. The dreams had been a warning, but he'd not had one of late. What had he involved Gwendolyn in—?

"I am not leaving," she said, accurately reading his mind. "You are a formidable bodyguard, Mr. St—" She caught herself. She looked toward the hall door as if she had finally become aware of the danger if they were overheard. He wished he'd listened to her and shut it when she'd suggested. At the time, he'd been more concerned over suspicious minds if they were discovered alone behind a closed door together. Golden-brown eyes returned to him. "—Mr. Curran," she said as she corrected herself." Her voice very quiet, she continued, "Your presence seems to have ruffled feathers and in a surprisingly short period of time."

He nodded.

"Then let us sow doubt. Let us continue as if we are who we say we are. If there is a connection between you, this portrait, and Colemore, someone will show their hand. They always do. That is a bit of gambling wisdom my father taught me. Best of all, Lady Orpington's campaign to reinstate the whist tournament will keep everyone stirred up. There is nothing close company like a house party enjoys more than a contretemps."

"Contretemps?" he echoed. He smiled. Her

sensible words and patient tone were helping him to recover a sense of balance. Dreams were strange things. He didn't believe anyone could see the future, but he had experienced moments he thought he'd lived through before. Moments he'd believed he'd dreamed. Now, looking at the picture, he wondered if he was merely imagining this was his singing woman, possibly because she sat at a pianoforte. In his dream, her hair was as dark as his own, and hundreds of women had lively eyes and determined chins. He felt himself relax.

"A quarrel," Gwendolyn said as if, from his silence, he needed the word *contretemps* explained. "An opportunity to watch two old friends bicker back and forth. It will keep the other guests amused. Meanwhile, we discreetly ask questions."

"*I* can ask questions. You don't need to be involved further. I mean those words, Miss Lanscarr. No more prying on my behalf."

"But I have been successful, haven't I?" She nodded to the portrait, proof that she had helped him. He might have discovered the painting on his own, but not the story behind it.

She'd also calmed him down when his inclination was to bolt, to drag her out of Colemore if need be. But now, well, she was right. He could appreciate a sounding board. "Come, we are required at dinner." He offered his arm, but she didn't take it.

Instead, she confronted him, her voice low.

"Understand this, sir. This is the most excitement I've ever had in my life. *You* are not going to run me off. Especially since I can ask the questions you can't. Frankly, I think Lady Middlebury is not happy you are here because she knows you are her husband's son."

She could be right.

And he realized a truth—he wanted to collaborate with her. He hadn't liked seeing Ellisfield cozying up to her. It had made him want to pack her up and send her back to London. However, Gwendolyn was also an antidote to Violet and those pesky debutantes.

He wasn't in danger of reigniting an old flame. Violet had jilted him. She could send all the longing looks she wished his way. They would have no impact on him. The door had closed between them. As for Miss Purley and her friends, he preferred a more spirited woman.

"What did I overhear that drunken fop say to you?" Beck asked.

"Do you refer to Lord Ellisfield? He seems to have sobered considerably from this afternoon."

"The name still fits. You knew who I meant." He took a beat and then added, "Except . . . he did call you 'quite extraordinary,' Miss Lanscarr." He paused and then said, "He's right. You are."

Gwendolyn blinked as if startled by the compliment. Her lips spread into a smile so broad, he had a desire to compliment her every day and every hour.

And then she almost destroyed his regard for

her by saying, "To be honest, I find Lord Ellisfield rather charming."

"In what way?" Beck challenged her.

"He is capable of introspection, something that isn't common of his set."

So she thought kindly of Ellisfield? That was no excuse for Beck to hope the man roasted in hell, but it was a start.

She continued, "He understands that his title and his wealth don't come from his work or by way of his hands or his brain. It is just a happenstance of birth. And of death. He has a title because someone died."

"That is the way of all inheritances."

"It is still weighty, isn't it? One person's good fortune depends on another's misfortune?" She gave a shiver at the thought.

"He can always do whatever he wishes with his life. His family is rich enough. There is the military, government service, the clergy. Many things he could do besides spending his days drinking with his mates."

"Except he is the oldest son. Many families don't wish for the heir to be in danger."

"No, that is just for lads like me who had to put their lives on the line to make something of themselves. A marquess's son is not put on the front lines. He would have been more in danger in the clergy or wandering around Parliament."

"I told you it weighs on him. He confessed to me that he shouldn't have been the heir. That his father was a younger brother who inherited the title after a child died. This was the tragedy Lady Orpington spoke of earlier."

Beck doubted Ellisfield was as sensitive as she believed. And yes, the death of a child was tragic but war had taught Beck the world was full of such heartbreaks.

He nodded to the door. "We should join the company for dinner before it is noticed we are late."

"You are right. I have no desire to earn a reprimand from the marchioness."

Beck checked the hallway. It was empty, but he could hear voices drift up the stairways. That meant the other guests had left the reception hall. "Come," he said.

Gwendolyn nodded and followed him out the door. As they walked, she had to finish her thoughts on Lord Ellisfield. "I do give his lordship credit that he realizes he has advantages others do not have."

Beck grunted a response. He didn't like Ellisfield—not if Gwendolyn was going to defend him.

By the time they reached the ground floor, the main hall was empty. Sounds of conversations and chairs being scooted across the parquet could be heard from the dining room.

The butler stood by the dining room door, apparently watching for stragglers. "Mr. Curran? Miss Lanscarr?"

They hurried toward him.

"Please come with me. We are ready to serve." The butler didn't wait but led the way, assuming their compliance.

In the paneled cavern of a dining room, the longest table Beck had ever seen had a setting for everyone. All forty to fifty-some guests. Many were neighbors who would not be spending the night. However, they would be taking part in the activities.

Beck couldn't help but be impressed. The linens were white. The glassware sparkled under the candlelight. The silver was heavy and expensive. Some of the female guests wore colorful ostrich plumes in their hair as they would in London. Lady Orpington's onyx jewels reflected the light. Magpie was not there, Beck noticed . . . although he wouldn't be surprised if she was under the table.

Everyone stood behind their chairs, waiting for the nod from their hostess to be seated. A footman was in position behind each guest to help pull out chairs and to cater to their individual needs.

Lady Middlebury remarked upon his and Gwendolyn's tardiness as they took their places. "Ah, the last of the guests." She addressed the butler. "Now all we need, Nathaniel, is my lord, and we may begin." The butler went off to search for his master.

Beck noticed that Ellisfield was seated close to the head of the table where his mother and Miss Purley would sit. The marchioness obviously hoped for a match between her son and the wealthy banker's daughter. So Beck did receive a bit of satisfaction when Miss Purley sent a welcoming smile in his direction. Ellisfield appeared not to notice. Instead, his lordship's gaze wandered down the table to where Gwendolyn stood between the admiral and the local rector. Beck couldn't remember his name. However, both men were aged and, he was certain, boring. He couldn't have chosen better companions for her. As for himself, he was across from Violet. Her husband was located near Ellisfield.

Gwendolyn was right. From the seating arrangements alone, he deduced Lady Middlebury knew he wasn't Nicholas Curran.

On Beck's left was a giggling Lady Julia, and a very interested Lady Beth was at his right. They greeted him eagerly, ready to flirt, while Violet sent him heartfelt, searching looks as if yearning for a sign that his affection for her had never died. He wasn't interested in any of them. No, his interests lay in the woman he should leave alone if he truly cared for her . . . Gwendolyn.

He shifted to look down the table at her. She appeared to listen intently to the admiral, her expression one of interest. And of grace . . . with the candlelight giving her cheeks a golden glow and the shadows highlighting her expressive brows, the line of her lips, the curve of her neck . . . and the curve of her breasts . . .

Beck wasn't one given to the nuances of a person. A woman attracted him, or she didn't. A situation benefitted him, or it didn't. Life was as it was.

But with Gwendolyn, he noted all the subtleties. He heard the sound of her voice in his head, her earnest suggestions, her retorts when she felt he didn't value her . . . but he *did* value her. He trusted her.

The room around him buzzed with the conversation of guests introducing themselves and making small talk while they waited for a sign from their hosts. Gwendolyn glanced his way as if she sensed he watched her. Her lovely lips twisted in a rueful smile, and it was as if she knew he was happy her dinner partners were not Ellisfield, but old men. He raised his brows in a show of mock sympathy, and her smile widened to one more genuine, just as he anticipated.

And in that moment, something hard around his heart cracked.

It was a strange sensation. He hadn't even realized he'd closed himself off. He'd thought he was fine, that he was good on his own.

Had he sealed himself off after Violet's betrayal, as Jem had suggested?

Or had he always been that way—a child rejected by a mother who hadn't wanted him and a father who had minimally acknowledged him?

He wasn't certain. He had never been one for deep introspection, until now. Until Gwendolyn.

And losing her, because he must let her go eventually, would be crushing. But he would manage. Didn't he always manage . . . ?

Violet said something to him. He smiled without bothering to understand what she said—

"The Marquess of Middlebury," the butler declared, his voice carrying over the conversation that came to an abrupt halt.

All turned toward the door.

Beck would have to look behind him. His thoughts had been so occupied with his quest for the singing woman—and with Gwendolyn—he'd not had a moment to ruminate on coming face-to-face with his sire for the first time. Perhaps purposefully? He now prepared himself. He was no longer a boy with childish dreams of a parent. He hadn't needed the marquess then; he didn't need him now.

However, he was curious as to what the man looked like.

The gathered company waited. The announcement had been made. The marquess should walk through the door.

Instead, nothing happened. No one entered the room.

The marchioness was not amused. She looked over to the butler who, almost comically, stood silent, expectant . . . for a man who did not appear.

It was decidedly odd.

At last, Beck broke down to glance behind him just as a figure appeared in the doorway. *Middlebury.*

Beck apparently had his father's height. The man was lean, his body silhouette far less muscular. He was too thin, almost as if he was ill. On the other hand, he and Beck did share a nose. As did Ellisfield, Beck realized, truly grasping for the first time that Ellisfield and his brother and sister were his half siblings.

However, there were more physical contrasts than similarities. Beck was not a younger version of his sire. His lips were thinner, his jaw more square, his shoulders broader.

Then there was the coloring. All of the Middleburys were fair. Beck's hair was black. Not as dark as Gwendolyn's but the color of shadows with more brown tones.

Even more curious, or perhaps not, Beck felt no connection to this man. In fact, if they had met on the street, they would have passed each other as strangers.

He'd had more of a reaction to Lady Middlebury than his father.

The marquess went to his chair at the head of the table. He stood, taking in the room. His gray eyes rested on Beck. He frowned.

The world around Beck stilled. Did Middlebury see the similarities as he did? Did he recognize some element of himself in Beck?

For his part, Beck felt a detached indifference, even as the man studied him.

Lady Middlebury broke her husband's concentration, saying, "My lord, we are famished."

His attention turned to her. He smiled, and Beck could almost believe he'd imagined his sire's scrutiny. Certainly no one else in the room appeared to notice. "So sorry, my dear." Lord Middlebury raised his voice. "My regrets to all of you. I lose myself in my research. Please, take your places." The footmen pulled out chairs.

The marquess waited until all the guests were seated and, while he still stood, said, "I wish to welcome you."

He had a raspy voice. His words were measured as if parceled out.

Lady Middlebury had also not taken her chair. She stood close to her husband. Beck suddenly had the feeling that he had seen them standing together before.

But he couldn't have. Was his mind again playing tricks?

"Enjoy Colemore," their host encouraged them. "I shall not be hunting. My sons and son-in-law will happily lead you." He nodded to Ellisfield and to Lord Martin, his youngest son, and to Lord Grassington, who was married to his daughter, Miranda, Lady Grassington.

"However," the marquess continued, "I look forward to enjoying your company at dinner every evening. My wife and I take *delight*"—he put emphasis on *delight* as if he had been rehearsing his speech—"in your presence."

Beck noticed his hand shook as he gestured, and his fingers were ink-stained. Up until then, he had kept both hands at his sides in tight fists. The man was not well.

"I shan't stay," Lord Middlebury informed them. His guests groaned their disappointment. He made a tight smile to express his appreciation of their mild protests. "My research needs me. You understand. Now, if you will excuse me?"

"My lord—" Lady Middlebury started as if to encourage him to stay, but he was already walking toward the door.

Beck frowned. What the devil was wrong with Middlebury? Because something was not right.

He was also not the only one to think that way. Looks around the table were exchanged.

Eyebrows raised. Did that mean that this was the first year he had behaved in this manner?

Then, to Beck's surprise, Lady Middlebury took her husband's chair. She signaled to the butler, and service began. From the other side of the room, two doors opened, and footmen charged out, carrying tureens of soup as the first course. The footmen lining the walls began pouring wine into glasses. There were more servants than there were guests so that every need could be met.

The conversation picked up its previous tempo. Everyone carried on as if the marquess's behavior had not been strange. Beck looked over at Lady Orpington and caught her instructing a footman to butter her bread. Apparently she could not be bothered with such a mundane task.

Perhaps, for this group of people, Lord Middlebury *had* seemed normal. He marveled at the resilience of the English character.

Dinner became an interminable affair. It seemed to take ages for the courses to be served. Beck found his impatience growing. He wasn't one for sitting for long periods of time, and he did not like small talk about matters of no consequence. In between all the flirtatious comments and Violet's many attempts to reminisce about the past, a man down the table from him wished to know where he'd gone to school.

Beck thought that a silly but common question. He answered "Faircote," and reliably predicted the man would be unimpressed, which was true.

The man wondered if Beck was interested in where he went to school. Beck ignored him.

Ellisfield appeared just as annoyed with the dinner as Beck was. There was a tightness to his jaw and, most telling of all, he'd stopped drinking. Beck wondered if his dissatisfaction was caused by his father's appearance or the fact that his mother, instead of offering the seat at the head of the table to her oldest son and the heir, had taken it for herself.

Finally, dinner was finished. The women wasted no time in withdrawing so that the men could enjoy their port in peace. Ellisfield jumped into that seat at the head of the table the moment his mother left it.

Beck was not interested in lingering.

Excusing himself by saying he felt a need to check on Lady Orpington's servant, who had been injured in the fall off her coach, he escaped the room. What he really wanted to do was find Jem and hear what he'd learned over the past week. He wanted the rumors and the bits of gossip servants shared.

As he was leaving, Randell remarked he didn't understand why anyone worried about a footman. Beck kept walking. Arguing with the entitled was pointless.

Out in the passage, he shut the door on the dining room and moved toward the grand hall. A footman had informed him that if he went through the West Wing and out a far door, there was a path that led to the stables.

Beck had just reached the main hall when he overheard Lady Middlebury and Lady Orpington arguing in low, angry tones. They sounded as if they stood on the staircase closest to him. He took a step back, hoping no one came out of the dining room and caught him eavesdropping.

"I told you there will be no whist play this year," Lady Middlebury said.

"You can't stop us playing whist," Lady Orpington answered. "We'll play it if we like."

"Not under my roof."

"You are being ridiculous, Franny. Or do you fear losing to me?"

"What is the matter with you, Ellen? I've lost to you in the past. I am not that petty."

"Then prove it. Let us play."

"No."

"Why are you denying me? Why are you denying my husband?"

"And *there* it is."

"What?"

"Another accusation that I was unfair to Orpington."

"You were."

"And that I may have precipitated his death?"

"He was greatly upset by your—" Lady Orpington paused and then said almost defiantly, "Gloating."

There was a heated beat where Beck could imagine Lady Middlebury not appreciating such an accusation. Then she said, a chill in her tone, "And so your answer is to betray *my* husband?"

"What does Middlebury have to do with this? Middlebury is not a player."

"You don't have a nephew."

Beck sucked in his breath. She knew Curran was an impostor.

However, Lady Orpington didn't flinch at the accusation. "I do. He was at the table tonight. Miss Purley found him quite entertaining." Beck could have kissed her for her courage and aristocratic hauteur. She sounded convincing.

"I know who he is," the marchioness assured her.

"Nicholas?" Lady Orpington was very good.

"I don't know his name. Except it is not Curran."

"Franny, are you feeling well . . . ?"

"No whist."

"You don't have the power, even under your own roof, to keep us from playing," Lady Orpington calmly responded.

"Don't anger me, Ellen. I am never good angered."

"We are guests, and a number of us enjoy cards."

"Then you can leave."

"Franny, *come back here.* Franny, we are not done."

Except they were. It was hard to hear footsteps on the stairs' thick carpeting, but Beck could imagine their hostess marching away to join the ladies wherever they were.

Lady Orpington still lingered. "She is the one being ridiculous," he heard her mutter to herself. "And we will play cards. We will," she added childishly. Then he heard her follow Lady Middlebury with a heavy sigh.

Beck stepped out from the nook where he'd secreted himself. He was lucky that all of the servants were apparently busy with a full house so he'd not been caught.

He swiftly found the door to the outside. The grounds were lit with lamps, a nice touch and probably more of a sign of the Middlebury wealth than anything else Beck had seen.

Out in the stables, he found his man, Jem Wagner, in good spirits. A large group of drivers and stable lads sat around a fire, talking horses and swapping stories that were probably lies but good to hear.

Jem noticed Beck immediately when he made an appearance at the edge of the circle of light. He'd probably been watching for him.

They walked into the darkness.

"A good group?" Beck asked.

Jem chuckled quietly. It wasn't lost on Beck that the tip of his friend's nose was red, as it always was when he was a bit foxed. "Probably better than what you have up at the house."

"I'm certain you are right. So, anything interesting?"

"We've been telling ghostie stories. They claim there are spirits here."

"Such as?" Beck asked, only mildly interested.

"Did you know about a drowning years back?"

Beck's interest was piqued. Another mention of a drowning. Or was it the same one Gwendolyn had spoken of? "The last marchioness?"

"Ah, you heard of it already, have you?"

"Only that she drowned." Wanting to hear Jem's telling, Beck said, "What do the servants say?"

"That she haunts the forest down by the river. After her husband died, she built a cottage on the river's banks. That is where they say she can be heard singing . . ."

Wagner's voice trailed off, tellingly. He waited a bit and then said, "They say she sings. Like the woman in your dreams."

"Singing is a common activity, especially amongst women."

"True," Jem replied easily enough. "Course, I grow suspicious when I hear about a family of deaths all at one time. Did you hear about how her husband died?"

"Her husband? I heard them say he collapsed. Probably his heart."

"Maybe. He wasn't that old. That's what the lads say. She had just given birth. Her son was a babe when he took the title."

Seeing Beck listened, Jem continued. "They claim she grieved deeply after her man's death. She and her husband's relatives didn't rub along too well. Our current Lord Middlebury complained she didn't listen to his advice. They had rows over it. She wouldn't listen to any of the family and said she didn't need to because her son was the marquess. Supposedly for that reason, she built the cottage. It was a place to escape. Or at least, that is what the servants and villagers believe."

Beck thought of his father's behavior at dinner, the marchioness's abrupt manner. "I can see that."

"She was also heartbroken. Merton, the stable head, knew her. He said before her husband died, she was always the merriest of women. Frankly, I think Merton was half in love with her. They all were. The lads said she was a looker. However, after her husband died, the only things that made her happy were her music and her son."

Beck thought of the woman sitting at the pianoforte in the portrait. The artist had caught her optimism in the light of her eye and in her smile. In that moment captured in paint, she trusted that her future would be everything she expected of it. Apprehension for her tightened his gut.

"Now remember," Jem said, "this is a ghostie story. She would go to that cottage often. She'd take her son, and they would stay there for hours. However, one day they didn't return. They also weren't at the cottage when someone went to look. They had just vanished. A search party was formed. Merton and a few of the others over there"—he nodded to the fire—"were a part of it."

"What did they find?" Beck asked.

"That river isn't a big river, but the waters move fast. The mother and son had disappeared shortly after a spring storm, and the banks were swollen over. Her little boy, the marquess, was said to be always going for a tumble or finding trouble—I have one like that. He is rarely where he should be and often where he shouldn't. Makes me want to hang him up on a peg until he learns some sense." He shook his head in parental disgust before saying, "They think the child may have fallen into the water. It would have been like him. They believe she might have gone in to save him and drowned. They found her body downriver a few days after she went missing."

"Who is the 'they' who says these things?"

Jem shrugged. "I don't know. '*They.*' Merton. The others. The searchers."

Beck nodded, frustrated by the lack of details.

"This is just a story," Jem reminded him. "Well, except it is true the marchioness drowned."

"And her son?"

"Gone. I asked. Merton said they never found his body. A small child doesn't stand a chance in a heavy current. Not much weight to him. He was only like three or four. The lads argued about his age. His wee body could have been swept clear to the sea. Merton said that the family searched for weeks for some sign of him. Nothing. Fish could have eaten him." He shivered at the gruesomeness of the thought.

"Is that it?"

"Of course not. I told you this is ghostie story, Major . . . and I ask you, have you noticed something is not exactly right here?" Jem lowered his voice and stepped closer. "No one likes the current marchioness. She's feared. This is not a happy place. However, most of the lads have families that have been here for generations. They won't leave no matter how they feel about her. Their loyalty is to the Chaytor name." He referred to the Middlebury family name.

"Have they said anything about the marquess?"

"Only that they believe he is an odd one. He stays to himself, but sometimes he is seen walking the estate, muttering gibberish. We have been ordered to not give him a horse if he requests it. It was my first instruction upon my taking the position. Lady Middlebury will only let him ride in a vehicle, and she has someone watching him at all times."

"He's her link to power, isn't he?"

"'Tis said her sons are not as biddable as her husband."

Beck thought of the delay in Middlebury's appearance at dinner. The way his hand shook. "Any gossip about why he is the way he is?"

"They say he has always been weak. Trust me, sir, she is the true Tartar. However, Major, I've seen that behavior before."

"The shaking?"

"Aye, palsy. It will get worse. They say that over the past six months or so, he has lost two stone as well."

Beck nodded. The man had not looked well, and yet the marchioness had not seemed overly concerned.

"Now for the ghostie part," Jem said. "The lad telling the story claims that the drowned marchioness searches for her missing child. They say she sings for him. A bit like your dream, ain't it, sir? Whenever you were having a nightmare and I woke you, you spoke of a singing woman, and I thought it strange that there is one here."

And that the marchioness in the portrait bore a remarkable likeness to his dream woman.

"There is more, sir," Jem said. "They say every

time the marquess escapes the house, he goes to the river, to that cottage. They always know where to find him. He stands there, talking to himself. Because, you see, he is the one haunted by the ghost. He is the only one who has ever claimed to hear her singing. And not always by the water. He has dreams, sir. Dreams of a singing woman."

CHAPTER ELEVEN

$\mathcal{G}$wendolyn wished she was anywhere except in this sitting room with a host of other women waiting for the gentlemen to leave their port and join them.

Worse, once the men made an appearance, Miss Purley, accompanied by Lady Julia, was to perform a few song selections she had chosen. Gwendolyn idly listened to Miss Purley, her mother, and her friends gathered around the pianoforte, furiously whispering last-minute concerns and instructions. If they thought warbling a tune or two would impress Lord Ellisfield, then Gwendolyn believed they would be sorely disappointed. Ellisfield didn't impress her as one to be lovestruck by an amateur musical performance.

Nor was it lost on Gwendolyn that, in spite of her parents' and, apparently, Lady Middlebury's hopes, Miss Purley seemed to have swung her interest from his lordship to Mr. Steele. She'd made cow eyes at him all through dinner. Of course, Lord Ellisfield hadn't shown much interest either. His gaze had wandered toward Gwendolyn.

Meanwhile, except for that moment before the company had taken their seats, Mr. Steele had appeared to ignore Gwendolyn. She wondered if she'd done something to vex him.

Suddenly Lady Orpington burst through the door, Magpie under her arm. She charged straight for Gwendolyn and plunked herself upon the settee, taking the space that Gwendolyn had been hoping to save for Mr. Steele. Magpie sat in her lap.

"She is refusing to let us play," Lady Orpington said in a whisper that could have been heard across the room.

"It is her party," Gwendolyn pointed out. "She is allowed to make decisions about the activities her guests enjoy."

Lady Orpington snorted her response. "I need to know *why* she is refusing us. I will get to the bottom of this. We *will be playing*. Be ready."

On those words, she picked up Magpie and came to her feet. Her personality changed from outraged cardplayer to serene gentlewoman. She smiled at Gwendolyn. "I will have everyone won over to my side by morning." So saying, she waved one of Magpie's paws at Gwendolyn and walked over to the table loaded with sweetmeats and drinks. She began making small talk with the women gathered there while Magpie leaned over and, sticking out her tongue, tried to snag one of the small cakes. The other guests listened respectfully, but Gwendolyn didn't sense they saw a prevailing need for a whist tournament.

Or appreciated Magpie eating the desserts.

She turned an impatient eye to the door again. Where were the gentlemen?

Gwendolyn was now very glad that she had requested a horse to go riding in the morning. She needed the freedom. Fresh air would clear her head. She sensed she was being watched all the time. Lady Middlebury would stare at her in the most discomforting way, and the servants all seemed too aware of her—

Lady Rabron plunked herself down on the settee in the space Lady Orpington had abandoned. "I hope you don't mind if I sit here?" she asked. Her red-gold curls caught the light and created a halo of sorts around her head.

"Of course, please," Gwendolyn answered, because she had little other choice. However, if Mr. Steele walked into the room, Gwendolyn would be tempted to elbow the woman off the settee. She instinctively did not trust her.

"We were introduced earlier. I'm Violet Rabron."

"Gwendolyn Lanscarr."

Lady Rabron smiled, her gloved hands folded in her lap.

There followed an awkward moment of silence. Gwendolyn sensed the woman had a purpose in searching her out. She waited.

"Have you heard Miss Purley sing before?"

Lady Rabron asked as if she'd been racking her brain for a topic of conversation other than her true purpose.

"Unfortunately, I have not," Gwendolyn replied politely.

"It shall be a first for both of us."

"That is so."

"This is also my first visit to Colemore," Lady Rabron said. "Have you been here before?"

Gwendolyn shifted in her seat. They had discussed this earlier when they were first introduced. Did Lady Rabron have no recollection? "This is my first visit as well. I'm Lady Orpington's whist partner."

Lady Rabron's eyes widened in mock horror. "I'm shocked that our hostess has refused to allow anyone to play whist. I'd understood it was an important game at Colemore."

Remembering her husband's earlier rudeness, Gwendolyn decided to let the topic be. "The weather is nice this evening."

Lady Rabron nodded. "I suppose." She fell silent.

Gwendolyn didn't choose to fill the void. Polite conversation was so trying.

Suddenly Lady Rabron asked, "Is there a connection between you and Mr. Curran?"

Lady Rabron was finally showing her purpose, and Gwendolyn was vastly annoyed. Was there any woman in this room uninterested in him?

"We are friends," Gwendolyn answered, hoping she sounded somewhat cool and detached.

"Ah," Lady Rabron said. She winced as the

rehearsing Lady Julia hit a note in disagreement with the pianoforte. "I noticed Mr. Curran kept looking in your direction during dinner. When he thought you weren't paying attention."

That news caused Gwendolyn's heart to do a little jig. "I don't know why he would," she managed to say.

"You do," Lady Rabron countered. Her limpid gaze met Gwendolyn's with a startling directness. "You have been watching the door with the patience of a hungry hawk. I know how that is." She waited two beats and added, "There was a time I watched for him as well. He was in love with me. And I him. We were devoted to each other. He asked for my father's permission to marry me."

Gwendolyn felt the smile on her face fade. Usually, when at a disadvantage for any reason, she was good at concealing her thoughts and disappointments.

But not this time.

She didn't speak. She couldn't. She didn't want to hear whatever story Violet Rabron had to tell. And yet she was powerless to stop her.

"Father said no," Lady Rabron said. Regret colored each of those three words.

She closed her eyes a moment and then put on a brave face to tell Gwendolyn, "I needed to marry for my family. I needed to marry for money and connections . . ."

Her voice died away. She studied some point on the floor as if lost in the memories. Gwendolyn sat silent. She suddenly found it hard to breathe, let alone comprehend what the woman was saying to her. In all of her musings about Mr. Steele, she'd never imagined that he'd had a grand passion for another, especially such a watery miss like Lady Rabron.

Her ladyship gave herself a little shake as if to rally and accept life as it was. "I'm certain you understand, Miss Lanscarr. A military captain, which he was at the time, and even one so dashing and brilliant, would not suit." She paused and then added softly, "The decision broke my heart. Beckett and I were so in love."

In love? It took a moment for the implication of Lady Rabron's avowal to sink in. He'd asked *this* woman to *marry him*?

It was in that moment that Gwendolyn realized how neatly she had discounted the conversation in Lady Orpington's coach. The one where he'd warned her not to fall in love with him. She had assumed that meant Mr. Steele had never been in love before. Therefore, he could not appreciate the depth of Gwendolyn's feelings for him.

How could she be so utterly naive?

The strangest part of Lady Rabron's confession was that she had *refused* Mr. Steele. If it had been Gwendolyn's choice, she would have run off with the man she loved, her family be damned.

But that wasn't completely true either. Gwendolyn had been prepared to marry a portly squire with a host of unruly children if it had meant that her sisters would be safe and free to marry men of their station. She understood the choice Lady Rabron made.

That didn't mean Gwendolyn liked this new

information. Mr. Steele had been in love, and not with her.

She thought of him standing with Lady Rabron and her husband when they were first introduced to her. Now she saw Mr. Steele's unease in a new light. She'd been so wrapped up in "helping" him, she hadn't noticed.

And then a new panic seized her—Lady Rabron knew that Mr. Steele was not Nicholas Curran. She had even just called him by his given name, Beckett.

As if reading her mind, Lady Rabron placed a hand over hers. She brought her head close to Gwendolyn's, her voice low. "Don't worry. I shall not denounce him. But why is he pretending to be someone else?"

Gwendolyn thought quickly. She widened her eyes and behaved as if this was news to her. "Someone else? What are you saying?"

"Oh, dear." Lady Rabron removed her hand. "I thought—" She paused, glanced around the room. The door had opened. The gentlemen came streaming in to join them. She forced a cheerful smile and came to her feet. "I need to find my husband."

The men's voices were boisterous as if the port had flowed freely. Lord Rabron was hanging on to Captain McGrath. His hair was slightly mussed and his cheeks ruddy.

And Gwendolyn watched Lady Rabron register disapproval and then resigned disappointment in what she saw. She caught Gwendolyn's expression. Her chin lifted as if ready to inform Gwendolyn to not pity her, but then her expression softened. "He is not that bad a sort." Her words lacked conviction.

Lord Rabron didn't approach his wife but swooped down on the sweetmeats table along with his drinking companions. Lord Ellisfield shouted for a whisky. A footman went running.

Meanwhile, Mrs. Purley and Lady Middlebury attempted to ask for quiet so that "the very talented Miss Purley" could sing. And over in a corner, Lady Orpington had the rector's ear and was talking away, most certainly, about whist.

But there was no Mr. Steele.

"He's not here," Lady Rabron said, more to herself than an answer to Gwendolyn's unspoken question. "He'll appear." Then she leaned close to Gwendolyn, her focus sharpening. "You have an attachment for him, don't you? I understand why. He makes the other men here tonight look like children. However, I want you to know, he's *mine*. He loves me. And now that I have found him again, I will not let him go."

"You are married."

Lady Rabron gave a dismissive wave. "I've honored my vows. I've given my husband two sons. The time has come for me to seek my own happiness. He was *devoted* to me." Gwendolyn knew she spoke of Mr. Steele. "He told me I was his sun, his stars and moon. It isn't my fault that we couldn't be together. Or his."

Her assumption that apparently all she had to do was snap her fingers and Mr. Steele would fall to her feet outraged Gwendolyn. The woman had rejected him. She even sounded smug about it. What right did she have to expect anything of him? "I believe Mr. *Curran* can and will make decisions for himself." She emphasized the fake name deliberately, a reminder to Lady Rabron. If the woman truly had feelings for him, she would be cautious.

Lady Rabron's gaze narrowed as if she'd caught the reprimand, and wasn't pleased. She walked off.

Gwendolyn watched her weave her way to find a place to sit for Miss Purley's performance. Would Lady Rabron betray Mr. Steele's identity? Would she expose Mr. Curran as a fraud?

Of course she would. She was in a miserable marriage, one of her own making. Seeing her former suitor had raised her spirits. But if Mr. Steele rejected her, how might she react?

And if she thought Gwendolyn would docilely stand by and do nothing to protect him, she was wrong.

The problem was, Mr. Steele had not returned with the gentlemen. Gwendolyn wondered where he was. She hoped he appeared in time for her to warn him of Lady Rabron's intentions . . . that is, if he wished to be warned.

Doubt began to worm its way into her thinking, especially as time passed and he didn't make an appearance. She remembered Mr. Steele's warning to her that day in the coach when he'd chastised her for being attracted to him. Was it possible he had cautioned Gwendolyn not to have feelings for him because he still carried a torch for Lady Rabron? He hadn't acted as if he did since they arrived at Colemore.

Gwendolyn looked over at Lady Rabron and wanted to believe all the way to her bones that Mr. Steele now had better taste. He'd obviously been very young when he'd made his offer. Why else would he fix his attention on such a shallow woman?

A wave of loneliness rolled through her. She wished her sisters were here. They would commiserate with her over this unwelcome information, even though Dara might secretly rejoice.

Finally, Lady Middlebury commanded the room's attention to introduce Miss Purley. The singing began. Lady Julia accompanied her while Lady Beth turned the pages. Miss Purley did, indeed, have a lovely voice. Her parents smiled indulgently, their chests puffed with pride. They kept looking over at Lord Ellisfield to see if he noticed how talented their daughter was.

Gwendolyn doubted if he did. He leaned against a wall as if it held him up.

As for Gwendolyn, she couldn't carry a tune. But she did have a talent—loyalty.

Mr. Steele needed to be warned of Lady Rabron's intentions to claim him at all costs. And that she could expose him, if she so desired.

Or at least, sitting there listening to Miss Purley warble on, Gwendolyn convinced herself that was what she must do . . . because confronting him would also give her the opportunity to gauge his reaction to Lady Rabron, one she hoped would be as enraged as her own.

BECK TOOK HIS time as he made his way back to the house.

Colemore raised more questions than it had answered. Nothing made sense.

Most of all, his father.

His dreams had been vivid but disjointed and scrambled. What if they meant nothing? What if they were just the delusions of a head wound?

He stopped at the edge of the garden and looked up at the great house. A bank of rooms was well lit. Apparently most of the guests were still up. Beck didn't hurry to join the company. He liked it out here in the dark. He could hide here. He could think.

Beck was not pleased to have run into Violet. He'd learned a great deal about human nature, and about women, since those tender years of his youth. Violet had let him declare his love for her, approach her father . . . and all the while, she'd known that her father would never give permission for them to marry. She'd *known*.

Love had been hard for Beck. He'd never experienced it until Violet. Part of his attraction to her was that she had a family. Families were both a mystery and the Holy Grail. He'd wanted to be included.

He wasn't. Her father had made that clear. In spite of Beck's commission, Danvers had referred to him as little better than a mongrel and not worthy of his daughter.

Beck had never met Lord Rabron, the man who had been chosen. Beck had been fighting the French in Portugal when he'd heard that Violet had married. He hadn't been as devastated as he'd anticipated. Then again, he'd been rather busy.

However, Violet's rejection had convinced him that life was easier spent alone. No one had ever wanted him; why should he want them?

He now walked around the house to the far wing, the East Wing, keeping in the shadows. His room was located in this section. He found a side door and the servants' stairs. The stairway was lit with wall sconces, not ones as fine as in the hallway but serviceable. He climbed his way to the first floor and then cracked a door open, pausing to listen.

A woman was singing. She was a far cry from the glorious voice in his dreams—

He heard a step on the stairs above him. The person couldn't be a servant. He moved like a child did, a step and a pause to bring feet together, then another step. The progress of the old, the crippled, or the anxious.

Beck waited. If it was a servant, he needn't say anything. If it wasn't a servant, he wanted to know who else had reason to take these back stairs. Beck turned as if occupied with looking out into the hall.

He could feel the person come up behind him. A hand clamped down on his shoulder.

Beck whirled around, grabbing the man's wrist, only to find himself looking at Lord Middlebury.

The marquess's eyes widened at how quickly Beck had moved. "I didn't mean to alarm you," he said. Beck didn't answer at first. He couldn't.

Laying eyes on his father for the first time had been a bit unnerving earlier, even though he had told himself he had been prepared for the meeting.

But here, in the very close confines of the servants' stairs, the full impact of his father's presence threw him completely off guard. He had thought Middlebury almost as tall as he was. He wasn't, not up close. He was several inches shorter.

The man smelled of brandy. That must have been his "research," and the reason he shook as if with palsy or moved so carefully. A drunk had to be wary of stairs.

Being this close, Beck noticed in the candle's thin, flickering yellow light the places his father's valet had missed when he'd shaved him. His forehead was furrowed with deep worry lines.

"Here, here, here now," the marquess grumbled, tugging on the wrist Beck held. Beck let go.

"My lord, you surprised me," Beck said respectfully.

"Did I?" Delight came to his eye. "That is good? Yes?" And then suspicion. "What are you doing here?"

"Avoiding being forced to hear a young woman sing."

"The Purley chit. My wife said she was to entertain the company. Is she any good?"

"I don't wish to be trapped with the others to find out."

The marquess nodded as if that made sense. Then he abruptly changed the topic. "Would you like to see my research?"

"Yes," Beck said without hesitation.

"Come then." He motioned for Beck to follow him as he started up the stairs to the next floor. His movements were easier going up the staircase. He opened the door and held it for Beck to join him in the passageway.

A trio of servants were standing there. One didn't wear livery and was probably the valet. He spoke. "My lord, we were looking for you."

"I'm right there." The marquess said this brusquely and with the consequence of a noble. He no longer sounded confused. The valet and servants stepped back, and the marquess led Beck toward a set of double doors at the end of the hall.

Beck half expected the servants to attempt to stop him. Instead, they too followed in the marquess's wake.

"This way," his father said, opening one of the double doors himself.

Inside, another valet was preparing the room for bed. He nodded in deference to his lord but, again, did not act alarmed to see Beck.

Lord Middlebury led him into a side room that served as a study but reminded Beck of an apothecary shop with stacks of what appeared to be dried herbs and flowers on the side table and filling sections of shelves lining the walls. There were also stuffed birds and small animals, their glass eyes reflecting the light of candles in the black iron chandelier. The chairs and desk were covered with books cracked open to certain pages. In the middle of the desk was a stack of papers that resembled a manuscript. The pages were covered with cramped handwriting, splotched with ink stains. There was no window, and the air was smoky from the burning of tallow candles and laden with the smells of old leather, glues, and whatever plants he was harboring.

The marquess walked around the desk and sat. "Now, here is my research." He looked up as if expecting Beck to be impressed and then pointed an impatient finger at a chair stacked with books on the opposite side of the desk, a silent order for him to sit.

Beck looked askance before moving the stack.

"Yes, yes," his lordship said. "Move it all."

Placing the stack on top of another pile of books on another chair, Beck sat. "What does your research concern, my lord?"

"I'm doing a complete history of all the flora, fauna, and insects at Colemore."

Only then did Beck notice the board on the wall with insects stuck to it. "That sounds like an interesting study, my lord," he replied politely.

His father nodded agreement. "Very important, very important. I've even been tracking the river's course. It is constantly changing. Oh, not in a way that a yeoman would notice. However, a scientist looks at incremental differences. I study to see if the changes have an effect on the natural habitats of all living creatures." He pointed to a stuffed pink-footed goose looking down on them.

Beck had not anticipated such a direct and sensible answer. "I'm certain they do."

"You would be right." There was no shake in his lordship's hand now even though a wine cup was close at hand. He dipped a pen in ink. He prepared to write. "I also keep track of everyone who comes to visit Colemore. We, too, are living creatures. I forgot a few names of our guests. You were one of them. You are?"

For a beat, Beck was tempted to say, *Your son.* But the man obviously didn't see any resemblance. To be fair, Beck must favor his mother.

He wanted to ask Lord Middlebury her name, to have plain speaking and be done with this . . . but something warned him that now was not the time. He didn't wish to upset his father. Not if he didn't have to. "Nicholas Curran. Lady Orpington's nephew."

"Curran. Is that with *i-n* or *a-n*?"

"*A-n.*"

"Ah, good. Do you have an education, Curran?"

"I attended Faircote." Lord Middlebury had paid for it. He did not seem to recognize the school even as he wrote it down, saying aloud, "Fair-*cote.*" Curious.

Lord Middlebury blew on the paper.

A valet appeared at the door. "Are you wishing to go to bed soon, my lord?"

"I am. Had to catch this Curran fellow and document him." He nodded to Beck. "Glad to have a moment of your time, sir. Good of you." He stood.

Beck realized he was being dismissed. He rose to his feet. "I am happy to be of service, my lord."

"See your way out on your own, will you? I am tired. Too tired." A second ago, he'd been energetic, even forceful. Now, in a blink, his shoulders sagged.

Beck gave a bow. One of the valets led him out of the marquess's rooms.

Out in the hallway, Beck said, "His research seems intense."

"It is, sir," the impassive servant answered.

"Does he go afield?"

"He has in the past, back when Winstead was with us."

Beck kept his voice carefully neutral. "Winstead?"

"Yes, sir. He was Lord Middlebury's personal servant. He went with the marquess on each of his endeavors."

"Where is Winstead now?"

"He went to visit his family. He did that from time to time. He has not yet returned."

"Has he been gone long?" Beck had to ask, curious as to the answer. His confrontation with Winstead had been close to ten months ago.

Instead of answering the question, the servant said, "I believe the musicale has ended. However, the young lords are in the billiards room. You may wish to join them?"

Beck had no desire to spend time drinking, especially with Ellisfield. Besides, he, too, was tired. It had been a long day. "I can see myself to my room from here."

The valet bowed and returned to the marquess.

Beck took the main stairs to the next floor,

where his bedroom was. He thought of taking another look at the portrait, but there was a small group in the library, talking among themselves. He could hear Lady Orpington complaining about having all card games banned in between ordering Magpie to stop "snapping at Lord Killenhall."

Lord Killenhall's deep rumble of a voice said he was ready for his bed, and Beck hastened his step to avoid being pulled into a conversation with Lady Orpington.

He wondered what was truly behind Lady Middlebury's edict. This was a question to puzzle over in the morning. He went to his room further down the hall. He was glad he didn't need to fuss with a valet. However, because he didn't have a personal servant, and because he forgot to ask the porter for a lit taper, his room was dark.

Beck didn't mind. Moonlight streamed through the window, throwing silver panes across the bedclothes. He shut the door and began tugging at his neckcloth, wanting to at last be free of it—when he realized he was not alone. A person dressed in white sat in the shadows. He thought of Jem's ghostie story, although he recognized the silhouette.

"Violet?"

The moon highlighted her reddish-blond hair flowing over her shoulders. She stood so she was silhouetted against the window. "Beck," she whispered. There had been a time he had dreamed of such a moment. Of her coming to him. Of her being his.

Now he was too damned tired to care.

Or *was* he that tired?

He frowned, and then realized that if she had been taller with raven-black hair, golden-brown eyes, and an obstinate nature, he wouldn't have been weary at all.

"Violet, your husband—" he started, using the easiest excuse available.

"My husband is busy drinking with his sporting friends. He hasn't been interested in my bed or me for the past year or more. Ever since our second son was born." She held out her arms. "I'm lonely, Beck, and I've never stopped thinking of you."

But he'd stopped thinking of her. In fact, even the resentment, the sense of betrayal he'd nursed for years was gone. Instead, he was glad she had rejected him. He didn't want a wife who crept around to other men's beds.

Now the question was how to convince her to leave, because at any moment, the group in the billiards room could break up. A husband full of brandy and whatever else never made sound decisions.

A soft noise out in the hall caught his attention. A folded sheet of paper started to slide beneath his door. He stepped on it with his boot, and the person on the other side pressed the note forward as if determined to deliver it. Beck knew before he opened the door who was there— Gwendolyn.

She still wore her dinner clothes, but her hair was down in one long braid over her shoulder. She looked up in surprise as if she had not expected to be caught on her clandestine mission.

And he'd never been so happy to see her. Granted, she wouldn't have been his optimum choice. He would have preferred a maid or even Lady Orpington—but he was in a touchy situation. Violet apparently expected him to fall into her arms. He was in no danger from her attempt to seduce him. The ship on that matter had sailed long ago when she'd rejected him.

However, a scorned woman who knew his true identity could upset all his plans. He needed to be careful . . . and Gwendolyn was the only diversion available to him.

Beck reached for her arm and pulled her into the room.

CHAPTER TWELVE

The more Gwendolyn had thought about Lady Rabron's possessiveness toward Mr. Steele, the more she found the woman's words unsettling. Would she truly expose him as an imposter if he didn't cater to her desires? Was that love? Gwendolyn thought not.

So she had written a note. The message was simple.

Lady Rabron may betray you. Be careful.

This was not a message Gwendolyn could give over to Molly to be delivered. What if it ended up in the wrong hands?

What if Molly mentioned to Tweedie or Dara that she had been passing notes to a Mr. Curran? In the late hours of the night? That would inspire a host of lectures Gwendolyn didn't wish to hear. She would be expected to explain herself.

No, she could only trust herself.

And so, she'd waited until most of the guests had sought out their rooms and the hallway was quiet. For a coin, the porter had told her which room was Mr. Curran's.

Her plan was simple. She had let Molly prepare her for bed. Once the maid had left, Gwendolyn put on her dress and snuck out of her room. She would slip the note under his door and then run back to her room and no one would be the wiser.

She hadn't anticipated the door opening and Mr. Steele pulling her inside.

His room was dark save for the moonlight. He shut the door behind her, and they were *alone*.

Gwendolyn's stomach curled with the enormity of what was happening. She was alone with Mr. Steele *in his bedroom*. In the dark.

And he smelled of fresh night air, the smoke of burning wood, and that hint of spiciness that she associated with him. He gripped her arm as if he was happy to see her, as if he'd never let go.

She readied to explain about the conversation with Lady Rabron and her needing to warn him—but she was alone with Mr. Steele . . . in his *bedroom* . . . in the *dark*.

Rules could be bent in the dark, or broken completely. Reputations were ruined in the dark, even happily given up.

And wasn't this what she truly wanted? To be alone, *with him*. She looked up at him. The lines of his face, the strong jaw, the straight nose, the firm mouth, were highlighted by the silver in the moonlight. He was the most perfect man she'd ever seen, and they were—

Her peripheral vision detected movement.

It took a second for her to register that he was *not* alone, even as a woman gasped her outrage.

Gwendolyn recognized the source. Lady Rabron.

No wonder he'd dragged her into his room, and his grip holding her was tight. He needed help. Just as the moonlight had fallen romantically upon Mr. Steele, it now unromantically outlined Lady Rabron's figure in the cotton lawn of her nightdress. It shone off her blond hair that curled past her shoulders. She was a woman ready for bed.

Or a bedding.

Her ladyship was trying to compromise him, just as Gwendolyn had suspected.

The problem was . . . Gwendolyn's reputation was far more fragile than his or Lady Rabron's. And now, whether she liked it or not, she was involved. Her scratching at his door was certainly a mannerism of the hopping around different beds that was whispered to be common at house parties.

"Did you need me, Miss Lanscarr?" he asked as if they were standing in the library down the hall and not his bedroom. He reached for the door handle. "Very well. I will come with you," he said as if she'd spoken. He opened the door and practically pushed her through it. He followed, taking her arm again. He marched her down the hall to the small library before he stopped. Some guests had been in there earlier, but now they were gone. Not even the porter was there to see Mr. Steele rush her into the room.

The room was dark save for the moon's light through the window. It fell against the wall, highlighting the portrait of the musical young woman. He closed the door before releasing the breath he'd been holding. "Thank you—"

She cut him off. "You need to return and tell her that we did not have an assignation planned."

He gave a small, unworried shrug. "I acted as if you needed my immediate attention."

Gwendolyn made an impatient sound. "Do you truly believe Lady Rabron is so gullible? If so, you know nothing of the feminine character. That woman didn't have bubbles for brains. She knew you were running, and she will blame me."

"Because you needed my help?" he questioned densely.

"Because she will assume I was sneaking into your room for the same reason she was there. She'll believe I stole you from her."

"It wasn't my attention she wanted. She was looking for a romp," he assured Gwendolyn with cool dismissal—and something inside her snapped.

"Maybe *I'm* the one with bubbles for brains," she announced.

"Why do you say that?"

She took a step away from him, her eyes scanning the deep shadows of the bookshelves as she attempted to sort it all out. "She told me you asked for her hand."

Silence met her words.

Gwendolyn waited. When he didn't speak, she turned to him. Silvery light from the window hit the hard planes of his face, the breadth of his shoulders. Had her words turned him to stone?

"I did." Another beat. "I didn't—" he started, but she interrupted.

"Don't tell me you have forgotten any of the feelings you must have once had for her? Marriage is an important step, sir. Don't tell me you didn't care for her. You aren't that sort of man."

He released his breath slowly as if just gaining the right of things. "I worshipped her," he said.

Gwendolyn didn't want to hear that. "Your sun and stars," she said, repeating Lady Rabron's words.

"So I thought. She had me convinced I mattered to her as well." He shifted his weight, but he did not move toward Gwendolyn. "She rejected me, and I was humbled. Not for the first time. Not for the last." He fell quiet and then added, "Satisfied? Is that what you wished to hear?"

"You don't mention brokenhearted." She turned her head, noticing the black binders of music on the bottom shelf. She focused on them, her own heart heavy and sad and peevish, her mind trying to sort out the reasons why.

"No. I overcame that. I always *overcome*," he stressed bitterly. "I wanted so much, Miss Lanscarr. I wanted roots and a feeling that I mattered, and that the future would be good. When Violet noticed me, all of that seemed possible." He paused before concluding bitterly, "I wanted *more* than a mere romp. I *wanted* someone to believe in me."

Gwendolyn swung her gaze up to him. "I believe in you. You rejected me . . . without giving even the idea of us a chance. And there is something between us. You can't deny it—"

She stopped, frowned. Then admitted, "You can deny it. You have."

Her own culpability threatened to overwhelm her. Gwendolyn leaned over, stunned.

"Gwendolyn?"

She held up a hand to stave him off. She didn't want him near her. Not now. Not ever. She started for the door.

Dara had been right. Her sister had warned her. She had sensed in that way siblings have that Gwendolyn might have been lost in her own hopes and imaginings.

Well, why not? Gwendolyn had never been in love before. She'd read about it, dreamed of it, longed for it, but had never experienced it—until him.

Or was it love? Something about him called to her, and it was more than mere lust, or so she believed. She liked standing beside him. She felt safe near him. She'd trusted him . . . or had that been, as Dara suggested, her own inexperience?

Gwendolyn didn't know. But the man had been forthright with her. He'd told her there was nothing between them. She'd just believed that he'd not understood the depth of her feelings, of her loyalty and her admiration. She'd been wrong. Shame burned through her. If Lady Rabron hadn't been in the room when he had pulled Gwendolyn in, she would have happily climbed into his bed. She wanted to believe the best of him, even when he warned her not to.

"My sister was right," she said.

"About?"

"You. She said I was being ridiculous pining over you—"

"Gwendolyn," he started to protest.

He used her given name again. She still liked

the way he said it, but she was seeing clearly now. She winced, and he fell silent.

She moved toward the door. She didn't speak. Her throat was too tight. She needed to find her room before she disgraced herself.

"Why did you come to my door?" he asked.

Gwendolyn drew a breath, faced him, forced herself to talk past the slithering emotions roiling inside her. "I wished to warn you that Lady Rabron wants her talons in you. She made her intentions very clear to me, and I sought to help. Ironic, isn't it?"

"You did help," he insisted quietly.

She tilted her head, believing she was seeing the full measure of him at last. He was wildly handsome, but also a bit feral. And, perhaps, damaged. Was it because of his base birth, something Gwendolyn would have happily overlooked out of her attraction to him? Or did he nurture resentments? Was he incapable of letting someone love him?

Gwendolyn frowned. Did she want a man who made her do all the work?

"You are a fool, Mr. Curran," she said, and left the room.

Shame burned through her. Gwendolyn hurried her step toward her room. The porter had not returned to his post. She was grateful for that small favor.

He did not follow, and she told herself that was good.

But disappointing.

This was what was behind Dara's warnings. It was what her sister had feared.

Gwendolyn also knew that no matter the consequences, her family would stand beside her.

She climbed under her bedcovers without undressing, a mortal sin for someone who stitched her own clothing. She even wore her shoes until she realized how silly she was being and kicked them off.

But sleep didn't come, not with guilt hounding her.

Lady Rabron was no fool. She knew Mr. Steele had put her off. The sting of rejection would bring out the worst in her, as it did all women. Her ladyship would look for a scapegoat and focus on Gwendolyn. She'd find willing allies in shredding Gwendolyn's reputation in Miss Purley and her friends. The story would be bandied around London in less than a fortnight. Once that happened, not even the loyal Viscount Morley would be interested in Gwendolyn's hand. Truth was not important when rumors were juicy.

And while she'd laughed at Dara's fears of her being a spinster . . . being ruined was not a pleasant prospect.

Her only solace was that she was truly and completely done with Mr. Steele.

He was right. She was too good for him.

"Miss Gwendolyn, you must wake. *Miss Gwendolyn.*"

Gwendolyn tried to bat Molly away. She pulled the bedclothes higher up over her and gave Molly her back.

"Miss *Gwendolyn*." Molly began shaking her shoulder. "You need to rise. I have to help you dress."

"Am dressed," Gwendolyn informed her.

"In your riding habit," Molly replied patiently, giving her another shake. "You want to go riding. You requested a horse."

"No, want to sleep."

"You promised to go riding with Mr. Curran this morning."

Mr. Curran. The name took a moment to wiggle its way into her exhausted mind. When it did, Gwendolyn didn't need to open her eyes to bite out, "I made no such promise." She buried her nose in her pillow.

Molly made a frustrated sound before trying a different tack. "Miss, you adore riding. You planned to ride this morning. And he's waiting for you."

Gwendolyn threw herself onto her back, her eyes still closed. "He can wait forever for all I care."

"But the horses can't. You hate to see saddled horses just standing around for their riders. You've told me that before. You think it is rude when riders don't consider their mounts."

This was true. She slitted open her eyes. "Molly, I will not ride with him. Tell him that." Although she was tempted to ride. A horse *had* been saddled. She missed riding. She could arrange for one of the stable lads to escort her.

"I'd rather not, miss. He tracked me down in the servants' quarters. Stood over my bed and ordered me to come fetch you."

That woke Gwendolyn. She sat up. "Who is he to tell my maid what to do?"

"If you had been out there to meet him at the appointed hour, he would not have had to do that," Molly muttered.

"Excuse me? Did he claim we were to meet this morning? *That* is not true."

"He said you would say that. He said I should not believe you."

Gwendolyn's temper exploded, fueled by lack of sleep and her very recent resolve to rip Mr. Steele out of her life. "Who does he believe he is?"

"Oh, I can't say, Miss Gwendolyn. However, I have your habit right here." She held up the garment.

"He is telling lies."

"That he might," Molly agreed before pointing out, "but you look so fetching in your new habit. 'Twould be a shame to not wear it. Please, Miss Gwendolyn, it is only a wee ride. Can't you do it?"

Gwendolyn wanted to shriek her frustration. She swung her legs over the side of the bed. "*Why* are you pushing me to do this?"

"He promised me a gold crown if I could rouse you out of the room to ride with him," Molly said evenly. "He's waiting on the front lawn with two horses. Please, miss, I would like that gold crown. I've never even seen one."

"What if I paid you a gold crown to tell him to—" Gwendolyn broke off before she said something she shouldn't. Besides, Molly knew she didn't have any money to call her own.

Abruptly Molly's eyes widened. She grinned as if she'd made a discovery. "I've never seen you like this over a gentleman, miss. You *like* him."

"I do not." Purging him from her system had been what last night was all about.

"Now I really think you should ride," Molly insisted.

"I'm tired."

"You don't look like you slept well," Molly commiserated.

Gwendolyn shot a glance toward the looking glass in the room, and frowned at what she saw. Her hair had come loose from its braid and was every which way. Her eyes looked like tiny, angry slits—

"I can make you look as if you slept like a princess, all fresh and relaxed," Molly offered seductively.

"You could?"

"He won't know you gave one thought to him," Molly answered, revealing that she understood the situation.

Gwendolyn considered a moment. She hated that she hung on his every word, looked for him in every gathering, shared what she was thinking at every opportunity, and he didn't return one ounce of the same regard.

This trip to help him unlock the mystery of his past had been the single most exciting adventure of her life—because she was helping him. She'd wanted to believe he'd chosen her.

Except he hadn't. Mr. Steele didn't need anyone. He'd told her as much in Lady Orpington's coach. She just hadn't wanted to accept it. She preferred to trust *her* instincts. To believe he was as attracted to her as she was to him.

And yet he had continuously dismissed her, and she was tired of it.

She looked stunning in her new riding habit. If she dazzled him and behaved as if his actions were of little interest to her, could she not reclaim a bit of her pride back?

He might also be pressing her to ride so that he could apologize for what happened last night. The idea of seeing him grovel was worth getting out of bed.

"What of the circles under my eyes?" she questioned Molly.

"Miss Gwendolyn, for a gold coin, they will magically disappear—" The maid wrinkled her nose. "You are wearing your dress from last night. Now I must iron it. That muslin is not easy to keep the creases out of."

"I know, I know," Gwendolyn said. Then she caught another look at herself in the mirror. "You should earn two gold coins if you can make me look brilliant."

"I'll settle for one. Take your dress off," Molly ordered, busily pouring fresh water into the basin bowl on the washstand.

Within a half hour, Gwendolyn did appear brilliant in the deep blue habit. Her hair was twisted and pinned at her nape, the better to wear the dashing riding chapeau with its pheasant feather at a jaunty angle. She caught the loop sewn in the overlong train of her skirt in one hand and left the room, confident that she looked better than good. She sparkled.

She didn't meet anyone as she went down the stairs. The hour was still too early. She was glad her footsteps were muffled on the carpet, because her riding half boots were a bit stiff.

A footman bowed and opened the front door for her, and there *he* was. Mr. Steele held the reins of two horses that he'd patiently been walking. He had his back turned to her as if he enjoyed the morning, and it was a glorious morning. There was that almost-crisp autumn feeling to the air as the sun filtered through scattering clouds. The light fell upon his person as if the whole universe singled him out.

A sudden case of nerves threatened Gwendolyn's resolve. To combat it, she pressed her hand against her stomach. He meant nothing her, she told herself. Repeating those words over and over to herself, she walked out onto the gravel drive.

He heard the crunch of her footsteps and turned. His hat was low, but it did not hide the appreciative gleam in his eyes at the sight of her. Yes, Molly had earned that gold coin.

"Are you a rider, Miss Lanscarr?" he said in greeting, holding up the reins to his bay and a gray gelding with a black mane and stockings.

Her answer was to put a foot in the stirrup before the stable lad could reach her with a mounting block. She lifted herself up in the sidesaddle. It was good to have long legs. It gave one an advantage. She arranged her skirts, took the reins from him, and gave the horse a kick. Her fear was that the horse might have a plodding gait, a "lady's horse," that would make her desire to demonstrate her skill ridiculous instead of confident.

Fortunately, the gelding surprised her. He set off at a smooth trot. "You will be fun to ride," Gwendolyn cooed, giving his neck a pat. He released his air as if agreeing.

A beat later, she heard Mr. Steele coming after her. He brought his horse alongside hers. "Does this mean I've been forgiven?"

All the angst concerning him came roaring back, and she was doubly annoyed. She wanted to say something sharp, to put him in his place . . . but then, in that strange way that things happen, a filter lifted, and she saw her actions clearly. She'd idolized Mr. Steele, and that wasn't wise.

He was a man like any other. Well, obviously more buffle-headed than most since he behaved as if he could control any situation. It was part of his mystique. However, there was one thing he could not control, and that was allowing someone to care for him. Or, even more dangerous, to love him.

"I'm a loner, Miss Lanscarr," he'd told her. *"I like my life the way it is."*

Mr. Steele couldn't value what he had never known.

And her battered little heart softened because the problem was him, not her. She didn't know all that had transpired between him and a young Lady Rabron years ago, but she intuitively understood in this moment that it had crippled him. As had being an orphan.

"No," she said lightly, "my riding with you means that you owe Molly a gold coin." And with those words, she gave the gray a kick. There was a surge of muscle beneath her, and then the horse shot off like a bolt.

Gwendolyn leaned low, letting the animal decide where they should go as long as it wasn't back to the stables. The gray gained speed, especially as Mr. Steele and his bay thundered after them.

They rode across the lawn and tore up a path along the ridge, and then Mr. Steele turned the bay in a new direction, but not back toward the house. He slowed to a trot. Her horse instinctively fell into line.

For a few minutes, they rode in companionable silence. Gwendolyn felt her blood sing with the joy of being out on such a beautiful morning.

"You have a good seat," Mr. Steele said.

"I'm a country lass. I've always enjoyed riding. I've missed it."

His expression turned serious. "Miss Lanscarr—" he started, but she stopped him.

"I don't wish to discuss whatever it is you are about to say. I want to just savor this moment."

Of course he didn't listen to her. "Violet will not gossip."

And just like that, all goodwill evaporated. "This was a bad idea. I'm returning to the house." She would have swung her horse around, but he reached over and caught her reins.

"You said you wanted to help with my purpose here."

She gave him a sour smile. "You told me to

play cards. You said that was *all* you wished from me."

A muscle hardened in his jaw. His eyes were a very dark blue this morning, bluer than she'd ever seen them. He'd shaved. She caught the scent of the soap he'd used. That spicy, spicy aroma of bazaars and places beyond her reach.

Gwendolyn braced herself, wanting an apology, not wanting an apology, wanting him to say he cared for her as much as she did him. And then hating herself for abandoning her night's hard-won convictions. She didn't need him. She didn't want him. She'd already sacrificed enough of her sanity and self-respect for him—

He let go of the reins. "Follow me." He set his horse off down a path into the forest.

"Where are you going?"

He drew his horse to a halt. The forest created a background of green and gold behind him. "There is a river in this direction. I heard a story last night about a cottage located on its banks. I wish to have a look at it."

"What sort of story?"

"A ghost story. The last marchioness built the cottage. It was her sanctuary. She drowned there. I want to take a look at the place. They say she haunts it." He gave a half smile, a canny one. He knew he'd baited a hook that she would find hard to resist. It bothered her that he believed he knew her.

And he was right. He had hooked her on the word *ghost*. She kicked her horse forward. "Where did you hear this story?"

"I thought you were returning to the house?" he said as she drew up beside him.

She could have shoved him out of his saddle for that remark. "You are annoying."

He reacted with genuine surprise. "What have I done?"

"You want my help. You don't want my help." *You look like you wish to kiss me. You don't kiss me.* Gwendolyn shook her head, not wishing to speak *those* thoughts aloud.

But they were true.

They rode in silence a moment. Then he said, "I have a man who is a Middlebury servant. He told me the story."

A shared confidence . . . it was a start . . . maybe. And once again, Gwendolyn had to pick up the thread. "Does the story tell us how the accident happened?"

"It is the same as we've already been told. She had a young son, and the thought is that he may have gone into the water the way children do, and she went after him. They found her body, but he was washed to the sea."

"And now the last marchioness haunts Colemore? I do believe in spirits, Mr. Steele. My family home in Wiltham is full of them. My sisters and I hope they keep our cousin Richard up at night."

"It is claimed some have heard her spirit singing for her child," he said.

"The singing woman." Gwendolyn could barely contain her excitement. "Is it every night? Or just some nights?"

"According to the tale, told by men trying to out-impress each other around a fire, the marquess is the one who can hear her. Interesting, no? He is an odd one." He told her of his meeting with the marquess the night before.

"But you didn't ask him about the ghost."

"There were servants around. He behaved differently than at dinner."

"In what way?"

"More sure of himself, although he is definitely eccentric."

She nodded. "He didn't recognize you? Or see a resemblance?"

"Any resemblance is slight. Thank God."

"It is the nose," Gwendolyn answered. "You, the marquess, and Lord Ellisfield have the same nose. Also, a bit of the same jawline."

Mr. Steele shrugged. "Perhaps. I don't see it all that much. But now you understand why I wish to see the cottage."

And he'd asked Gwendolyn to come with him.

She found herself smiling.

He smiled back . . . and all the promises she'd made to herself in the middle of the night seemed to fade away.

They came to a fork on the bridle path. He turned to the left. "It can't be much farther to the river. I can feel it in the air. Wagner said the marchioness used to go to the cottage every chance she could."

Wagner must be his man. "Is there a reason why?"

"They say she and Lord and Lady Middlebury did not rub along well."

"Unsurprising," Gwendolyn said. "She was foreign. She would have had difficulty with any of the Top One Hundred families of England."

"True. Wagner was told the marquess considered her stubborn. He found her independence annoying."

"Most men would," she replied dryly.

Mr. Steele burst out laughing. The sound echoed around them, and she realized she'd never heard him laugh before. And he was laughing because of her quip.

She couldn't recall one time when any of the men courting her ever caught her little witticisms. Usually they weren't paying attention to anything other than her bosom or the next sentence they wished to utter instead of listening to anything she said.

But whether he admitted it or not, Mr. Steele did pay attention.

And she smiled at him. She couldn't stop herself—because in this moment, the love she felt for him came roaring back with breathtaking force. It was not sane. It was not sensible. But it was there . . .

He spoke. "I did not invite Violet to my room. I don't dally with married women. It is not something I do."

"That is *not* the issue." Although it was good to hear that he had standards.

"Then *what* is it? I'm attempting to apologize."

He spoke as if she was being difficult. "Apologize—even though you have no idea why I am—" She hesitated. She was about to say "disappointed" but realized she actually had no right to expect anything from him. He wanted nothing from her. So, what sense was there in an apology . . . ?

"Speak your mind, Miss Lanscarr. You usually do. I don't believe I have flinched yet." Early morning sun filtered down through the leafy canopy of the trees. It was an idyllic place for confidences, or a fight.

She turned in her saddle to face him. "You have ruined my reputation. By pulling me into the room—"

"It was an impulse—" he started.

"—you gave Lady Rabron grist for the rumor mill."

"But you came to my room," he pointed out with unreasonable male logic.

"My purpose was to slide a note under your door warning you of Lady Rabron's interest, not to be publicly humiliated. If I'd wanted that, I would have pulled my skirts over my head at dinner."

He blinked as if either her words or her vehemence surprised him.

She released her breath in aggravation. Men were obtuse. "Your sex seems to value chastity, even though few of them are chaste at all. As an unmarried woman, I must be careful. One terrible rumor or spiteful word can not only ruin me but also reflect upon my family. I was attempting to warn you, and in doing so, I have compromised myself." She could have added, *with your help.* She didn't. If he didn't understand the role he played, then there was no hope for him.

He sat silent, his brow gathered. Then, "She won't say anything."

Gwendolyn knew he referred to Lady Rabron.

"I'm not so certain." She kicked her horse forward.

Mr. Steele grabbed her reins. "Do you regret helping me?"

The question annoyed her. Her horse had stopped at the touch of his hand. An urge to lash out at him built inside her, but in the end, the truth won out. "No. I believe you needed to be warned." Her gaze dropped to the worn path through the late summer foliage ahead of them. "I told you, I wanted to help."

He released his hold. "You have. You saved me from an ugly scene last night."

Gwendolyn mentally debated that. "You would have managed. My warning was actually unnecessary."

"But the attempt was not wrong," he vowed to her.

"Except, it cost me my pride."

He rocked back in his saddle at her statement. She could feel him study her, and suddenly, she was tired of the game. He did not feel what she felt. Even if he did, he denied it. "We should move on," she said, and would have kicked the gray forward, but then he spoke.

"I don't . . . know another way than being . . . alone."

"Or is it just safer?" Gwendolyn answered. If she'd slapped him, he could not have looked more stunned. "I understand, Beckett." Using his Christian name felt right. "I was orphaned. I grasp that some fears start early in life—"

"It isn't fear—"

"Then what else would you call it? You don't

trust. Fine. You want to be alone. Very well. A woman rejected your suit for a man who may have a title, but a *boring* character." Gwendolyn couldn't imagine tossing aside a young Mr. Steele for someone so fond of brandy and his own conceit like Lord Rabron. It made her question Violet's intelligence.

But she didn't say this. Her focus was on Beckett. "It is hard to trust, but *worth it*." She let the last two words hang in the air before saying briskly, "Now, where is this cottage?" As far as she was concerned, the subject was closed. She lifted her reins, ready to ride.

He didn't move. His jaw tightened. He appeared as if he was trying to form words and questioning their wisdom.

"If you are going to tell me," she warned him, "that you are denying any feelings for me because you aren't worthy of me, then you'd best keep quiet."

"But it is true, Gwendolyn," he snapped back. "You can do far better."

She released a heavy sigh. "Now you are the one who is being boring. Don't tell me what I think, what I feel, or what I want. I have no pretense to nobility. I'm a half-sister. My mother was the daughter of a British civil servant. I have no fortune. But I have a family who loves me and whom I love dearly in return. That makes me vastly wealthier than anyone back at Colemore. So mark my words. If I turn up at breakfast this morning and my reputation has been compromised, then you will have to step up to the mark, Mr. Steele. I won't let my family suffer because you wish to sulk through life alone."

For the briefest of moments, Mr. Steele—Beckett—appeared speechless. And then he said, "Challenge accepted, Miss Lanscarr. I will make an honest woman of you."

She believed he was jesting, but she also knew he was an honorable man. The tension knotting her shoulders over what would become of her when the rumors started eased. "That is not a strong declaration," Gwendolyn noted. "But you didn't argue with me. I consider that a win."

"I will always protect you, Gwendolyn. When I asked you for my favor, I promised no harm would come to you. I meant those words."

She looked away from him. This was what she wanted—she'd dreamed of a promise of any sort, actually.

But it was not *how* she wanted it.

She loved him. Was it too much to wish he loved her, too?

Tears stung her eyes. She blinked them back. Self-pity was a shameful emotion. She gathered her reins. "Where is this cottage?" Had he noticed her reaction? Possibly.

However, he did not mention her lapse of spirit, and for that, she was grateful. Instead, he pushed his horse ahead. They rode through the forest with only the sounds of their horses and the morning bird calls. A squirrel scrambled down a tree, saw the riders, and skittered back up to safety. He sat out on a limb and chattered warning of their invasion to everyone else. She and Beckett didn't speak. Their silence was like a spell around them. It was actually companionable.

Beckett straightened. "The cottage," he said. "We found it."

And there through the trees she caught a glimpse of silver water, a small clearing, and the stone facade of a building.

CHAPTER THIRTEEN

$\mathcal{L}$ooking at the cottage through the trees, an unexpected foreboding fell over Beck. He had an impulse to turn back.

But Gwendolyn was already making her way toward the cottage. She reached the clearing and looked back at him with a smile. "We found it," she said happily. And then she tilted her head as if listening. "Do you hear singing?"

"I don't." He was surprised how hoarse his voice was.

"I don't either. Come, Beckett, let's explore."

He was relieved her good humor had returned. She'd been very quiet the last leg of their ride in spite of his promise to see she came to no harm. And he'd meant those words. In fact, riding beside her, he realized how deeply he'd intended them . . . and he began to allow himself to consider that perhaps, he could trust her? That she was honest with him about her feelings?

That he could allow the spark between them to grow?

His sense of unease lifted. He did not believe

in ghosts. Or in allowing his imagination to run rampant. He kicked his horse forward.

The cottage was a charming stone building covered with vines and the last blooms of summer roses. Someone tended the place. Probably one of Colemore's many gardeners. A path from the front steps led to the riverbank. The water appeared placid and deep at this particular juncture of the river's course. A piling with an iron ring attached stuck out of the water as if waiting to tie up a skiff.

In fact, Beck could imagine the boat. It was white and yellow with oars painted to match. There was a mast in case the boater wished to use it as a sailboat.

The vision was so fanciful, so vivid, it took him aback . . .

There had been a boat like that here. He did more than sense it. He *knew*.

"Shall we go inside?" Gwendolyn asked.

Beck slowly pulled himself from staring at the water to see that she had dismounted, tied her reins on a post there, and waited by the step. Beyond the corner of the cottage, he could see the line of another road, this one wide enough for vehicles. It led to the main road through the estate.

And they had taken a cart here. It, too, was yellow and white and was pulled by a chubby gray pony. Everything was yellow and white, *like daisies* . . .

He heard *her* say those words. They echoed in his ears. *Like daisies*, and then she would laugh because yellow and white together made her happy.

But who was she?

"Beckett?"

He looked over to Gwendolyn. His horse stamped impatiently beneath him, as if he, too, felt something was not right.

I don't think we should be here, he wanted to tell Gwendolyn, but he didn't. Because . . . *she* was here.

The marquess wasn't the only one who heard her.

Gwendolyn looked at the door. The top of it was arched. The wood had been painted white but had grayed with age. She glanced back at him. "I'm going to look inside."

She paused as if expecting an answer.

Beck found it hard to speak. He could hear his blood in his veins. He forced himself to breathe deeply. To relax. His reaction was madness.

And then he realized Gwendolyn was opening the door, and he felt alarmed. *"I want to enter first."* His words came out in a rush. She stopped and cocked her head as if concerned.

Beck dismounted. He led his horse to the post by the door. He knotted his reins around the ring beside hers.

His chest was tight, his movements stiff.

"Beckett?" Her voice was a whisper.

He stopped, one foot on the top step.

"Are you all right?" she asked.

He gave a curt nod. This uneasiness was ridiculous. He'd faced French cannons. And so he reminded himself repeatedly as he stepped between her and the door and lifted the latch.

The cottage was unlocked. He pushed the door open, revealing a large sitting room. Morning light streamed through charming lace-covered windows. The pattern fell upon the stone floor. There was an arrangement of wooden chairs with upholstered seats, but the colors weren't white and yellow, and he realized he hadn't expected them to be. The blue on the upholstery was faded. The stuffing was loose in a few places. They hadn't always been this way.

Gwendolyn slipped past him and walked to the center of the room. "I like this. Look at the view of the river. Lovely." She moved toward the doorway on the other side of the room— and Beck felt his knees buckle with fear. He needed to stop her, except he choked on his own breath.

She walked inside. "It's a music room," she exclaimed gaily. "You should see this."

He did not want to see it, even as his feet, as heavy as iron weights, began moving toward that door.

Images rose in his mind. Violent images. Images that didn't belong to his dream.

The singing woman was screaming at him. *Run. Don't let him catch you.*

And yet Gwendolyn was in there.

He put a hand on the doorframe. Common sense told him that all was fine, and yet tension was winding inside of him, tighter and tighter. *He used to go in and out of this room, using the windows along the far wall as doors if he so chose. He'd been small enough to climb through them easily—*

"I could spend my life in this room," Gwendolyn said, her words cutting through his growing panic. She stood by a pianoforte, basking in the scene out those windows. A sliver of the river could be seen through the far corner. The rest of the view was of the surrounding forest.

Gwendolyn smiled over at him. "It is all lovely and peaceful."

Was it? Beck wasn't certain. He leaned against the doorframe bombarded by doubts and unnamed fears. Details were emerging—but not from his dreams. No, these were memories. *His* memories. It became hard to breathe as he recalled foraging among the leaves, sticks, and pine needles in the woods, creating buildings and even people out of them while she worked on her music. He could see her there now, bent over the pianoforte. She spent hours writing and practicing. Day after day. His world had been the wind in the trees and the melodies, the notes, the rhythms, the sound of her soft laugh of approval when she thought she'd had it right.

When he discovered something truly special, Beck would bring it to her—acorn caps, snails, a chewed-off rabbit leg, all things he'd scavenged from the forest. She'd made him throw out the bit of rabbit and then had kissed his forehead because he was so like his father, she'd said, curious and fascinated by everything.

So like your father.

"Are you feeling well?" Gwendolyn asked. She moved toward him, and she walked *through* the pianoforte, and that was when Beck realized he was imagining it, although it seemed real and solid.

He thought of the black leather folios in the small library, the ones Gwendolyn had noticed.

That had been *her* music, *her* songs. She'd written them . . . in this room—*she had died in this room*.

Suddenly, and with startling clarity, Beck remembered everything.

"The man, he came through the door." He moved into the room, following the path of the intruder. His body no longer held him back, but he felt as if he was not himself. He was that small boy who busied himself while his mother worked.

"What man?" Gwendolyn asked.

"Olin Winstead. The marquess's man." Yes, it had been Winstead. Beck could see him now. Huge and hulking. Beck hadn't been afraid. "I knew him. I liked him. I was playing by the front of the cottage. He picked me up and carried me into the room with him."

"You?" She frowned as if she couldn't picture it.

Beck shook his head. He didn't have time to explain. The tightness was leaving his chest as what seemed like doors in his mind sprang open.

"He held me. Mother was at the pianoforte right here." He framed the space with his hands for Gwendolyn. "She knew something was wrong. She told him to put me down. She spoke sharply. She could be that way. Not with me but with others. She wanted to know what Winstead was doing here. She didn't like him. I could feel her anger. I—I didn't understand why she was upset. It was just Winstead."

Beck walked a pace to the left, then two to the right. He searched the stone floor as if it would help him understand everything.

"What happened next?" Gwendolyn asked.

"He gave me to her. She wrapped her arms around me, but then he put his hands around her throat and began choking her. I thought he was playing at first, and then I realized she was upset. So I yelled for him to let her go. I hit him. I slapped his face. I had to be—what? Four, maybe?" He looked to Gwendolyn. "I have no idea how old I am now, let alone then—but I remember what he did. Gwendolyn, I *remember.* This is what the dreams were trying to tell me."

"This doesn't sound like a dream, Beck. This sounds as if it happened."

"It did." He stared at the window and then said, "When I hit him, Winstead looked down at me. I told him to leave my mother be. I was angry. He had loosened his hold. My actions gave her a chance to bite him so she could break free. I was surprised because one shouldn't bite. I had bitten my cousin—" He paused in surprised realization. "I bit Ellisfield and had been punished for it."

He moved around to the door, seeing it as it was years ago. His mother had raced to the shelves and started throwing anything she could get her hands on at Winstead. "She shouted at me to run, to go find help. I didn't run to the door but out one of the windows. They were all open. Winstead was a big man. He couldn't follow me, but he didn't want me. I heard mother scream." His muscles tightened up and down his back. "I should have helped her." He felt the horror of what he'd failed to do. Tears welled in his eyes. "Or I should have found someone who could have come to her aid, but I was afraid."

"What did you do?"

"I hid. I didn't go for help. He was murdering Mother, and I was shaking so hard my teeth chattered." He flinched at the realization, even as he could remember fear paralyzing him. "She was fighting for her life . . ."

"You were a child," Gwendolyn said crisply, as if brooking no nonsense.

Beck frowned, puzzled by another hard realization. "I didn't recognize Winstead when he came to the brothel for me. I didn't recall him at all. I feared him, but only because he was big and angry. Gwendolyn, I've had no memory of any of this"—he raised a hand to the right side of his head, to the scar hidden by his hair right above his ear—"until I was wounded." Carefully he lowered his hand. "This happened, Gwendolyn. I remember it all now. But how could I have ever forgotten?"

She crossed to him, her voice gentle. "Maybe you didn't *wish* to remember it? You were *a child*." She said this last as if wishing to impress the knowledge on him. "You didn't know how to handle it."

Beck wanted to push the terror of the memories out of his head. At some point, his hat had tumbled to the floor. He hadn't realized it when it happened, but now he didn't bother to pick it up. Instead, he walked out of the room, *that* room, shocked by what he now knew . . . and his own guilt. Why had he not helped his mother? Why had he hidden?

And why had it taken a French bullet to his temple to make him remember?

Now that he did, he wished that bullet had done its job.

Gwendolyn followed him, hovering as if worried.

He moved to the front window that overlooked the calm, deep waters of the river. "He strangled her and threw her into the river."

"Did you see the murder?"

"No, but I heard her die. I peeked from where I was hiding. I saw him pick her up. Her arms, her legs, her head dangled loose. Her hair had come undone. She always had her hair pinned. Then I heard the splash. He came back for me. He knew I hadn't left. My hiding place was amongst those junipers at the side of the cottage."

Beck remembered holding his breath, shocked by what Winstead had done. It had been summer. He and his mother came to the cottage every day. "She didn't like Colemore. She and my aunt argued all the time. It was about money. My aunt and uncle wanted more. Mother refused."

He had liked to escape to the cottage. He enjoyed riding in the yellow-and-white cart, and sometimes his mother let him take the reins.

Funny that he could recall the arguments. He remembered his mother talking to him, explaining that his uncle and aunt needed to live within their means. Her English was excellent, but there was a hint of the country of her birth.

Just as Gwendolyn had the smallest lilt of Ireland in her speech—

"Beck?"

He faced her, glad she was here. The memories, as shocking as they were, were slowly settling into mere facts.

"Winstead lifted me out from my hiding spot. He held me by the scruff of the neck, like a cat does her kittens. I was crying. He asked me if I was scared, and I said I wanted my mother." He looked back at the water. "He carried me to the river's edge. Mother's body was in the water, face down. I reached for her, and Winstead let go of me. I dropped into the river. It's deep there, just off the shore. The boat was tied up, and I tried to reach for it, but my clothes weighed me down. My hand hit the hull. I dug my nails into the boards, trying to find a hold."

The sensation of drowning fell over him. He'd tried to kick his legs, to stay up. Winstead had leaned down with one meaty hand as if to push him under . . .

"He pulled me out." This image was very clear. "He grabbed me by the arm I'd stretched out to the boat and yanked me up onto the shore. He was crying. He said he couldn't do it. He couldn't murder me. Then he held me and sobbed while I coughed up water."

"Did he say what changed his mind?"

Beck shook his head, and then remembered the words. "I'm not a killer." He scowled. "Except he killed her, didn't he? I don't remember him hesitating in taking her life. And she was beautiful, Gwendolyn. Just like in the portrait."

"The portrait?"

"The one in the library." Tears filled his eyes. Not the tears of a frightened boy but the emotions of a man's sorrow. Grief filled him, not just for her death, but for all that he had lost. His mother hadn't been a whore. She hadn't abandoned him. She'd loved him.

Gwendolyn moved to his side. She placed a hand on his arm. He was glad she was there.

"He told me I had to shut my mouth about what I saw. I had to forget everything or he'd throw me back in the river as he had my mother. He then gave me to a woman who was on her way to London."

"Did you know the woman?"

Beck shook his head. "He did, but I don't think I'd ever seen her before. The woman took me to London, but I was unhappy. I was grieving and scared. She told me I was too much trouble. She passed me on to Madam. I learned then that I had best be good because nobody cared about me. No one was left."

It all fell into place. The turbulence inside him that the cottage had created subsided. What had been dark and heavy took on purpose. He glanced back at the river with its water reflecting the morning sun. There was the dark green of the grass, the trees, and the sound of horses impatient to return to the stables.

He'd had a mother . . . and she had loved him very much.

And someone had her murdered.

"I feel as if something exploded inside of my head." He gave a short laugh. "That *is* what a French bullet did." He turned to her and noticed the marks of tears on her face. "Gwendolyn, I didn't mean to burden you."

She swiped at her cheeks with her gloved hand. "What would have happened if you had been here alone and had those memories? I'm glad I was here."

"You don't think I'm mad? What if that was all made up?"

"It's not."

"I was too young to remember—"

"Beckett," she said, grabbing his arm. "I remember when I was about the same age and they put me on a ship for Ireland. My mother was dead. My grandfather had just died. And I was placed in the hands of a woman from our church who was returning to Britain. I can tell you what the captain looked like, what the weather was for that day, who was at the pier when I left, what we ate for meals . . . it is all burned into my memory because it was that important. I was leaving the only home I knew. I felt lost and frightened, and I will never forget."

"But I did."

"No, your mind protected you. It helped you survive. I was traveling toward a family who cared for me. You had nothing."

He shook his head. "What would have happened if I had run for help . . . ?"

"This Winstead would have caught up with you and wrung your neck to protect himself," she answered briskly. "The question is, did he act on his own? You said he was the marquess's man?"

"I don't believe the marquess is behind this. After all, at some point, he learned I was alive and sent me to school—"

He broke off, struck by a new realization.

"What?" Gwendolyn asked.

"The current Lord Middlebury is not my father.

I'm not a bastard." This thought was truly novel. He slowly lowered himself to the nearest chair as the implications began to sink in.

Gwendolyn pulled a chair around to sit next to him. She appeared as stunned as he was.

She broke the silence first. "You are the true Marquess of Middlebury. The title was stolen from you."

This was almost too much for Beck to grasp after years of shame, of feeling unwanted.

Another memory stirred. There had been a portrait in the main house. It was in one of the family rooms. His mother would point out his father. *He was so very proud of his son.*

She'd say that to him.

His son . . . the heir.

Beck shook his head. It was too much. "I'm not certain. What if the murder is my mind playing tricks with me? Or the head wound has me mixed up inside my brain?"

"What we need is confirmation," she agreed. "I don't believe we can ask Lord and Lady Middlebury for this information. Because if your memories are correct, one or both plotted a murder."

"But why had they kept me alive? Why did Lord Middlebury send Winstead to put me in a school?"

"Those are excellent questions," she said. "Especially since everyone thought you were dead." She sat a moment and then said, "You also are not Beckett Steele. You have another name."

He did. Beck searched his mind. "I don't remember it. I also don't think I can ask the marquess or anyone at the house party what it is. In fact, we need to keep my identity a secret more than before."

"Lord Ellisfield referred to his cousin as Robbie."

Beck scowled, not liking the sound of it. The name didn't even feel familiar to him . . . or did it?

Gwendolyn rose to her feet. "There is a place where we can find answers. I believe we need a trip to St. Albion's."

"St. Albion's?"

"It is the village church. One of my dinner companions last night, Reverend Denburn, is the rector there. I'm certain your birth was recorded in the church register. Shall we go? It can't be far." She started moving to the door.

Beck came to his feet. "I believe I should see you back to the house. I don't want you involved in this."

"Too late, Beckett," she replied. "I already am involved. I'm half in love with you, remember? Now, are you coming, or do I need to go by myself? I'm curious even if you aren't."

She marched out the door, ready to do battle—and that was when he fell in love.

It had been coming. It had hovered around him, and he'd kept pushing it away. Ignoring it, calling it by another name—respect, attraction, lust. It was the reason he'd boldly promised to protect her reputation with his name if it came to that.

But now, he fell into "it," shoving reservations and excuses aside.

He loved Gwendolyn Lanscarr. And he found the realization both illuminating and terrifying.

The breadth of what he felt for Gwendolyn shook him to his core.

Had he warned Gwendolyn off because he didn't want her? Nothing could be further from the truth. She had been right in her claim. There had been a connection between them from the moment he'd first laid eyes on her in that Dublin gaming hell.

And his fascination had grown, even when he didn't wish to admit it. He'd told himself it was because he'd been rejected by a woman once, and he did not wish to experience that humiliation again.

Except he knew Gwendolyn's heart, her courage, her intelligence. *Her honesty.* She didn't act thoughtlessly.

She met him as an equal, as if *her* feelings, *her* desires . . . her *opinion* mattered because *he* was important to *her*. He understood that now. Never once had she wavered in her admiration of him . . . even when he hadn't admired himself.

And there wasn't a moment when he'd not been aware of her—the way she tilted her head up to listen to him, the light in her eyes when he approached, her empathy when memory overtook his sanity. She'd been right there beside him. She'd not questioned his quest to find his mother or the horror of what he said had happened.

And if a man didn't value such a woman, if he didn't open his heart to her, then he was a bloody fool.

Beck was no fool.

He rushed for the door. She was checking the

gray's girth. He was struck anew by her grace, her beauty, but he'd known beautiful women, and none of them had Gwendolyn's strength of character.

She was a cut above. She was unique. Precious. *His.*

Beck moved down the steps to her.

"You don't believe we will be too early to call on St. Albion's—" she said as if she thought he hadn't left the cottage yet. Then, realizing he was there, that he stood close, she turned in surprise—and that is when Beck swept her up in his arms and kissed her.

CHAPTER FOURTEEN

The kiss caught Gwendolyn off guard.

Ever since he'd almost kissed her in Dublin, she'd dreamed of this moment. She'd even hugged her pillow and rehearsed for when he'd finally take her in his arms—what she'd say to him, how he'd respond, how she'd answer. She had a conversation of comments planned out.

Except now all those careful, brilliant words flew from her mind . . . because he was kissing her. And words were inadequate.

That didn't mean that another part of her brain wasn't panicking. Gwendolyn had never been kissed by a man before.

Yes, there had been dutiful pecks from boring suitors and the sloppy, quick kisses of the too bold. But this was different. Beckett knew how to hold her in his arms, and there was no timidity about him.

Her breasts flattened against his chest. Her thighs pressed against his. She felt his desire, his passion. It was strong and bold, and she abruptly stiffened, overly conscious that she was going to embarrass herself. She didn't know what she was doing. She would disappoint him and then he'd pull back, and all would be lost.

As if giving credence to her secret fears, Beckett paused, lifted his head. She wrapped her arms around his neck, not wanting to let him go.

"Gwendolyn? Is something wrong?" he asked quietly.

She felt her forehead crinkle in alarm. "I—I—" She stopped, and then confessed, "I don't know what I'm doing. Not when it comes to kissing someone like you."

"Like me?" His features softened. "Then let me guide you. Close your eyes."

She did as instructed.

"Now." His deep voice hummed through her body. "Part your lips and breathe deeply."

As she took the breath, his mouth covered hers, and it was magic. His hold around her tightened. She melted against him, breasts to chest, thighs to thighs, the juncture of her legs against the juncture of his. He didn't push. He kept himself still . . . and all was good.

Because she was safe, she realized. She didn't need to guard against Beckett.

No poet, no writer could have prepared Gwendolyn for what this kiss meant. If she hadn't been in love with him before, she would have tumbled into it now. Who knew that patience in a gentleman was so attractive?

And while Beckett might deny being in love with her, this kiss said different.

An impatient horse nickered.

The kiss broke, but Beckett still held her tight.

"Gwendolyn." His voice was hoarse, as if he struggled with himself.

She held up a stern finger. "If you dare to say I am too good for you—" she threatened.

His lips twisted ruefully as if that was exactly what he'd been about to say. "You'll what?"

"I shall stomp on the toe of your boot so hard you will hobble around for days. Then every time you take a step, you'll think of me and how I don't appreciate nonsense." She paused. "Don't spoil what this is," she whispered.

Beckett nodded. He lifted her hand and pressed his lips against her gloved fingers. Heat flew through the leather, up her arm, right to her heart.

"When this is done," he promised. "When we have all the answers, we'll talk."

She nodded, accepting his plan. "Then let us hurry."

He helped her mount before swinging up into his own saddle. They followed the cart path and came to the road that led through the estate. Some stable lads were exercising their horses. Beck stopped them and asked if this was the direction to the village.

They nodded and told him it was some two miles down the way, not a far distance. Beck and Gwendolyn set off at a trot.

Gwendolyn suspected it was close to half past nine when they reached the village outskirts. It was built around a Norman church, St. Albion's. The church was a small one and relatively unremarkable.

They dismounted and tied their horses to a

post, then walked up the stone pathway through the graves buried in the churchyard. The narrow front door was open.

Taking Gwendolyn's hand, Beckett led her into the church. Their footsteps echoed against the stones. The nave was cool and dark. A candle had been lit as if for prayers, but there was no movement, no sign of anyone.

"Hello?" he called.

Silence.

Beckett frowned. "Someone must be here." He went outside. Gwendolyn followed but stayed in the doorway. From around the corner of the building, she heard Beckett speaking to another man. A beat later, he and a short man with a bald pate and dressed in the clothes of a workman came walking toward her.

"This is Mr. Tucker," Beckett said. "He is the warden. This is Miss Lanscarr."

Mr. Tucker blushed when Gwendolyn smiled at him and bobbed a bow. She was a good four inches taller than he was. "It is a pleasure to meet you, Mr. Tucker."

"My pleasure, my pleasure," the man mumbled. He kept his head ducked as if too shy to look up at Gwendolyn.

Beckett took charge. "We are interested in your church registry of births and deaths."

"You mean the parish record. Yes, it is over here." Mr. Tucker walked to the front of the church where, off to the side, a stone shelf had been built into the wall. The closed ledger sat on it. "Is there anything in particular you would like to see?"

Beckett hesitated, and she understood. They knew the information they wanted, but how to find it? What date were they looking for? He had told her he did not know his exact age.

"We will be looking for a range of dates," she said. "We are searching for information on Mr. Curran's mother." This was actually true. "We aren't certain of the details." Another truth.

"Well, you can look through here." He opened the registry. "We have listings back to the early 1700s. Births and deaths are in the front. Christenings have a section in the back. If you need an earlier date, Reverend Denburn has that registry in his home."

"This should do," Beckett answered.

"Very well. I am trimming around the headstones. I like to keep them neat. Please let me know when you are done."

"Thank you," Beckett said, and Mr. Tucker returned to his task.

Gwendolyn began turning pages. "I can't read anything here. It is too dark, and the writing is very cramped. Or completely illegible."

"Let us go stand by the door."

St. Albion's did not have pews but wooden chairs. They pulled two to the doorway, ignoring the rope to the bell above in the tower. Beckett opened the front door wider. They settled into their chairs, and Gwendolyn reopened the registry.

"Where to start?" he said.

She studied his features, the lines at his eyes from years in the military and squinting into the sun, the masculine maturity of his jaw, his cheekbones, the line of his mouth. "Lord Ellisfield is just over five and thirty, and he told me he remembered the marchioness's son. How old do you believe you are?"

"Thirty-one. I think. I could be younger or older but, I suspect, by not more than a year or so either way."

She made a quick calculation. "Let us start at 1783. That gives us a good range to search." She went to the front of the book. "It starts at 1710."

"It is a small community."

She paged through the 1700s, conscious that he leaned toward her, his arm protectively on the back of her chair so he could read over her shoulder. Births were listed with the names of the parents. That was convenient.

"It shouldn't be hard to find a listing for the Marquess and Marchioness of Middlebury. I imagine they were written with a flourish."

"It still feels strange to me," Beck murmured.

"That they are your parents?" she asked, running a finger down a page, lingering on any births and then moving on.

He didn't answer.

They kept reading.

Ten minutes into their search, she felt Beckett stiffen. He looked out the door. "What is it?" she asked, and then she heard Reverend Denburn's voice. He was saying something to the warden.

A few moments later, he appeared in the doorway. "Hello, Miss Lanscarr." He turned to Beckett, who had risen to his feet out of respect. The reverend regarded him a moment and then said, "I am sorry, sir, I know we've been introduced—"

"Nicholas Curran," Beckett said. "Not a problem. There are a number of guests at Colemore."

"That there are. More than I have ever seen. Like the old days."

Gwendolyn placed a finger in the registry to mark the page. She stood. "You have been to several of the Middlebury house parties?"

"Oh, yes. I am one of the disappointed whist players. What brings you to church this early in the morning? Looking for some spiritual guidance?" He chuckled as if he jested.

"I forced him to join me," Gwendolyn said. She held up the book. "I enjoy genealogy."

"Do you now? Are you searching for anyone in particular?"

Gwendolyn paused. She'd forgotten what they had told Mr. Tucker. However, Beckett was thinking quicker than she was. "My late mother was rumored to be from this village. Or somewhere in Kent. Miss Lanscarr is helping me in the search."

"Family is very important," Reverend Denburn said solemnly. He had a double chin that made him seem older than he probably was. "Well, search away. I hope you find something in your perusal."

"We shall put the registry back on its stand when we are finished," Beckett said respectfully.

"Yes, please do. All right. I'm on my way to breakfast with the marchioness and her guests. Will I see you there?"

"Hopefully," Beckett answered. "I'm famished."

"As am I," Gwendolyn said. The reverend

started to turn, but then she realized she had another question for him. "Reverend?"

He stopped, looked back at her.

"You have been the marchioness's whist partner in the past, correct?"

"I have had that honor. I was playing with her when she defeated Lord and Lady Orpington. Good players. They had been the reigning champions."

She thought of what Lady Orpington had said about her husband's health beginning to fail during those games. Had Reverend Denburn sat quietly and not offered help to an obviously ill man? If so, he wasn't what she would consider a true servant of the Lord.

So she pushed. "Can you tell me why Lady Middlebury refuses to let anyone play this year? It is as if she has banned cards of any sort."

He waved a dismissive hand. "You can play charades, that sort of thing. I also hear the young people wish a dance. The marchioness will even be inviting a few prominent parish families to attend. Nothing like a Colemore country dance to stir the blood."

"But whist?" Gwendolyn pressed. She would think Lady Middlebury would prefer her annual card game over a dance that included locals to increase the number of young people.

Reverend Denburn made a sonorous sound as if considering what he should say before sharing. "Lady Middlebury has had a difficult year. You saw her husband last night. He was—" He paused as if debating a word.

"Slightly erratic?" Beckett suggested.

"He's always been that. He didn't weather the death of his brother well, even though it has been decades. Then Death kept knocking."

"What do you mean?" Gwendolyn asked, wishing to hear the reverend's knowledge of all that had happened.

"Nothing untoward. After his brother, his brother's wife and young son drowned. Did you hear of it?"

"No," Beckett lied for both of them.

"Sad story. He fell into the river, and she died trying to save him. I wasn't here back then, but I've heard stories. I also have a sense," he continued, warming to his topic, "that last year's death of his good friend Lord Orpington stirred up old memories. None of us wish to be reminded of our own mortality. Then again, Lord Middlebury has always been—well, let us say the responsibilities of the estate have rested heavy on his shoulders."

"You have known him long?" Gwendolyn wondered.

"Ever since I took the livelihood here some twenty-five years ago. I met Lady Middlebury first. We are distant cousins. She's been very good to me. To my whole family."

"She seems nothing but kindness," Gwendolyn agreed perfunctorily. "So, I don't understand why she wouldn't let her very good friend Lady Orpington play whist."

He clasped his hands. "What can I say? She is our hostess. Must be going. I shall see you at breakfast if you hurry." On that note, he left the church.

Gwendolyn had, of course, been hoping for more. She looked to Beckett. "He's not a deep thinker." She was quiet a moment and then she said, "What I don't understand is how Lady Middlebury can be so petty as to deny her childhood friend a chance to play her favorite game and win back her title?"

"You ask a question when you already have the answer. Yes," Beckett said as if it was obvious, "she also took advantage of her childhood friend's husband's ill health. *Petty* is a nice description. Of course, Lady Orpington is not letting this go gracefully. They are both like two dogs with one bone."

Gwendolyn nodded. "Something is terribly wrong here. I mean, her behavior is—" She paused, tapped the book, and then she tried a different tack. "If we were talking about my cousin Richard, who took over the family house by declaring our father dead, then I could see such manipulations. But Beckett, these people, all of them, have too much money to be greedy." She frowned. "Don't they?"

"Greed doesn't have a social class. Then again, Gwendolyn, what if my memories of a murder are true? Winstead, the murderer, was the marquess's man. I don't believe he acted independently. If that is true, they risk losing it all. Now, back to the book."

They returned to their search.

And there it was—the third of May 1786, a boy was born to "Marquess and Marchioness of Middlebury." To Gwendolyn's disappointment, no name was recorded.

"The third of May," Beckett said. "I've a birthdate."

"And you are thirty-one, just as you'd thought."

On the same page was the entry of the child's father's death. That writing appeared bleak and somber. The marquess died on the tenth of September 1786

Gwendolyn stared at those entries. "He only had a few months with his son."

"But no name for the child."

"Let us look at the christenings." Gwendolyn turned to the back of the registry, where the baptisms were recorded.

Beckett leaned against her as if anxious for the information. He ran his finger down a few more lines. "Robert Ellicott Dumas William Chaytor, christened on the seventh of May 1786." Beneath his name were the signatures of his godparents, Lord Walter and Lady Chaytor. Walter was the marquess's given name.

His uncle, his godfather, had his mother murdered?

"That is your christened name," Gwendolyn said. "Robert. And from that, Robbie."

"If it is true. How do I know I'm not making up the memories?"

"We will find out," Gwendolyn assured him.

"What do you suggest? Should we ask Lady Middlebury? Accuse her husband of murder? Corner poor, befuddled Lord Middlebury?"

"We will find a way to confirm what did or didn't happen," she answered. "We just have to keep our ears open." She turned back to the births and deaths. "Here is Ellisfield's brother," she murmured. He, too, was at the house party, as was Lord Ellisfield's sister—although it was clear to anyone they were not of any importance. Their brother, the heir, was the person everyone watched and gathered around. She kept going and found the information she wanted.

"'6 June 1790, the death of Catalina Marianna Borromeo Chaytor, Fourth Marchioness of Middlebury, by drowning.' Below it is the entry of your death." She looked up at Beckett. "Even though they never found the body, they have you listed here."

Beckett took the book from her and studied the passages. He shut the ledger and sat a moment. Gwendolyn kept a respectful silence. She could not fathom how he felt. These events were so traumatic. His child's mind had shut them out to protect him.

"I'm not this person," he said as if trying to understand his reactions. "I'm not Robert." He stood.

"Actually," she answered, "you are."

At that moment, Mr. Tucker appeared in the doorway. "How is the research going?"

Gwendolyn forced a smile. "We are done."

Beckett—or Robert . . . or, actually, Lord Middlebury—turned and walked into the sanctuary to return the book to its shelf.

"What did you learn?" Mr. Tucker asked.

Gwendolyn made a little face. "Nothing," she lied. "There is no mention of his family. We had hopes, but you know how family lore is. Memories are never reliable."

"True," Mr. Tucker agreed heartily. "Here, let me help you put back these chairs. I'm done cutting around graves. I have to do it every week. Keep the place tidy."

Beckett joined them. His expression was impassive; however, she was beginning to know him well enough to realize how good he was at hiding his true emotions. "Thank you for letting us look at the registry." He offered the man a coin.

"No need for that, sir. Well, I suppose, yes. Thank you, sir." The coin disappeared into Mr. Tucker's pocket. "You are welcome, sir."

Beckett offered Gwendolyn his arm. "We should return to Colemore. Reverend Denburn claims the breakfast is worth being at the table."

His voice was distant as if he was distracted. She gave one last smile to Mr. Tucker, and they went out into the day. The sun seemed very bright after the dimness of the church.

However, Beckett didn't move toward the horses. Instead, he let go of her arm and began walking among the graves.

Gwendolyn joined him, taking another line of graves instead of the ones he searched. She knew what he was looking for.

Mr. Tucker left the church and watched them for a few minutes. Then he called out, "Is there something else I can help you with?"

To Gwendolyn's surprise, Beckett said, "The marquess's family plot? Is it here?"

Mr. Tucker frowned, and Beckett quickly explained, "We heard a ghost story." He said this as if they were curiosity-seekers.

The warden made a dismissive noise. "The singing marchioness. I imagine the current Lord

Middlebury wishes that story would go away. And yet," he confided, moving closer to them as if not wishing to be overheard, "they say Middlebury himself hears her often. Reverend Denburn wouldn't like me telling you this. He calls it gossip. Course, he gossips plenty."

"Has anyone else in the village heard her?" Beckett asked.

"I best let that alone, sir." He started to back away. "I've said too much already."

"Understood," Beckett said as if it was of no matter. "However, we would like to see the graves. Even if the story isn't true, it is a matter of curiosity." Another coin appeared in Beckett's hand.

Mr. Tucker slipped that one in his pocket to join the other. "Follow me, sir."

He led them around the building. The headstones on this side were larger and better cared for. Some tombs, especially the ones covered with lichen, were dated almost two hundred years ago. Mr. Tucker directed them to three relatively new headstones. One was proudly in the open, next to the family monument. The other two graves appeared almost hidden. They were located under the overgrown branches of a giant hemlock tree.

Mr. Tucker pointed to the larger headstone in the open. "That is the fourth marquess, my lord's older brother."

Beckett's expression was somber as he approached the site. Gwendolyn respectfully followed him.

"His wife is next to her son," Mr. Tucker said. He nodded to the half-hidden graves. "I saw her a few times when they first married. Lovely woman. Always laughing. And that there is the tragedy." He nodded to a much smaller headstone. It was the child's, carved so that it appeared a miniature of his father's.

"Course, the lad's not in there," Mr. Tucker said. "Chances are the fish ate him. Gives me chills to think of it. We tell our children the story to remind them to be respectful of the river. It doesn't appear dangerous, but water can always claim lives no matter how shallow. It did that day."

"Yes," Beckett agreed absently. He turned to Gwendolyn. "Shall we go to breakfast?"

"I don't know if I have an appetite," she murmured, shaken by the sight of the smallest grave . . . and what it meant.

He understood. He took her arm. "Come."

They were quiet as they rode down the road. She waited until they were well out of the village before she said, "What are you thinking?"

"That I know why Middlebury feels guilty. Murder is grim business. What I don't understand is why he rescued me from a brothel in London? I would have grown up not knowing anything. I'd probably be a rat catcher or some such low trade today. And why did he give me an education and see to my commission?"

"Guilt. It makes people do strange things."

He appeared to mull over her words. Then he said, "None of this can be proven." He looked to her, his expression bleak. "How can I claim to be Robert Chaytor? I'm not even certain myself.

I don't want the money or the title. I just want answers. And if someone ordered Winstead to murder my mother—I want justice."

"Who do you believe gave the order?"

"The only person who stood to gain—the Marquess of Middlebury."

"Unless this Winstead was a rogue who acted alone," Gwendolyn suggested.

His glance said he thought she knew better.

She nodded an acknowledgment. "Well, then, I would place a wager on Lady Middlebury. She strikes me as ruthless. So, what is our next step? What are our plans?"

"Our plans are to move you, Lady Orpington, and Mrs. Newsome to someplace safe. And then? *I* will have a conversation with the Marquess of Middlebury."

CHAPTER FIFTEEN

Colemore's front drive was far busier when they arrived than when they had left. Other riders were setting out to enjoy the morning air, dogs were barking, and a swarm of gardeners were busy keeping the grounds pristine. A stable lad took their horses. Beck escorted Gwendolyn into the house.

The butler, Nathaniel, bowed a greeting. "Breakfast is set up in the blue dining room." He indicated the room was down the main hall.

Gwendolyn looked to Beckett. "I need to change outfits." She didn't want to fuss with the overlong train of her habit while trying to eat breakfast. "I shall see you there?"

He nodded, and she went up the stairs. She didn't take long. Molly was waiting for her. She was quite happy to have earned a gold crown. The bribe had been a well-played move. Beckett would have known that Molly would have done anything for such a fantastic sum. Once again, Gwendolyn reassessed her knowledge of Beckett. The clothes he had purchased for his disguise as

Mr. Curran were from some of the finest tailors and bootmakers in England. She had thought him poor, but perhaps not? It made no difference. Her love was clever enough to do anything he wished, and the thought made her proud.

Gwendolyn chose a day dress out of green muslin with white stripes and boasting a low, lace-edged bodice. The color was a good one on her.

Molly restyled her hair high on her head in two blinks. Gwendolyn made her way to the blue dining room.

The Reverend Denburn was still at the breakfast table. Gwendolyn wondered how many plates he had enjoyed. Otherwise the room was empty save for Beckett, who had waited for her. Instead of letting the footman pull out her chair, he did so.

They were just tucking in to the plates they had filled among the choices on the sideboard when Lady Orpington barreled into the room, Magpie in her arms. There was a small yellow bow in the pup's hair and a larger one around her neck for a collar.

"*Prepare*, Miss Lanscarr. We are playing cards. I just received the word."

"Lady Middlebury changed her mind?" Gwendolyn asked, a bit thrown off by the change after their hostess's earlier edict.

"Of course she did. She had no choice. Not in fairness. She is also playing. Reverend, you are still breakfasting?" She reached out to the sideboard to choose a piece of ham to feed to Magpie. "He was here when Vera and I broke our fast earlier," she explained to Gwendolyn and Beckett.

"I do enjoy the marquess's hospitality," the cleric admitted.

"Well, we will need you as well. Did Lady Middlebury mention playing to you? No? Then take this as your invitation. We meet at half past the hour in the music room, where we were last night," she tacked on, an instruction for Gwendolyn's benefit. "Come, come, *come*."

On those words, Lady Orpington started to leave, but stopped. She shoved Magpie into the nearest footman's arms. "Here, take Magpie out—and don't let one of those heathen hounds near her." On those instructions, she dashed out of the room to continue her card preparations.

The footman's impassive expression suddenly changed to one of alarm. He held the dog up, and everyone could see a Magpie spot on the chest of his livery. His fellow servants snickered as he marched Magpie out of the dining room. The dog hung her head, but Gwendolyn didn't sense she was sorry for her transgression.

Reverend Denburn pushed his plate away. "I am summoned. I shall see you upstairs," he said to Gwendolyn. He followed Lady Orpington.

Gwendolyn turned to Beckett. He did not appear happy. "How are you going to convince her to leave now? This is what she has been waiting for."

"I'm not certain."

She shrugged. "Will one day of play hurt?" She looked around the breakfast room, empty save for themselves and three footmen standing ready to see to their every wish. The walls boasted prints of songbirds. It was a far cry from the horror of the cottage. "It all seems distant, doesn't it? Almost unreal."

"Oh, it is real," he assured her. He seemed to weigh his options.

At that moment, Miss Purley and her friends and their mothers entered the breakfast room. They didn't speak to Gwendolyn, and she didn't offer more than a nod as a greeting . . . although she knew Miss Purley and Lady Beth had noticed how close Beckett sat to her. She took pleasure in stiff shoulders and their bitter, jealous frowns. Let the rumors fly. Mr. Steele's kiss had cemented the two of them together. He was *hers*, and she'd not apologize for disrupting their designs on him.

Beckett stood. "I'll walk with you to where they are playing cards." Out in the front hall, as they climbed the stairs, he said in a hushed tone, "Be ready to leave at a moment's notice."

Gwendolyn came to a halt. "Lady Orpington will not go. Not now that we will be playing cards."

"I won't give her a choice." He placed a hand on her waist and encouraged her up the stairs.

She liked the weight of his touch, especially since it drew her closer to him. "What of our maids, and then we must include Mrs. Newsome, as well?"

"The servants are safe. I can see them returned to London once I know I have you and Lady Orpington safe."

"And Mrs. Newsome."

He seemed to consider a moment. "I'll speak to her." A group of people gathered outside the music room. Inside, servants were setting up tables, organizing refreshments, and hastening to do as Lady Middlebury commanded. She noticed Beckett and Gwendolyn. She paused, smiled, the expression tight-lipped. The expression told Gwendolyn that their hostess was not pleased with the turn of events. So why was she doing it? Lady Orpington stood close at hand, watching all with a self-satisfied smile.

Mrs. Newsome sat outside the room on a bench with her knitting. She smiled up at Gwendolyn and Beckett. "It is happening," she said, her eyes lively as if she enjoyed the scrambling of servants.

The footman returned with Magpie. His jacket was still stained. He gingerly carried the dog into the room and offered her to Lady Orpington. She took her pet without comment or a thank-you and marched right out the door, where she dumped Magpie onto Mrs. Newsome's lap. "Watch her, Vera." She looked toward Gwendolyn and Beckett, clapping her gloved hands together with a smile of anticipation. "The time has come," she said with great relish. "Come inside. I will show you where we will sit." She didn't wait for an answer but marched back into the room.

Gwendolyn shot an overwhelmed glance at Beckett, but then noticed Mrs. Newsome shove Magpie off her knitting and off her lap. She even attempted to give the dog a small kick. Magpie, her large eyes resentful but unsurprised, scooted under a chair. She eyed Mrs. Newsome warily, and Gwendolyn could almost hear the dog "grumbling" over her mistress being preoccupied with cards.

Gwendolyn wasn't fond of the spoiled Magpie either, but she would never hurt a dog, or take out her hostility on one. And Mrs. Newsome's behavior when she believed no one was watching alarmed Gwendolyn. The companion was not as sweetly docile as she wished to seem. Then again, Magpie, and Lady Orpington, could try anyone's patience.

Beckett leaned close. He'd apparently not seen the little dog drama. His attention was on the whist room. "How long will the card playing go on?"

"Most of the day. Perhaps into the night. At least, that is what Lady Orpington told me."

"Very well. At least I will know where you are. You'll be safe with so many people around."

"Are we becoming a touch too vigilant?" Now that she was at the house and among the guests, the danger didn't feel real as it had in the cottage.

"No," he answered succinctly. "Be watchful. I shall check on you later."

"Yes, sir," she answered back, smiling to soften the words. "And you will be?"

He looked to the stairs. "Attempting to see the marquess."

Lady Middlebury announced loudly, "We are ready. Ellen," she said, addressing Lady Orpington, "do you know how you wish the pairs organized?"

"I do," Lady Orpington answered. "Come inside, everyone. Let us begin."

Gwendolyn sighed. It was going to be a long

day. She nodded to Beckett and walked to the music room door. She glanced back.

He was already gone.

BECK STARTED UP the stairs to the next floor and the family quarters. He could knock on the marquess's door and request an audience . . . and say what? *Did you have my mother murdered? Did you steal my inheritance?*

That last thought stopped him. He was halfway up the stairs. He stood, one foot on the next riser.

If what he suspected was true, at one time, all of this—the paneled walls, the gardens, the stables—was supposed to be his.

A footman walked down the stairs, giving a small bow toward him as he did. Lady Orpington's voice drifted up to him as she chastised one of the cardplayers for dallying. "We are ready to play," her ladyship declared, the tone strident.

This was *not* his world.

And yet it might have been.

But was it now? Did he wish it to be?

Beck didn't know.

He was thankful that Gwendolyn was here. He needed her cool head as he tried to decipher the mysteries of the past. As he attempted to understand the challenges of the present.

He continued up the stairs, but then Ellisfield came down the stairs toward him. His eyes lit up. "Curran, just who I needed to see. I'm off to see Squire Miller about a gelding he has for sale. A hunter. If he is any good, I thought I'd try him tomorrow. Ride with me? I could use a second opinion."

The invitation surprised Beck. His guard went up. "What of your friends?"

"They are still in their beds. Besides, they aren't good judges of horseflesh. I like that bay you ride."

He sounded friendly. Course, he was sober now. And Gwendolyn had also mentioned that Ellisfield had known him as a boy, as cousins would. He wondered what stories the lord could tell.

"I hoped to have a moment with the marquess," Beck said, curious of Ellisfield's response.

The man acted surprised. "My father? Whyever for? I keep my distance as much as possible."

That was an interesting response but not a shattering one. The marquess's family did not seem close. "I heard about his research on the flora and fauna of Colemore. I'm a bit of an amateur botanist."

Ellisfield seemed to accept the excuse. "Well, you are three hours too early. He doesn't like being interrupted before one. I'm a lark myself, obviously. Like you. I saw you riding with Miss Lanscarr earlier."

"You should have joined us." Beck was glad he hadn't.

Ellisfield shook his head. "I was well in my cups last night. I needed a bit of time in my bed. However, I'm ready to ride now. So, will you come?"

Beck hesitated. Was Ellisfield tasked with keeping track of him?

His lordship noticed Beck's uncertainty. "It isn't a long ride. We shall return well before midday. However, you are free to stay here, if you wish."

There was no guile in his tone or expression, and in that moment, Beck decided to go. Ellisfield was spoiled like many oldest sons, but he also wasn't a bad sort. Beck had run into his type in the military. They were men searching for a purpose, and he found he wouldn't mind a bit of time with Ellisfield. They were family. In spite of all that had transpired over the years, Beck discovered the yearning to belong was still there.

"I will," Beck answered. Gwendolyn would be playing cards for most of the day, and Beck was curious to know what Ellisfield knew. "I hear there is a portrait of the last marquess and his family. Do you know where I may view it?" He wanted to see his father.

"Why?" Ellisfield asked.

Beck shrugged with a nonchalance he didn't feel. "I heard a ghost story," he offered.

"The singing marchioness." Ellisfield shook his head. "Those deaths were a tragedy, but if she is haunting us, I've not heard her. The best portrait of her is upstairs in the small library."

"I was told there is a portrait of all of the family."

Ellisfield nodded. "In the main library. Come this way." He continued down the stairs, and Beck fell in line behind him.

"This house has more than one library?" Beck asked conversationally.

"This house has multiples of everything. There is a library on each floor."

On the main floor, Ellisfield walked through the house to a cavernous room lined with bookshelves and art. The shelves weren't all full. A man would have to collect books for more than one lifetime to fill this room. Sunlight poured in from arched windows that overlooked the back gardens. Groupings of chairs, desks, and settees created places to converse or read. Gwendolyn would be in heaven.

"We use this room for balls," Ellisfield said, "but I can't remember the last time we held one. Perhaps it is better to say, we could hold balls in this room."

"The marquess does not like to entertain."

"No." Ellisfield did not elaborate.

Over the mantel was a portrait of the current Marquess and Marchioness of Middlebury. They sat in this very room with its patterned draperies. Their children were grouped around them. In the portrait, Ellisfield was a school lad.

"The one of my aunt and uncle is over here." Ellisfield pointed to a portrait beside an exit door. This painting was not as light and bucolic as the one over the mantel. The colors were dark, wooded. The woman in this picture resembled the musical woman in the upstairs library; however, now she appeared matured although not much older. She wore a lace cap over raven curls. Her eyes burned with pride, and her arms were wrapped around a rosy-cheeked babe too young for hair.

But it was the man behind her who commanded Beck's attention. His father was a tall man, like himself. He appeared very much a man of his time with his powdered hair and the lace falls of his neckcloth. One hand rested protectively on his wife's shoulder. His expression was also one of pride. He was older than his wife, much older, and yet the two appeared ready to face whatever the world brought them.

"The fourth and fifth marquesses," Ellisfield murmured. "Now, if you don't mind, I need to break my fast before we ride."

Beck turned away reluctantly. He could have spent hours studying that portrait. But to what purpose? "Did you know the last marquess?" he asked Ellisfield. "The adult one."

"I don't remember much," his lordship said as he walked out of the room. "I remember the funeral. He was greatly admired."

The two men went to the breakfast room. Ellisfield made a sandwich of two slices of bread and a beefsteak, shaking his head to ward off the footmen overly anxious to serve him.

He then flirted a bit with Miss Purley. He even complimented her singing before giving a nod to Beck, and the men left the room together.

After collecting Beck's hat from where he'd left it in the entry hall with a footman, Ellisfield led them out the side door of the West Wing, the one with the path leading to the stables.

"You don't have your horse brought to the house?" Beck wondered.

Ellisfield shook his head. "I enjoy visiting the stables. I find it restful compared to the activity of the house. I can be alone with my thoughts. I also like to saddle my own horse. That's why he trusted me to jump your coach team. We are a bonded pair."

"The jump was still foolhardy."

His lordship took a big bite of sandwich. "But I lined my pockets with the money I won off of my friends," he answered, munching away.

"You could have crashed."

"Not with Ares. He hasn't let me down once."

Of course, it had been Beck who had walked his horse to the house. He wondered how the animal was today or if he still had the hint of a limp.

They reached the stables. Horses were being taken out for exercise or up to the house for their riders. The handsome chestnut knew Ellisfield had arrived. He nickered a greeting.

As they walked to the stall, Beck said, "With your family, one wouldn't think you'd need to perform dangerous endeavors for your spending money."

"My parents use money to keep us in line. My brother and sister conform. I don't. I purchased this horse with my own money, I trained him, and he has repaid me handsomely. He is the fastest I've ever owned. Certainly the smartest. When he was a year or two younger, there wasn't anyone who could beat him."

"You raced him?"

"Aye, and I purchased an estate in Yorkshire recently with the money we made. It isn't large. Not a Colemore. But it is mine. And Ares's." Ellisfield opened the stall gate and patted Ares on the neck. The horse gave him a nuzzle. He showed no sign of the previous day's lameness.

So that explained where Ellisfield spent most of his time instead of dancing around London drawing rooms. Beck began to change his poor opinion of his cousin, especially since he appeared to be a more respectful man when he was sober. Yes, Ellisfield was arrogant, as all lordly sons were, and the trick jumping the coach was foolish, but at least he was doing something for himself.

"What of you, Curran? What are your interests?"

"The usual," Beck replied, evasively. "Excuse me, my lord. I need to saddle my horse." He walked away, not giving Ellisfield a chance for more questions.

He discovered Wagner and the bay together. He let Jem know that he was riding out with Ellisfield. He also let him know he planned on moving Gwendolyn and the ladies to safety. "Be vigilant. We'll have to use the coach," he warned. "And keep your eye on Miss Lanscarr."

"Aye, sir. I'll be ready. Will you be all right with Ellisfield?" Jem asked.

"I think so. I don't know."

"One of those, eh? All right, sir. I'll keep watch."

His horse saddled, he met Ellisfield out in the yard. They mounted and rode off in the direction of the village called Chislet.

Beck kept the conversation cursory, biding his time, waiting for Ellisfield to reveal his true motive in inviting him for the ride. And yet his lordship didn't seem to have one. He didn't pry into Mr. Curran's past and certainly didn't make accusations.

At one point, Beck did share that he'd been in the military. Ellisfield had a number of questions, and there was a longing in the man's voice as if he envied Beck's adventures.

"Did you think about a commission?" Beck asked.

"I might have." Ellisfield shrugged. "However, it was not to be."

"So you are in the Lords?"

"I go in for Father on occasion. I have some interests, but . . ." His voice trailed off. He was quiet a moment, and then he confessed, "I should do more."

Beck agreed. Ellisfield surprised him. There was some substance to him, if only he would act on behalf of himself.

"My family is not political," Ellisfield said.

"Why not?" He'd assumed all of the great families had political ambitions. Wasn't that the way of the world?

"The last marquess was, but Father prefers the family stay in the background."

Beck had been waiting for him to mention his father. "What does that mean?"

"That we give money." Ellisfield shot him a knowing look before saying, "They also serve who pay the way."

Beck didn't know if he agreed. "Is the marquess's health good?"

"What do you mean?"

"He didn't stay at dinner last night. I thought he was not feeling well."

Ellisfield looked away, studying the trees lining the road before saying, "My father is fine."

Beck raised his eyebrows but said nothing.

They rode in silence for a few minutes, and

then Beck's patience was rewarded when Ellis-field said, "Father doesn't socialize well. Never has. Nor is he aging well. To be honest, the man has only cared for one thing in his life, and that is my mother."

"Many men are fond of their wives."

"True, but few always do their bidding. Father is one of the few. Whatever she wants. I will say they are well-matched. She supports him as fervently as he supports her."

"They are a love match?"

"Not necessarily." He looked over at Beck. "And yet they do well together. However, he has started having these spells. They began a year ago. I believed he was getting better, but I don't know. Did you notice his hand shaking?"

Beck nodded.

"I try not to think on it," Ellisfield said.

"Did something happen a year ago to upset him?"

His lordship frowned as if uncertain he should say anything. Then, "He lost Winstead."

Beck kept his tone neutral. "Winstead?"

"He was my father's personal"—he waved a gloved hand in the air—"everything. Winstead was both friend and bodyguard. His dogsbody. Both of my parents trusted him. I heard he dis-appeared. Just left. It is a pity, because he used to force Father to leave the house."

"It must be difficult to see a parent growing frail," Beck said.

Ellisfield nodded. "Mother warns me to be ready to take over the title." He added quietly, "I don't like having the weight of my father's death hanging over my head. It is macabre."

"It is also the way of great families."

His lordship acted as if ready to say something, but instead chose, "Listen to me. I asked you to come look at a horse with me. Not listen to the family woes."

"I don't mind," Beck answered honestly. "Besides, your family has had its share of tragedy. I understand your reluctance."

"There are hundreds of people who would be happy to be in my boots, Curran," Ellisfield said. "I can't feel too sorry for myself. Are your parents alive?"

Beck thought of the laughing woman in the portrait, the three graves. "No."

"That is right," his lordship replied as if just remembering. "There isn't much to Lady Orpington's family. Mother was surprised when she learned Lady Orpington was bringing a nephew."

"We weren't close," Beck offered as an excuse. "Family estrangement."

"It is probably simpler that way. Money tears a family apart."

"Has it taken a toll on yours?" Beck dared to ask, hoping he wasn't appearing unreasonably nosy.

He also found he wondered what he had missed.

"Of course. My brother has his resentments, as one would, knowing he is always considered the second-best. He would be happy to step into my place and inherit it all. When *I* am in control of the estate, I will increase his and my sister's allowances." He patted his horse's shoulder, something he did often. "The irony is that I can remember how angry my parents were with my aunt, the last marchioness. They claimed she never gave them enough for expenses, and yet they do the same to their children."

"Her death was what? Years ago?" Beck said carefully, not wishing to sound too enthusiastic at this new information.

"Decades," Ellisfield agreed. "But they were the sort of battles one remembers. I hid under a table when their rows were too much."

"What were they truly fighting over?"

"I said, money. Isn't everything about money?"

"Colemore has plenty of money."

"Does anyone ever have enough? But as I remember, my aunt held her own. I keep that in mind when I choose my own counsel over my parents' wishes." He lifted his reins and gave the chestnut a kick. "We are almost to the squire's place."

Beck feared the time for confidences was over, but after turning down a side road, Ellisfield said, "My late uncle was an innovator—what I hope to be. What I'm trying to be in Yorkshire. My aunt tried to continue his plans, and that is why, I suppose, she wished my parents were more frugal."

He was quiet a moment and then said, "And I pray I'm more like my uncle than I am my father. I also hope to find a woman with my late aunt's qualities."

"Your mother has someone in mind."

"Ah, Miss Purley, who is very attractive, and very *young*."

"She is an heiress."

Ellisfield laughed. "You sound like my mother." Then he sobered. "I don't want to end up like my sister and brother. Jane's husband is a bore, and my brother, Martin, married Mother." He rode a bit in silence before confiding, "I know that marriages of convenience aren't all bad."

"Were your parents a marriage of convenience?" Beck asked.

"Certainly. They barely knew each other when they married, and now I believe they have high regard for each other. Mother protects Father in spite of his increasing eccentricities. She could let him be, but their lives are entwined. And, strange as it sounds considering what a bastard he can be, I believe she loves him." He fell silent a moment and then said, "I just don't want to wait thirty years to finally learn I'm in love."

Beck heard the last statement as if from a distance. Instead, he was caught up in Ellisfield's confidences about his parents. Up to now, everyone had claimed that Lady Middlebury was the force to be reckoned with . . . but what if she acted on behalf of her lord? Few women were as independent-minded as Gwendolyn or her sisters. Most did as they were instructed. Especially if it would protect the family.

Furthermore, Ellisfield probably did feel trapped, because he was. He had responsibilities to his lineage, to the title he *could* inherit, depending on what more Beck learned about his past. He was expected to marry, and soon, considering his age. Miss Purley was probably not the first woman his family had dangled in front of him like bait. The expectations would be over-whelming.

That he had so far managed to be his own man spoke volumes for him—

"I have noticed Miss Lanscarr."

Ellisfield's statement snapped Beck to attention. "Miss Lanscarr?"

"Yes," he said, the light of possibility coming to his eyes. "I find her remarkable. Beauty, intelligence. *Grace*."

She has faults, Beck wanted to say . . . although he hadn't noticed any. Well, she was stubborn. And headstrong. No one could deny those two qualities.

Yet what some would see as flaws, Beck actually enjoyed. Because she was also loyal—and when those characteristics were matched with beauty, intelligence, and grace, it made for a very attractive package.

One that he didn't wish to share.

Ellisfield shot him a glance and continued, "However, I sense a bond between the two of you. Is that true? Because if there isn't one, I'm interested."

At that moment, the bay stepped into a rut in the road and stumbled slightly. Beck appreciated the interruption. It gave him a moment to sort out his response to Ellisfield.

The man was handsome, well-connected, titled, and spoke of wanting love . . . he was everything the Lanscarr sisters had come searching for in London.

Except, Beck realized he didn't want to let Gwendolyn go.

"We have an understanding," he lied to Ellisfield.

And those words meant that he needed to be certain they did once he returned to Colemore. Of course, he had no idea what he would say to Gwendolyn. Especially after he had told her in London that she should expect nothing from him—and yet, he had kissed her.

It had been a good kiss, too. The sort that left a man hungry for more.

No, the sort that told a man, he had fallen in love.

The truth of that statement rang through Beck. He loved Gwendolyn Lanscarr. It was a simple statement, and yet it changed *everything*. Especially him.

His lordship's head seemed to sink a bit between his shoulders as if he'd received a setback, but then he straightened. "I thought as much. I saw you riding together this morning. Still, if I thought I had a chance—" Ellisfield started.

"You don't."

His lordship laughed and then confessed, "Now you see the challenges of my love life. The ones I want are taken."

"You will find yours," Beck answered. Although he didn't care if Ellisfield found happiness or not. Beck loved Gwendolyn Lanscarr, and that made him one very lucky man.

THE HORSE FOR sale was lame. The squire hoped they would not notice. They did.

However, that didn't mean that Beck and Ellisfield had not enjoyed themselves. Beck had few friends. He told himself he liked it that way—except he didn't. He could be honest with himself now. Gwendolyn had opened him up and exposed the lie.

Now he rode with a man who was his blood. In another life, with different circumstances, as cousins, they could have been bonded as close as brothers.

Their trip took longer than anticipated. They arrived back at Colemore a good two hours before dinner to find Lady Middlebury pacing in the front entry, annoyed that they had not returned sooner. She apparently knew that her son had ridden out with Beck, and she was not pleased. Her glance rolled over him, and there was a flash of anger in her eyes before she turned her back on Beck to speak to her son. "I need you, Henry, to help with the guests. You know, your father—"

"I know, *my father.*" Ellisfield waved Beck on while he stayed to placate his mother and listen to her complaints about the marquess.

If Lady Middlebury was free to worry, that meant the cardplayers had quit for the time being. He wondered where Gwendolyn was. He checked the small library. Gwendolyn was not there with her nose in a book. He took a moment to examine the portrait more closely, seeing it differently now that he understood his connection to the happy bride. He'd decided they would leave this evening, after dinner and before the charades that were scheduled. Any sensible person would bow out of charades, and their absence would not be noticed, he hoped. He wished he could take the portrait with him. Perhaps he could claim it later.

He hadn't spoken to Lady Orpington about leaving yet. He met Mrs. Newsome in the hall. She held her knitting bag in one hand and appeared tired. "How was the whist?" he asked.

"Disappointing," was the crisp answer.

"Miss Lanscarr and Lady Orpington did not do well?"

"Oh, they were excellent. My cousin said that Lady Middlebury was very distracted and didn't even play as if she cared. She lost their match, and now, if my cousin wishes to play her, and she does, she will have to wait until tomorrow. To be honest, I was surprised at how badly Lady Middlebury lost her games. Her points were very low."

"She has a houseful of guests. She may have been distracted."

Mrs. Newsome made a face. "My cousin is in a mood. I asked a footman to take Magpie for a walk, and he hasn't returned. Meanwhile, my lady is furious she cannot have her pet immediately this moment. She has sent me out to look for the servant, but I can't remember which one took her. They all look alike in their wigs and livery."

Beck frowned. He knew he would have to take the dog with them when they left. For a second, he debated leaving Lady Orpington, Magpie, and Mrs. Newsome behind. Were they truly in danger?

Possibly. Whoever had sent Winstead after him was of a murderous bent. If something happened to even Magpie, he would blame himself.

"Mrs. Newsome, I'm going to tell you something in the strictest confidence." He looked up and down the hall. Muffled movement could be heard behind several of the doors, but they were alone save for the porter sitting at his station. And he appeared more interested in the carpet pattern than their conversation.

He took her arm and pulled her a few steps down the hall, leaning his head close. "We may need to leave this evening."

"Leave?"

"For reasons I can't disclose," he said.

Her brows lifted. "Oh. Yes. I understand." She looked away. "Do you wish me to see that my cousin is packed?"

"No, we will leave with what we have. The servants and clothing can be sent for."

"Do you truly believe it has come to that?"

"I trust my instincts, and the answer is yes. Please, pass this message to your mistress."

"She won't go," Mrs. Newsome said. "She is wound up in the shabby way Lady Middlebury has managed the whist tournament. She is thinking of taking it over herself on the morrow."

"She may choose to stay. However, I have sensed that Lady Middlebury and perhaps others know my identity. And may have been aware of it before I came."

"What makes you say that?"

He thought of Violet, but he didn't answer Mrs. Newsome. "We leave tonight. You and Lady Orpington will come with us if you are wise."

She nodded. "I shall tell her."

"Be ready. No luggage."

"That is a challenge."

Beck didn't respond. He expected his order to be obeyed. "I hope you find Magpie."

"I pray that dog is lost forever."

Her bluntness surprised him. Then again, he could never have survived if he'd been in her position. He watched her walk down the stairs before turning his attention to Gwendolyn. He thought about knocking at her door, but then reconsidered. He'd spent many hours in the saddle. He was certain he reeked of horses. He could spare a moment to make himself presentable.

Especially since, if he got nerve up, he was going to admit that she was right—he loved her.

And was it possible she might, possibly, hopefully return the feeling?

Beck had never known love but now, he found himself in awe of the depth of his feelings for Gwendolyn.

In his room, Beck hurriedly poured water into a basin, removed his clothes to the waist, and washed his face and hands and torso. He believed in the benefits of bathing and wished he'd had the opportunity of a bath. It had been a full day. He couldn't wait to find Gwendolyn and hear her thoughts about the tidbits of information he'd gleaned about Ellisfield or how she and Lady Orpington had fared over cards. He couldn't wait to tell her that he'd changed his mind: He wanted her to fall in love with him. He'd demand it, and he'd kiss her again and again until he won her over.

She was the only woman for him. He'd always believed he preferred being alone. He'd needed it, or so he'd told himself. People were a challenge. Few were dependable. No one was faithful, well, except Gwendolyn. He'd come to rely on her.

That idea was radical.

Beck stopped drying himself with the linen towel provided, stunned by how important Gwendolyn was to him.

The wariness, the deeply rooted anger that he would deny even existed in him, had faded away. In its place was love. It had finally found him and the Greeks were right—love was like being shot with an arrow. But he wasn't mortally wounded. No, he'd been given a new life. And so he would tell Gwendolyn when he made his declaration, except, he wasn't one for flowery words. However, his love for her made him want to spout poetry. It made him want to sing.

It made him want to hold her and never let her go.

Finished with the towel, he turned to the small chest where his clothes were stored, then saw a note on the bed. It was small, and the paper had blended in with the counterpane. He'd been so focused on preparing to meet Gwendolyn, he had not noticed.

Beck picked it up. The handwriting was feminine.

I have learned something Important. Meet me in the gazebo in the back garden as soon as you are able. Gwendolyn.

He quickly dressed. He had not yet had a chance to explore Colemore's gardens. They took up acres of land. However, a good number of the guests already walked the paths when he stepped from the house. He asked about a gazebo and was told to keep following the path until he saw a line of trellises shading the main pathway. "Watch for a thicket tunnel. Right before you reach it. It isn't far from there," a guest said.

The garden was a mix of formal and informal spaces. Passing the trellises, he walked down a row of yews that cut a border. He searched between them for any sign of a gazebo. He didn't see one.

Clouds gathered overhead. He was alone in the garden now as the other guests had gone inside to prepare for dinner.

At the end of the alley of yews was a winding path that led into a section of shrubs and over a brook, designed so it flowed into a series of good-sized pools. The pools had been filled with water lilies. Silver fish darted beneath them in the late afternoon light. He crossed a small bridge before he caught sight of a low thicket tunnel and the roof of a gazebo.

Anxious to see Gwendolyn, he hastened his step. The privacy offered by this splendid garden seemed the perfect backdrop for him to confess to Gwendolyn that he had been wrong—he loved her. She was his future. His reason for being. He *wanted* her beside him.

He didn't have all the right words in his mind. He trusted they would come to him once he had his arms around her.

The gazebo was of a Chinese design. The roof was red with curling points. The columns were carved wood painted white. It was a delicate-looking building and oddly fit the forest setting. The surrounding thicket tunnel made it very private.

He entered the gazebo and was annoyed to see that Gwendolyn was not there. Then he chastised himself for his impatience. He thought of the kiss that morning, the hunger that had been in both of them. He could wait forever for Gwendolyn if he could feel her arms around him . . . and know he was no longer alone in this world.

The gazebo floor was stone inlaid in the shape of a star. Just like the parquet floors in the house, he mused. Or, stars like the ones in Gwendolyn's eyes when some particular thought caught her imagination or fancy.

There was no seating. Instead, Beck leaned against the railing, watching the spot where the thicket opened to the gazebo entrance.

He couldn't wait to tell her of Ellisfield's confidences. His lordship's observations about his parents didn't completely make sense to Beck, but Gwendolyn would help reason it all out.

Gwendolyn, Gwendolyn, Gwendolyn. He rolled the syllables of her name in his mind. It felt good to be in love. It felt even better to trust again.

Beck was so caught up in his anticipation for Gwendolyn's arrival, he didn't sense the other man's presence until he had risen up out of the thicket and brought a hard club down on Beck's head.

CHAPTER SIXTEEN

$\mathscr{G}$wendolyn was frightened and yet curiously calm.

She had been tossed in a coach, her arms bound to her sides and her ankles tied together. A gag kept her from crying out.

It was vanity that had gotten her into this mess. Well, that, and a strong desire to help Beckett by discovering all she could about the singing marchioness's death.

The cardplayers had played whist for a solid four hours. She and Lady Orpington had done very well. They had not played against Lady Middlebury and Reverend Denburn, but that would happen, and soon.

Lady Orpington had been upset when Lady Middlebury had announced the end of card playing for the day. Lady Orpington had happily announced that they would continue after dinner as they always had. Lady Middlebury had told her no. She'd said the young people wished to play charades and other games. As a good hostess, Lady Middlebury insisted she must oversee the activities. As good guests, she expected that *all* the cardplayers participate in the evening's plans.

Of course, Lady Orpington had complained, but honestly, Gwendolyn was tired of whist. The play had not been all that challenging. No wonder Lady Orpington and her late lord had done so well.

Gwendolyn was also anxious to see Beckett, to have a moment for a few words with him. She wondered what he had been doing while she'd been cooped up inside on a truly lovely day. She had yet to inspect the gardens.

Shortly after the cardplayers left their tables, Lady Middlebury had sought her out. "Would you walk with me in the garden, Miss Lanscarr? It is a lovely afternoon. Seems a shame to not enjoy such good weather while we have it."

Gwendolyn had not been able to turn down such an invitation. This was the first time her hostess had singled her out, and Gwendolyn was curious as to why. Unfortunately, all Lady Middlebury had seemed prepared to discuss was a bit of the garden's history—that is, until they reached the lily pond.

Gwendolyn had watched fish flit around under the layer of water plants, wondering how to politely suggest they return to dress for dinner. She liked gardens as well as any woman, but she'd seen enough.

Suddenly Lady Middlebury had said, "Marriage isn't easy."

Gwendolyn turned, the change of topic catching her off guard.

Her ladyship continued, her gaze on the pond, but her mind seemed to be elsewhere. "I hadn't anticipated that my husband would ascend to the title. You must understand that. It was not foreseen."

Gwendolyn had kept her tone carefully neutral. "It must have been a shock to have his brother die at a relatively young age."

"So many deaths." Lady Middlebury had shaken her head as if it had still surprised her, and perhaps that was true. She might not have known the last marchioness had been murdered.

Murder . . . The word gave Gwendolyn a shivery chill.

"I've had a very good life," Lady Middlebury had continued. She'd nodded to the gazebo, and they had started moving in the direction of the thicket. They went inside. It was quite close, and the humidity mingled with the scent of earth and growing things. "Middlebury built the gazebo for me the year he came into the title. He designed it himself from a picture I admired of a Chinese garden. He combined the Orient with the English. He is clever." She'd said this last as if reminding herself. They came out of the thicket, the exit placing them right at the gazebo's open entrance.

"It is quite unique," Gwendolyn had murmured. Of course, she preferred the simplicity of the river cottage.

"See the flooring?" Lady Middlebury had said. "It took the masons weeks to copy the pattern of the floors inside the house."

Gwendolyn had looked down to inspect them.

But as she did so, she used the moment to change the subject. "Why did you decide we should play whist today?"

"I thought it is what you and Lady Orpington wished. Ellen has been most vocal."

"Absolutely, and yet you shut her down. But then you changed your mind abruptly. Why, my lady?"

The marchioness had eyed her. "Time was needed to make arrangements. Cards were the easiest excuse to keep you here."

"For what reason?" Gwendolyn had asked—just as two masked men had climbed over the railing from the thicket. She had caught their movement in her peripheral vision and had given a shout of alarm. The men had grabbed her arms. She'd struggled, but they had held her tight.

Lady Middlebury had watched the attack before shaking her head. "It is a pity I won't be able to play whist against you, Miss Lanscarr," she had said. "You may blame Mr. Curran for that lamentable fact." She'd left the gazebo.

Gwendolyn had fought to free herself from the men's rough holds. She'd doubled her fists and kicked and attempted to cry out for help, but she'd been overpowered. They had stifled her with a vile rag stuffed into her mouth. It tasted of sweat, and she wanted to spit it out but couldn't.

Once they'd had her trussed up, the men had carried her like a sack of grain to a coach waiting deeper in the forest. They had dumped her into it without even trying to be gentle. She'd found herself face down and half on, half off a coach seat.

After the door had been slammed behind her, she'd heard one captor say, "Now for the next one."

"Me shoulder is giving me problems," the other had complained.

"I'll 'elp ya carry the man," had been the answer.

The man. That meant Beckett. She was certain of it.

Gwendolyn had struggled to sit up, her mind frantic with the knowledge that Beckett was about to be attacked. Long skirts had not made the endeavor easy. She'd managed to push herself up and leaned back in the seat. She hated the gag to the point of tears, but before she could break down into angry, frustrated sobs, she realized she was in Lady Orpington's coach.

And that was when the strange sense of calm had descended upon her.

The coach shades had been drawn but she could crane her neck and see around the edges. She suspected she was being used as bait to trap Mr. Steele. That action confirmed that Lady Middlebury knew who he was. The true him. The supposed dead fifth marquess.

However, was Lady Orpington involved? Had her asking Mr. Steele to find her a whist partner been part of an elaborate ploy?

Gwendolyn's mind chewed on the possibilities. Lady Orpington had behaved oddly all afternoon. Even though she had nagged everyone to play cards, she had not been good-humored about it. A few times, she had played the wrong card when Gwendolyn had known she'd had a better card in her hand. It was unlike Lady Orpington

to be so distracted over whist. Had she been nervous about this abduction? Gwendolyn hoped if
she was involved, she experienced some remorse.
This was a betrayal, and she wanted Lady Orpington to feel the sting of it.

She also prayed that Beckett saw through
whatever ruse they created to lure him to this
coach. And that he was on his way to rescue her.

The bindings on her wrists were too tight.
Gwendolyn moved her fingers, trying to keep
the circulation in her hands. Evening was beginning to fall. The summer days were growing
shorter. Soon it would be time to sit down to dinner. Would anyone notice her missing? Or would
there be a plausible excuse as to why? She prayed
they didn't claim she'd had a fit of the vapors. She
was made of sterner stuff than that.

Of course, the worst part of her situation was
the waiting. She strained her ears, listening for
the slightest sound.

Nothing, save an occasional stamp of a hoof
or a snort of the nostrils from the coach horses—

She heard voices arguing. Were her kidnappers
returning, or was this Beckett coming to rescue
her . . . ?

"Will you move yer arse? He weighs more than
an ox," a grunting man complained.

Her heart sank. They had Beckett.

The coach door was yanked open. One of the
attackers propped it open with his shoulder as he
adjusted his hold on a bound and gagged Beckett. "Come on, shove 'im in."

"Shove 'im? He's not a sausage. He's dead-weight. You'll have to do some guidin'," the other complained.

With a growl of impatience, the man at the door climbed in and shoved Gwendolyn over, and they unceremoniously pushed and pulled Beckett into the coach. He was a large man, a long and heavy one. Carrying him must have been hard work. His hatless head hit the door-frame.

They didn't even give a care to Gwendolyn, so she ended up with the weight of Beckett's bound feet resting on hers. They bent his torso so he was propped on the seat across from her.

The man by the door caught her watching them and gave a toothy grin. "Yer a lovely one."

"Mouser, stop flirting."

"I kinna help it. I like 'em dark." ·

"Shut the door."

Before obeying, Mouser reached out and cupped Gwendolyn's left breast. Shocked, she tried to turn away from him. He laughed and gave it a hard squeeze before sighing. "'Tis a pity." He let go and shut the door.

Gwendolyn was furious. His fingers seemed to have left an imprint on her skin even through her clothes. If she hadn't had this gag in her mouth, she would have scorched him with her tongue. It would have been the last time he ever touched a woman uninvited.

The surge of anger did her good. Her spirits revived.

She was done with waiting. As soon as Mr. Steele regained consciousness, their two kidnappers would pay for their crimes—

The coach leaned as the heavy men climbed up into the driver's box. Then it lurched to roll forward.

She bent so she could see Beck in the coach's shadows. He was so still, she started to worry that he was dead, and then reason told her they wouldn't have bound him if he was. For whatever reason, they had kept them both alive.

That thought gave her hope.

She lifted her feet under his, wanting to nudge him to consciousness. He didn't stir.

That didn't stop her from repeating the effort until her legs hurt with the strain. Evening gave way to nighttime. She worried about where their kidnappers were taking them. She worried she would fail Beckett.

They seemed to have been driving for hours, but perhaps it was no more than an hour or so. Every minute seemed an eternity. The road was sometimes smooth and then full of ruts so she bounced around uncomfortably.

She could no longer make out Beckett in the darkness. The kidnappers had not bothered with lighting the coach lamps. They certainly didn't wish anyone to catch them transporting people trussed up.

The coach rolled to a stop. The brake was set. She braced herself for the door to open. It didn't.

What was happening? She listened hard and thought she caught the sound of water lapping the shore.

Gwendolyn tried not to think of the murdered marchioness. Drowning was not a way she wished to die. She knew how to swim, but bound as she was, she'd sink.

The thought of her sisters learning of her death brought the sting of tears to her eyes. She blinked them back angrily. She was not going to let herself be murdered. Or Beckett either. She would save them both—

Someone shouted, "Halloooo?"

He was answered by one of her kidnappers. "O'er here."

She heard the creak and soft swoosh of a paddle through water. They were near the river. She could smell the dankness of the water even through the walls of the coach.

"You have the cargo?"

"We do. We will need help liftin' one out."

"Let's do it, then. It's goin' to storm. I want to be on my way."

A few beats later, the doors on both sides of the coach opened.

"I'll take the lass." The man who spoke was Mouser, the breast squeezer. He reached in for her, and Gwendolyn leaned away from him. "Come on, pretty," he said with mock hurt. "Dinna be that way with me."

"Git over here and help us carry this bastard," his companion said, hissing out the last word. "She can wait."

The man left Gwendolyn alone to do as he was told.

They dragged Beckett out of the coach. There was just enough moon peeping in and out of the quickly moving clouds that Gwendolyn caught a glimpse of Beckett's head hanging as the three of them carried him into the night. She held her breath, praying she didn't hear a splash. She didn't.

Then one of her kidnappers came for her. He wasn't Mouser. She was thankful for small favors. The man picked her up and carried her down a bank to a lugger, a small sailboat big enough to move cargo. In Ireland, they were popular with smugglers. The boat was pulled up on a bit of muddy beach. The sails were tied down.

He had to wade a few steps into the water to hand her up to a man in the boat. They almost dropped her. The hem of her skirt dipped into the water.

The man handing her up said, "Stay with that coach and prepare to drive it. We have a long road ahead of us."

"Where are going?" the boatman asked.

"North," was the curt answer.

With a grunt, the boatman dropped her, none too gently, beside Beckett on the deck. Her back was to his. Her skirts clung to her legs, and her arms ached from being tied behind her for so long.

"What is the name of the ship in Portsmouth again?"

"The *Duke of York*. It's sailing in two days' time. These two had better be on it."

"What do I say when I deliver 'em?"

That seemed to baffle their kidnapper. "Don't know." He paused. "Do you need to say anything?"

"I dinna?" the boatman said.

"Tell 'em they are from Colemore," came the reply.

"Colemore? Aye, fine then. And my payment?"

"Here is half, and you will receive the other half when you have delivered the cargo."

"Do I come back here?" the man demanded, none too happy.

"See me in one week's time at the Riverhead in Gravesend. Do you know it?"

"I do."

"One week from tonight."

"And if you don't show?"

"You can trust me. I'm married to yer sister, remember? But either way, half of what was agreed is still good payment."

"I want it all now."

"Dint have it. But I will, in a week."

There was a long pause as if the boatman considered his options. There was movement at the bow, and Gwendolyn realized there was another man on the boat.

"Riverhead, then," the boatman agreed. "But if ye cheat me, it'll go bad for yer."

"I've never cheated you, Ezra. I won't start now. Don't like hearin' Betsy complain. Just be certain that the man is alive when he is put on the *Duke of York*. The captain will make a report."

"Wot? These are transports?" Gwendolyn understood he was referring to them. Transports were criminals being shipped to Australia for their crimes. "Ye know half that ship will be dead before they reach Queensland."

"Not our problem, mate. See you in a week."

The boatman picked up an oar and used it to push the boat into deeper water.

Gwendolyn tried not to panic over the knowledge that she and Beck were going to be loaded on a ship that transported criminals to Australia. This was almost worse than drowning. It could take years before she'd be able to let her sisters know what had happened and where she was—

Two strong fingers found and squeezed her hands bound at the wrists.

It was Beckett.

He was awake.

She started to roll toward him, so relieved she wanted to cry and laugh at the same time. The gag kept her quiet. His strong fingers stopped her motion.

The boatman walked by them to unfurl the sail. The breeze was picking up.

"It's going to rain," his companion said.

"We'll outrun it. Keep the course to the river entrance," was the reply. The wind caught and filled the sails. "Those two are all right where they lay. I'm going to close my eyes a bit."

"Aye."

Beck and Gwendolyn kept still during the exchange. The world fell quiet, save for the water against the hull and the creaking of the lines as they pulled against the wind.

That is when she felt his fingers begin working the knots at her wrists. She edged closer to him to make it easier. After several minutes, she realized she would be more successful untying his ropes because her fingers were smaller. He seemed to have reached the same conclusion because he let her take over.

Patiently she picked at his knots. She tried to keep her movements to a minimum so that the boatman wouldn't notice what they were doing. She was aware of time passing and felt frustrated that she could not move faster.

However, her persistence was rewarded when Beckett was able to slip one finger from his bonds. Then another. Elated, she continued to loosen the knots until he had a hand free.

With complete freedom of movement, Beckett made quick work of her knots. Their legs were still bound. However, Gwendolyn's first act was to pull the gag from her mouth. It took all her will to not cough in disgust.

The man at the rudder had not noticed a thing.

Beck tapped her arm for her to wait.

She felt his body curve as he brought his knees up to his chest and began untying his legs. She listened for a warning cry that the boatman noticed. There was none.

And then Beck slowly rose to his feet. She heard his faint, sharp intake of breath at his first attempt to stand. She imagined it hurt. The blood needed to circulate. She knew she'd feel the same when she first tried to move. She wiggled her toes in preparation, wanting to do what she must to stave off the inevitable.

She attempted to see the man at the rudder. His face was turned skyward. Was he navigating or woolgathering?

It didn't matter. Beckett moved with the slow, quiet patience of a panther. She watched his silhouette stay in the shadows. Three steps and then a yelp and a splash. He'd tossed the sailor overboard.

The man hollered. *"Billy. Billy."* He choked on water. Then he began swimming. Gwendolyn could hear the sound of his thrashing.

Billy could, too. He came awake with a start. He jumped to his feet. "Ezra?" He saw Beckett and grabbed an oar, which he raised over his head.

Gwendolyn sat up, wanting to call a warning. Apparently the sailor had forgotten she was there. Her sudden movement caught him off guard. He whirled on her with his oar—

Beckett grabbed the oar. Over her head, the two men grappled with it. They fell into the sail. The boat heeled dangerously as the sail shifted with the change of direction.

A fist was thrown and then another. The moon peeked out from the clouds, and Gwendolyn saw that Beckett held the sailor by his shirt. They were punching away at each other—Billy lost his balance.

He started to fall and would have landed on Gwendolyn save for Beckett grabbing him and pushing him over the side. There was another quiet splash. A beat later, a gasp and a curse.

The waves had started to pick up speed, a sign they were moving into open water and a warning of bad weather. The lugger seemed to skim along the way.

Beckett went to the rudder and tried to steady the boat. They lurched to one side, then to another.

"Do you know what you are doing?" Gwendolyn asked. She untied her legs.

"No," came the reply.

"Here, I can sail," she said, and started to move toward the stern of the boat. The sensation of a thousand needles pierced her muscles.

"Be careful," he advised her. "Take your time to ease your muscles."

"Keep the rudder steady," she advised back. Eventually she came to a shaky stand. Placing her hand on the lugger's rigging, she followed it sternward to the rudder.

Watching the wind in the sail, she slowly turned them in the direction of where she thought the shore was. The moon had disappeared behind the clouds. There were no stars. "We're free," she said, a bit surprised.

"For now." He sat beside her. "How do you know how to sail?"

"My sisters and I had a small sailboat back in Wicklow. Sailing on a lake is different than on open water." The latter took more strength. "I've never sailed at night." She looked to him. "Do we know where we are?"

"Were you awake when they drove us here?"

"I was."

"How long do you believe we traveled?"

"An hour, maybe more. It seemed forever."

He expelled a heavy sigh. "Let the wind take us," he advised. "We will sort it out."

Beckett sounded confident. Bold, even . . . and he gave her courage. They would manage.

"Show me how to do this," he said, referring to the mechanics of sailing.

"It isn't difficult." She explained the basics of keeping the wind in the sail.

He placed his hand over hers. "Let me try it."

She did. The danger that they had been in was just beginning to seep in, leaving her strangely lethargic body feeling disconnected from her head, and cold. "Why?" she asked at last.

Beckett didn't misunderstand what she meant. "Lady Middlebury wishes us gone."

"But not dead? Did you hear the coachmen say that we were to be kept alive?"

"I did, and that is the true mystery."

"Well, I'm actually thankful she didn't wish us murdered. But why did they plan to take the coach north?" Her teeth chattered slightly on her question. Her damp skirts didn't help keep her warm.

Beckett noticed and moved so that he was on the same side of the rudder as she was. He took off his jacket. The sleeves were torn at the shoulder seams. He put the garment around her.

And then he put his arm around her.

She burrowed into the haven of his body. He felt safe, secure, and warm. She tried to wrap part of the jacket around him.

"Perhaps Lady Middlebury realizes I am the true marquess," he said. "And she doesn't wish to have my death on her hands?" He shook his head. "What puzzles me is how she knew my true identity. Who gave me away?"

"Lady Orpington?"

"I find it hard to believe. I'm a good judge of character. I thought her trustworthy."

"You don't know about the coach," she remembered. "We were kidnapped in *her* coach."

"They used it to bring us to the river?"

"Yes. And then the men said they were taking the coach north. But what does that . . . ?" Gwendolyn broke off with understanding. "North," she repeated.

"North?" he echoed.

"To Scotland. To make it appear as if we eloped?"

He shook his head. "This doesn't make sense. Or does it?" He mulled the matter over. "We would be the center of all manner of speculation, none of it particularly alarming. Couples elope."

"Except we could have been missing for years if we were transported."

"Exactly. Lady Middlebury wouldn't have to worry about someone else claiming the title."

A shiver went through Gwendolyn. "I'm just surprised at Lady Orpington's involvement. Why go through the ruse just to turn you over?"

He had leaned back against the bulwark. She rested on his chest. A yawn escaped her. And was it her imagination, or did he brush his lips across the top of her head? She snuggled deeper in his arms, holding him close. "We are alive and safe because of you."

"Because of *us*," he corrected her. "You have more courage than a dozen men, Gwendolyn."

No praise had ever touched her so deeply. "Do you know, Beckett Steele—if I have to be kidnapped, transported, and passed off as having eloped to Gretna, I'm glad it is with you."

She expected him to laugh. Instead he answered, "This is *my* fault. I should have anticipated this. I let myself be distracted."

"Distracted by what?"

"You." He looked down at her. His arm around her tightened. "I received a message that you were waiting for me in the gazebo. I was anxious to—" He paused, shook his head, and then said, "A callow lad could have seen the ambush."

"Anxious about what?" she pressed, uncertain if she understood correctly. His tone combined with the way he held her and his words made her think that he had *wanted* to see her. But she needed to hear him say it before she'd let herself believe. The time had come for him to be the vulnerable one.

"Now is not the time. We still aren't out of danger."

"Beckett—"

"Gwendolyn. I'll see you safe. I promise."

And in that moment, the first big plops of rain came falling down on them.

$\mathcal{T}$he rain came down hard.

It dampened the sails and cut through the wind. It slashed them in the face like soft darts.

Worse, it brought an end to confidences.

Gwendolyn had been on water before in a storm. She knew the dangers of being in the open. She took the rudder, pulling it toward her. "To the shore," she said. "We must reach the shore."

The rain came down harder. It was all around them. "Is there an oar?" she asked. The current was growing stronger, rocking the boat as she steered against it. An oar would be useful.

Beckett crawl-walked along the edges of the boat, looking for one. He came back. "I couldn't find one." He placed his hand over hers on the rudder. "I'm a good swimmer. Don't be afraid. I'll take care of you."

His face was white in the dark, and his hair was plastered against his skin. She didn't look any better. "I swim, too," she said, and noticed his surprise. "Father made us learn. But he said I already knew from being in the Indies."

"Cards and swimming," Beckett said. "An unusual upbringing."

"But practical for right now." She gave a worried sigh. "I wonder how far the shore is."

"We will manage," he assured her, and she nodded. He took over the rudder, his superior strength needed to keep the boat on track, while she peered ahead of them as if she could see where they were going.

The lugger literally bumped into the shore. The boat shook with the force of hitting land. They were thrown forward, but Beckett didn't wait a beat. He jumped into the water, found his footing, and held his arms out. "Come, Gwendolyn. Jump," he commanded.

She leaned over the side. Beckett's arms grasped hers. He half swung and half dragged her toward him, even as wind and waves lifted the boat, freeing it from what little land was beneath.

He carried her the few steps toward shore while the current bore the boat away.

In spite of the rain pouring down on them, Gwendolyn wanted to collapse. Beckett refused to let her. He picked her up in his arms and held her until they reached the shelter of trees. He dropped to his knees, and the two of them fell to the ground side by side.

For a several long moments, all Gwendolyn

could do was catch her breath. The spot where they had sought shelter was relatively dry. A canopy of leaves protected them somewhat from the rain.

She listened to it, wanting it to stop. The air smelled of the shore, of rotting wood and fish mingled with grass and leaves. Her heart slowed from its frantic beating.

Beckett sat up on the wet earth. She joined him.

"Now what?" Her legs stretched in front of her. Her kid slippers were soaked, but at least she still had them. She could have lost them.

She sensed rather than saw him smile in the darkness. "We find someplace safe while we decide our next actions." He paused, then added drolly, "You wanted adventure." He was right. Had she not longed for anything other than the endless balls and social calls? Hadn't she longed for him?

And now she had both.

Suddenly Gwendolyn started laughing. He laughed with her, until a sob escaped her. She clapped a hand over her mouth, embarrassed, but that is when the tears started.

Beck didn't chastise her. He pulled her into his arms. He said, "You have been brave, Gwendolyn. So brave."

"I'm not afraid," she answered, but that wasn't true. Now that she was safe, what could have happened overwhelmed her.

He didn't press her to stop her show of emotion. He held her, her face against his shirt and her hand gripping the wet lapels of his jacket, and eventually she began to recover herself—but she didn't move. She stayed there in the haven of his arms, savoring his quiet composure. "You are safe," he whispered to her. "We're safe."

She didn't move but released the breath she'd been holding. "When do you think Lady Middlebury will know we escaped?"

"Who will tell her?" he asked. "The men she paid for a job that will not be done? Or the coachmen driving north, thinking their part is finished?"

"So, what are *we* going to do?"

"Find someplace safe for the night. Think over our next steps," he said. "And find dinner. I'm famished."

Gwendolyn realized she was as well. "Isn't it late?"

"Perhaps nine? Possibly ten?" He rose to his feet. She immediately felt the loss of his warmth. "The rain is tapering off. Let's discover where we are." He held out a hand. It touched her shoulder and she took it, letting him help her up.

He offered his jacket to her. She shook her head.

"Take it," he ordered. "The dress you are wearing wasn't made for the rain."

Only then did she realize how the damp muslin clung to her figure. She slipped on his jacket. The wool sleeves reached below her fingertips. The hem was heavy and wet from their adventure. She wrapped it around her. Her hair was a bedraggled mess down her back. She thought some of the pins still held out, but she didn't bother trying to find out. She couldn't waste energy on vanity.

In truth, he didn't look much better. The sleeves of his shirt seemed to be adhered to his arms. His waistcoat was intact but ruined. His boots squished as he walked. Hand in hand, they set off in search of help.

It wasn't easy, even when the rain stopped. There were branches that thwacked them in the face and vines across the ground that tripped them. She hated the thorns. They were feeling their way through the woods, but Gwendolyn refused to complain, even when she almost twisted her ankle. At another point, a rock in her shoe made her hobble a few steps. Her wet stockings had come untied and gathered at her ankles. She didn't try to pull them up because they would just fall again. Her kid slippers were not made for a trek through a wood. She longed for her walking shoes, and while she was making wishes, she would appreciate a warm fire and a roasted chicken.

They trudged along until Beckett noticed a light. They made their way toward it and came across a village of whitewashed cottages. Their walls stood out in the darkness. Beyond them was what appeared to be a small posting inn.

Beckett and Gwendolyn hurried toward it. Two men sat out on a bench under the torchlight of the inn's front door. Gwendolyn held back.

"What is it?" he asked.

"My hair." She reached up and felt a pin. She pulled it and two more out before quickly braiding the wet mess as best she could. "You might need your jacket." She shrugged out of it and handed it to him. "We don't wish to appear completely disreputable." She shook out her skirts. The muslin had dried a bit so it didn't cling to her legs.

"Or like what we are, two people who were caught in a storm." He pushed the jacket back to her. "Come, Gwendolyn. Don't worry. We'll be fine." However, he did comb his hair back with his fingers.

The arguing between the two men outside the inn came to an abrupt halt as they moved into the ring of torchlight. They watched with curiosity as Beckett opened the door and motioned her forward. She stepped into a low-ceilinged room with several long tables. The room smelled of cider and ale. A group of men were playing cards. Whist, she noticed.

All conversation stopped at the sight of her. The two men from outside followed them in.

Beckett put a protective arm around her. He appeared even taller than he was under the room's low ceiling. "Where is the barkeep?"

One of the men from the card game stood. "What may I do for you?"

"We need food and a room for the night. Our vehicle broke down."

"Where did that happen?" The barkeep had brown hair and a few days' growth of beard. The others in the room didn't appear any more respectable.

"Down the road," Beckett said easily.

"And your horses?"

"With a farmer. Do you have a room?"

"Aye. Two tuppence. Four if you want food."

"I'll take the four."

Gwendolyn was looking around. In spite of the innkeeper's appearance, the place appeared clean. There was also the lingering scent of baking bread in the air as if it had just been made that day. Beckett took coins from a pocket in his breeches and pressed them into the man's hand.

She was certain it was far more than four tuppence by the smile that spread across the innkeeper's face. "This way, sir."

Beckett took Gwendolyn by the elbow, and they followed the man out of the main room. He introduced himself as Mr. Stimson.

They went down a narrow hall and walked through a half-open door. It was the kitchen. An old man was half-asleep in front of the fire.

"Charles," Mr. Stimson said, "wake up."

The older man frowned as if annoyed to be bothered. Then he sat up. "I am awake."

"Anything for them to eat?"

Charles eyed Gwendolyn and Beckett. "Eggs. That is what I have."

Beckett spoke up. "Eggs are fine. And ale?"

"Always have ale," Mr. Stimson said. "I'm putting them in the back, Charles. They broke down and need a room for the night."

"And ended up here?" Charles didn't hide his doubt. "Looks like you were caught in the storm."

"We were," Beckett answered in a voice that

seemed to settle the matter. And then he added, "But we are lost. Where are we?"

"The Hare's Foot," the innkeeper said.

"And the village name?" Beckett answered.

"Sandston. Where were you heading?"

"Portsmouth."

"If you want to go there, you'd best take a boat."

"We thought about it," Beckett said dryly.

"You're not far from Gravesend," Charles broke in to offer helpfully. "You may have passed it depending on which direction you took."

Gravesend. That was where the boatmen and their kidnappers were to meet. Gwendolyn made a note to give Beckett that information.

Charles rose from the chair, stretched, and scratched his belly before walking over to a table to begin slicing bread. Gwendolyn's mouth watered. Eggs and bread sounded delicious. She also wouldn't mind an ale.

"This way," Mr. Stimson said. He lit a stub of a candle off the kitchen fire as he led them out into a hall. He opened a side door. "This is the room."

Gwendolyn braced herself, not knowing what to expect when she looked in. To her surprise, the room was lovely in its simplicity. The four-poster bed was made of dark wood that looked sharp and inviting against white walls and a white counterpane.

"You take your meals in the main room or in the kitchen. Whichever you want."

"Thank you," Beckett said.

The room was not large. The bed filled it with perhaps a foot or two between it and the wall on two sides. There was just enough room for the table at the foot of the bed. Mr. Stimson lit a candle on the table.

"Privy is outside. Wash bowl and water in the kitchen. Give a shout if you need anything." He gave a curt bow of his head and left them alone.

However, a beat later, there was a knock. It was Charles to let them know their food was ready. They ate in the kitchen.

The meal was delicious. Of course, anything hot was to be greatly appreciated, and she was starving. Saving themselves from wickedness was hard work. The ale helped wash everything down.

"I'll stand guard while you use the privy," Beckett offered.

Gwendolyn didn't even blush over the familiarity.

She and Beckett were alive. They were safe . . . and that was all that mattered.

It did not take her long to see to her business. Charles had left the kitchen when they'd started eating, but he'd shown her where the pitcher of water and a bucket alongside a bar of soap were located. She was alone. She washed her face and hands and removed her stockings that had been annoying her. She tucked them in the pocket of his jacket and put on her wet shoes. The plait of her braid was coming undone. She didn't bother to fix it. Her hair dried faster when it was down.

Beckett came in from outside while she was still in the kitchen. Their gazes met. His broke away first, and yet they were here together, and alone.

She stood and moved to the bedroom, giving

him a moment to wash. Giving herself a moment to escape this heavy awareness between them.

What had seemed easy earlier become awkward. She wasn't certain how to act. She knew what she wanted, and she also knew there would be no turning back, no matter what each of them wished.

Gwendolyn touched the bedpost. Her earlier exhaustion had vanished. Instead, her every sense seemed to hum with anticipation. She shouldn't feel this way. She shouldn't be eager.

A step sounded behind her.

She turned. Beck filled the doorway. The tail of his shirt was loose, and he held his boots. Apparently he'd taken them and his wet stockings off in the kitchen. Her gaze dropped to his bare feet. Like the rest of him, they were strong and masculine . . . the sight of them intimate. He whispered her name. She looked up. His eyes had never seemed bluer or more intense. They stood a mere foot from each other in the small space dominated by a bed.

The drawback was the grim line of his mouth. She knew what he was about to say. He was going to offer the bed to her while he slept out in the main room or in front of the kitchen fire . . . the way he had in decades past as the scullery boy.

Instead of disappointment, her heart filled with love and understanding. Beckett would always think of her needs first. That was the sort of man he was—a protector . . . in spite of all life had handed him.

And she must take matters into her own hands,

or else he might slip away again, convinced he didn't need anyone—no, that wasn't it. He didn't believe he was worthy of anyone. Nothing could have been further from the truth.

"You may have the bed. I'll sleep on the floor—" he started. Before he could finish his statement, Gwendolyn took a step forward, threw her arms around his neck, and kissed him, holding nothing back. She kissed him fully. Deeply. *Hungrily.* Begging him to kiss her back. To believe in them.

He'd gone very still. Then, just when she feared she was going to have to do all the work—his arm came around her. His lips met hers with a passion of their own, and he brought her close as if he could wrap his body around hers.

She felt his desire for her.

He could not hide that, any more than she could resist pressing herself against him.

Beckett broke the kiss. He looked down at her. She tightened her hold around his neck.

"I'm not going away," she said, her voice both husky and defiant. "No matter how many times you swear I must."

He looked into her eyes and then said the words she had longed to hear, speaking as a man who could hold back no longer. "I'll *never* tell you to go away. I love you, Gwendolyn Lanscarr. I've loved you since that night in Dublin."

She was loved. She *loved* in return.

Beckett started to turn. She tightened her hold, fearful he was going to leave. Instead, he closed the bedroom door.

She smiled against his neck. He brushed a kiss

against her hair and lifted her as if she weighed less than a feather. He carried her to the mattress.

The bed ropes gave under her weight. She expected him to join her. Instead, he pulled his shirt over his head. She kicked her shoes off, letting them hit the wood floor.

Candlelight turned the hard planes of his torso to gold. He had a long, lean waist. His arms and chest were well muscled. Desire, sharp and needy, spun deep inside her.

And then she noticed the scar along one shoulder. Another was on his right side, an incision no longer than an inch, the skin around it puckered.

He started to lean down to her, but she came up on her knees in alarm. She placed her fingers on that scar on his side. "So close to death," she whispered. "And here." She brushed his shoulder with her fingertips.

He caught her hand, raised it to his lips. His breath was warm against her skin. She kissed the scar on his shoulder, letting her lips linger. He was so precious to her.

Beckett drew her arms around his neck. She pressed herself against his bare skin. Her dress was still slightly damp. He kissed the sensitive place right where her collarbone met her shoulder. She felt his fingers unlacing the back of her dress.

Tears welled in her eyes.

"Gwendolyn?" he whispered, alarmed.

She looked up at him, her hair a dark curtain over her shoulders and down her back. "I love you," she said fiercely. She laid a hand against his jaw and felt the gentle scratch of his day-old whiskers. "Never doubt that."

"I love you, Gwendolyn," he answered, his gaze intent and solemn. "And we shouldn't do this—"

"No." She wrapped her arms around his neck, lest his conscience forced him to pull away. "You are the man I want. And besides, the damage to my reputation is done, even if we were kidnapped. No one would believe I didn't seduce you. You are stuck with me, Mr. Steele. I'm yours whether you want me or not."

She spoke the last with defiance and a hint of humor, although all of it was the truth.

He responded solemnly. "I want you, Gwendolyn. You are mine. I shall love you all the days of my life."

These were vows, she realized. Vows more holy than could be said before a cleric because they came from his heart.

And she could have wept from the beauty of it. Instead, she kissed him, breathing him in and thinking how blessed she was. Then she shifted so that her gown fell to the bed around her knees, leaving her in the thinnest of chemises over tight breasts. She slid her arms out of the thin lace ties and let that fall over her petticoats still tied at her waist.

"Gwendolyn." She'd never tire of hearing him speak her name, especially when he said it with such hushed, reverent delight.

"I warn you, Beckett. A Lanscarr will keep you busy."

"I'm up for the challenge," he assured her, and

then he found her mouth and kissed her deeply. Their tongues met as Gwendolyn wrapped her arms around his ribs and his back before her hands drifted lower. She stroked the curve of his buttocks before her fingers slipped under the material of his breeches. She followed his waist until she discovered the first button, the back of her hand against the hard flatness of his abdomen.

She twisted the button free.

As she reached for another, Beckett sat on the edge of the bed and swung her into his lap, where he kissed her neck, her shoulders. Her dress and chemise fell to the floor. He began untying the tapes of her petticoats and sliding them down her legs until she was gloriously naked in his lap. The heat of his mouth covered her breast. She gasped his name. She buried her fingers in his thick hair.

When his lips found hers again, she kissed him with all the growing passion in her being. She held nothing back. She drank in all she could of him, his taste, his scent, his warmth . . . his strength.

He eased her back onto the mattress and then started to stand.

"No," Gwendolyn said. They couldn't stop now. She had no desire to ever let him go.

"Let me undress." He hooked his hands in his waistband and pushed his breeches down.

Men didn't wear smallclothes.

And his body was beautiful in its strength.

A fierce pride fell over her. This was her lover. He desired *her*. Gwendolyn was not one for miss-ish airs. She yearned for his touch, his heat.

She reached for his hand and drew him down to the bed alongside her. The candle cast their bodies in a thin golden light. She settled against him in the crook of his arm. His hand with its long, tapered, masculine fingers smoothed over her belly.

Her hand ran over his hip, and she marveled how where she was soft, he was hard. It was the way the world was meant to be.

He kissed her neck, whispered in her ear, tell-ing her she was lovely, she was priceless. She couldn't speak. She was too overwhelmed with happiness, too lost in his touch.

Gwendolyn turned into his shoulder, inhaling the spiciness of his soap, the horses, the water, and the rain. He threaded his fingers through her hair and then rolled her on top of him.

She had imagined that for this "act" between a man and a woman, it would be just rote and done in a blink. She'd grown up in the country. She'd not been sheltered . . . but what was hap-pening between her and Beckett was something beyond the limited scope of her understanding. This wasn't just mating. They were lovers.

She liked being this free with him. She sat up, her legs bent to cradle his hips. His arousal, his desire for her, was not hidden. She leaned to nuz-zle his neck and kissed the rough texture of his chin. She wanted to be closer to him. She wanted all of him. His sex surprised her. It was hard and demanding and yet as feathery soft as the finest velvet. Her body wanted to move against him—

He caught her hands and rolled again, this time placing himself over her. They were notched together, her legs opening to accommodate him.

Their kisses grew slower and sweeter . . . and deeper. He braced himself as if saving her from his full weight. He didn't understand. She adored having his warm, naked skin against hers.

He nipped her earlobe. She laughed and did the same to him. Their movements took on more heat. He made her almost weep with wanting.

His hands lifted her hips. She liked feeling him cup her buttocks. She pressed a kiss on his shoulder, on the scar, on his chest—

Beckett entered her.

She felt him slide inside. Her body stretched to take him, but it was not uncomfortable. If anything, she reveled in being this close to him. It was what she'd wanted without being aware of the next step—

And then he thrust deep, even as his mouth covered hers.

A cry caught in the back of Gwendolyn's throat at the sharp pain in her deepest recesses. She hadn't expected it. Everything had been lovely until he did this. She would have bolted from under him if he had not held her.

He ended the kiss, sucking lightly on her bottom lip. He found her ear. "Easy, Gwendolyn. Easy. That was the worst," he promised. He held himself still.

The worst. Was it every time? Moments ago

she'd been wrapped in the joy of sensation, until this. It soured her. Although slowly the pain subsided. Gwendolyn felt wetness. Her whole being centered on where they were joined. Beckett began to move slowly, carefully. He whispered soothing words. He told her he was sorry she was hurt. He promised that the hurt would never happen again, and there would only be pleasure.

The strangeness of having him inside her began to ebb, as did the pain.

His movements became more directed. The thrusts deeper.

Raw sensation took hold of her. She found herself moving to meet him. She seemed to search for something she didn't understand and yet needed.

He lifted himself higher above her. He seemed lost in her, as if he had a need only she could fulfill.

And she liked that very much.

Heat built between them.

Beckett kissed her neck, her shoulders. He moved harder, faster. His breathing grew as labored as her own, because Gwendolyn was no passive partner. She wanted to be bonded to him forever—

A sensation so piercing, so intense, swept her up. It spiraled inside her, higher and higher until an instant so perfect turned her senses inside out, even as the joy of wonder burst through her. Now she understood.

"Beckett." His name was both benediction and praise. She clasped him hard to her and would

have held on—but then he rolled abruptly off of her with a guttural response.

His defection confused her. She wanted to follow him, and then she felt his seed, the life force, against her thigh. He had released his seed, but not in her.

And she felt robbed.

Cold air caused her skin to prickle. "Beckett?"

"A moment." He sat up, his back to her. He stayed there, breathing heavily.

She dared not move. He'd told her to wait. Was something wrong?

He turned to look down at her. Confused, she had come up on her elbows.

Then he said, "You are beautiful."

Gwendolyn felt herself relax. "*You* are beautiful," she countered, and he was. No artist could ever capture the perfection of his lean body in the candle's light.

"Stay here." Beckett rose from the bed and went out the door, naked.

Gwendolyn wondered what would happen if Charles was there. Apparently he wasn't. She didn't hear voices.

A minute later, Beckett returned with a basin and a rough cotton cloth. He held up the material. "This is all I could find. It is clean." He shut the door and crossed to the bed.

She didn't understand what he wanted it for, until he sat on the bed and dipped the cloth into the water. He wrung it out, placed the basin on the floor, and then used the cloth to gently clean her thighs and her body where they had joined.

At first she was shy. She wanted to take the

cloth from him. He kissed her into submission. "Let me do this for you."

She nodded, trusting him enough to turn herself over to his intimate touch. With great care, he washed the stains of their lovemaking, of her virginity and her passion, from her thighs.

His expression was so committed to her well-being, she didn't believe she could love him more.

Beckett rinsed the cloth out in the basin and set it aside on the floor. He blew out the candle and climbed into bed bedside her. He gathered her into the haven of his body, her back against his chest.

Their legs were intertwined. She adored having him all around her.

"Go ahead and say it, Gwendolyn," his deep voice murmured in the darkness. There was a smile in it. "I can hear the questions humming in your mind." His arm brought her closer to him. She could feel his spent desire against her buttocks.

"I thought I would feel differently," she said.

"In what way?" He ran his hand over her hip as if tracing the curve of it.

If she wished, she could pretend they were the only two people in the world. There wasn't a sound except for the beat of their hearts. "I thought that I would still be me."

"And?"

She rolled to face him, the cotton counterpane around them. "Now, there is us."

His hand had gone still. For a swift moment, she feared she had said something wrong . . . and then he spoke. "I love you, Gwendolyn Lanscarr."

Then he kissed her, so deeply, so sweetly, it sent her senses swimming.

He loved her. There was no better music in the world than those words.

And she realized that this act of intimacy, of trust they had shared, was the bond that forged them together. She'd noticed it at work between her sisters and the men they loved. It was what created a haven for a relationship to blossom and then deepen.

Especially as a woman, she was putting her being, her very health, into his hands. That was why he hadn't wanted to spill his seed in her. He was protecting her . . . because he loved her.

She moved closer, at ease with his body, knowing she was safe. She dared to touch him. He was hard. He wanted her.

"May we do it again?" she asked.

"Over and over again," he assured her. His lips curved into a lazy smile. He pulled a lock of her hair through his fingers as if enjoying the silky touch of it. "However, not tonight. You need time to heal," he said.

"That sharp pain goes away?" she wondered.

"Oh, yes."

Gwendolyn placed her palm against his chest, coming up on one arm to meet his gaze. "I love *you*, Beckett Steele. Forever and always. That is my promise." Could he see her expression in the dark? Did he know how happy she was? He *loved* her. Not just that he'd made love to her. He loved *her*.

It was all she'd ever wanted. He'd captured her imagination from the moment he'd rescued her in Dublin.

"Please, Beckett. Let us make love again." She needed to be joined with him once more. To know that it was the two of them against the world, forever and always. "I will not complain."

"Well," he said thoughtfully, "there are many paths to pleasure that would not cause you pain."

That was an enticing statement. "Other ways than what we just did?" She was intrigued. Apparently there were many things her country life had not taught her. She smiled. "Are you going to show me?"

His answer was to rain a line of kisses along her neck, across breasts that were now *very* sensitive to his touch, and down her abdomen. His head dipped lower still.

At first she was startled. She tried to move away.

"Trust me, Gwendolyn." His quiet, deep voice calmed her. This was Mr. Steele, the man who had never failed her. *Her* man. Her one, true desire.

And in the end, she was very glad she let him have his way . . . because this, too, she liked.

CHAPTER EIGHTEEN

*G*wendolyn woke the next morning to an empty bed. She sat up, confused. She'd slept deeply.

The room had one narrow window close to the ceiling. Judging by the angle of the light, the day was quite advanced.

Where was Beckett?

The sheets smelled of him. *Of them.*

From the other room, the inn's kitchen, she smelled roasting meat. She didn't hear voices but she knew she was not alone.

She stood, wrapping the counterpane around her body. Her gaze fell on the bed. There was a stain on the sheets. The proof of her virginity.

Gwendolyn stared at it, thinking it should mean something more. She'd finally gone through this passage of womanhood. And while the stain concerned her because she was conscious of her host's bedclothes, she had no regrets.

Or expectations, she realized as she noticed a peg in the wall with his jacket, much the worse for wear, hanging upon it.

There was a light knock on the door, just a

scratch really. It opened, and Beckett, dressed in shirt, breeches, and boots, looked in.

He smiled when he found her awake and entered, closing the door behind him. His blue eyes seemed to shine. There was tenderness to him. He crossed to her and let his fingers comb the tangle of her hair, pushing it over her shoulder.

"How are you?" he asked with genuine concern.

She shot a pointed look to the stain.

His lips twisted into a rueful but unrepentant smile. "Don't be embarrassed. I shall take care of it."

Of course he would. He'd always take care of her.

She hooked her hand around his neck. The curled edges of his hair brushed the backs of her fingers as she kissed him. He was her family now. There was nothing Gwendolyn wouldn't have done for her sisters, for her brothers in marriage, and for Tweedie, Dara and Elise's great-aunt.

However, she belonged with Beckett.

The kiss deepened. The counterpane dropped between them.

Later, lying in bed together, her head resting on her hand on his chest, Gwendolyn looked up at him. "You seem lost in thought. What are you thinking?"

He stretched as if her question nudged him out of his thoughts. He gave her a quick smile, one that didn't reach his eyes. "The whist tournament. Not having it didn't make sense. Unless Lady Middlebury wished to punish Lady Orpington for bringing me to Colemore. And Lady Middlebury knew in enough time to arrange for Lady Rabron to be in attendance."

"But why? Even if she knew you weren't Mr. Curran, why bring someone from your past?"

"To encourage me to leave . . . to warn me that the ruse was known."

"So she wanted you to leave. Well, we were going to do so until she changed her mind about the whist tournament."

"At some point, she changed her mind about what she wished to do. Agreeing to whist was a way of keeping us there. She knew Lady Orpington wouldn't leave if she had a chance for revenge."

"Lady Middlebury's mind was not on the game. She was very distracted." Gwendolyn thought a moment and then said, "Neither was Lady Orpington's. Do you believe she betrayed you? Could she have been feeling guilty?"

"I don't know. She always claimed she and the marchioness were childhood friends. I'm usually a better judge of character. But I do know that deciding to play whist was a way of keeping us at Colemore so Lady Middlebury could do away with us once and for all."

"Instead, we have learned the truth. Will you change your name and become Robert?"

"It doesn't sound right to me."

"Or me." She liked the name Beckett. "London is full of Roberts." She paused then asked, "What of Chaytor?"

"Next you will ask me if I plan on being the marquess."

Gwendolyn sat up. He followed suit, his back

against the wall behind the bed. "You very well could be," she said seriously.

He winced at her words.

She understood. "That doesn't make you comfortable, does it?"

Beckett pulled a strand of her hair through his fingers. He liked touching her, she realized. She liked his touch.

Then he said, "It is possible that all of this has a reasonable explanation."

"And that Lady Middlebury wished to ship you away to the other side of the world out of the kindness of her heart. She knew you had a desire to see a penal colony."

He shook his head with a quiet laugh at her sarcasm. "Does it make a difference to you how all of this plays out? Whether or not I am the marquess?"

She reached for his hand, lacing her fingers with his. "I'm surprised you ask," she said.

"I don't trust easily, Gwendolyn, let alone 'love.' It is a new word for me. And yet, you have both my trust and my love."

"And I value those gifts. I will never abuse them. I love you, Beckett, *whomever* you may be."

He drew her to him. She rested her head on his chest, listening to the beat of his heart.

"I can't prove I was the marquess," he said quietly. "Winstead is dead."

This was news to her. She pushed away from him. "How do you know he is dead?"

"He attempted to murder me in London. It

had not been my intention to kill him, but it was in my defense."

A thought struck Gwendolyn. "If she attempted murder once, why did she decide to let you live? Why go to the trouble of transport?"

"That is what I don't understand," he confessed. "It is as if she is at cross-purposes."

"Two different aims," Gwendolyn agreed.

"Two different people?" he suggested.

They exchanged glances as the possibility of his suggestion took shape. "Who could be her accomplice?" Gwendolyn wondered. "The marquess? Her son? Lady Orpington? The place could be crawling with murderous characters."

He grinned at her. "You say that with such delight."

"I told you I could be helpful with your investigation," she reminded him confidently.

"And you have been." He leaned over to kiss her brow. Outside the door of their haven, she heard voices. It was the world. She wasn't ready to face it. He'd heard them, too, because he said, "But now, we need to dress. There is work to be done."

She nodded. "You are right. We must return to Colemore." She started from the bed, but Beckett caught her wrist. She paused, one foot on the floor.

He met her eye. "Gwendolyn, *I'll* return to Colemore. I'm sending you back to London."

"Why?"

"I want you safe."

"I am safe." She stood. "I'm with you."

"And I almost had you transported to Australia. We were lucky to escape."

"Because *I* was there," she pointed out. "Because I helped you."

"If anything happened to you, your sisters would flay me alive." He put his legs over the edge of the bed and reached for his breeches on the floor. "Nor would I be able to live with myself."

She pushed her heavy hair back over her shoulders. "You need my help. You are outnumbered at Colemore."

"Not completely." He had risen and begun fastening his buttons. "I have a man there. I've already sent a messenger. He'll be ready." He picked up his shirt from the floor and started sorting it to put over his head. She grabbed ahold of the garment before he could.

"Will you stop?" she demanded. "You and *one* man can't go against all the family and servants of Colemore."

"We can. Wagner and I are wily. We will be fine. What I don't need is you as a distraction. They've already used you against me. We are lucky to have escaped." He released his hold on her hand and tugged his shirt over his head.

Gwendolyn frowned, aware that he was right. They had trapped him using her.

He began putting on his boots.

She pictured the three graves in St. Albion's cemetery. Her imagination quickly pictured the small one being expanded to contain him. Her chest tightened.

Gwendolyn sat next to him, heedless of her nakedness in the face of his dressing. "Beckett, I won't go to London. I'll stay here and not interfere.

It will be hard. I'll be pacing the floor, but I need to be close in case—" She stopped. She'd been about to push again that he might require her assistance, and she knew he would disagree.

He shifted his attention to her. His leather-covered thigh rested along her naked one. "I want you out of this." He wasn't angry, just firm. "I must handle this myself, Gwendolyn."

"What if they discover you are on the estate?"

"They will know I'm there. I sent a message requesting a meeting."

Gwendolyn rocked back. "Why would you do that? If you can't prove the title was robbed from you, and you don't sound as if you want it—"

He nodded. "I don't need them or their money."

"—then *why* are you telling them you are coming? Why even return?"

"For justice, Gwendolyn. I want the truth, whether I take action or not. *We* won't be safe until it is laid to rest. If what we suspect is true, that they have murdered for the title and all that it entails, they will do anything to keep power. They already have."

He was right.

She rose and reached for her dress and petticoats. They were folded on the footrail. Beckett must have put them there. "I don't want to be shuffled back to London." She faced him. "I'm not afraid to face them with you, Beckett."

"I know. However, I need to know you are safe. I won't let harm come to you, and they know that." His expression was bleak. She was not going to change his mind. She shouldn't because he was right. Her presence would interfere. That didn't mean she was happy about leaving.

"You are a stubborn, stubborn man."

"Then we are well-matched."

She almost laughed, but the sound couldn't slip past the sudden tightness in her throat. If she was completely honest, she did fear that Beckett *might* forget he loved her. That what they shared was merely one bubble in time, and he'd move on. *Like her father had.*

The thought startled her. She tried to push it away, but it returned, stronger than before.

John Lanscarr had always been an absent father. He would sweep into his daughters' lives with presents and a smidgeon of attention before just as quickly leaving again. She and her sisters had lived for those visits. They had believed they were a sign that their father did care for his motherless daughters.

But in the end, they had learned he didn't. It was that simple. He had other pursuits, another family, and daughters were unimportant.

At the time of this revelation, Gwendolyn had thought she'd handled it all very well. She'd accepted the facts and carried on . . . but that wasn't exactly true. Learning that he had just abandoned them had been one more betrayal in a lifetime of them. Perhaps his absence was the reason she'd kept her distance from men in general—until Beckett. The truth was, trust wasn't easy for her either.

His brows came together. He seemed to be trying to read her mind. "I will come—" he started.

Gwendolyn stopped him, raising a hand to

cut him off. "Don't. No promises." She looked at the bunched material of her clothing she held, preparing to dress. If something happened to him . . . ?

But that was out of her control. She had to let him be the man he was.

"I have faith in you, Beckett Steele. I'm not certain even a bullet could stop you."

"Some have tried." He tapped his head where a French bullet had found him.

"Is that supposed to be humorous?" Her words came out sharper than she'd intended. Her impulse was to reach for him, to fall into his arms and fiercely hold him close. Instead, she began dressing.

She didn't know what *she* would do if the Middleburys harmed him. There was no other for her, and there never would be. She felt a strange kinship with her mother, who had died waiting for her love to return. Oh, yes, John Lanscarr had fobbed her off as well. However, Beckett was a far better man than her gambler father.

"Gwendolyn?"

She didn't answer, keeping her back to him. What more could be said? She tied the tapes of her petticoats.

He waited a moment and then left the room to fetch fresh water. Without comment, she used it to do what she could to make herself presentable. She braided her hair and fashioned it into a knot at the nape of her neck. There was no piece of glass to check her appearance.

Finally she made herself face him. "You ask for me to believe in you, to do as you ask."

"I do."

She hesitated, not liking the choices. "Fine. I'll leave. But don't you dare let them kill you."

"They won't."

She pressed her lips together, biting back any retort. Her gaze fell on where his finely tailored riding jacket was torn at the shoulder seams. The material was the worse for wear after the previous night's adventures. She could make him a bit more presentable. "Ask Mr. Stimson for a needle and thread and I'll repair your jacket."

"We don't have the time," Beckett answered.

"It won't take me three minutes. Besides, do you have my transport to London arranged?"

He released his frustration in a heavy sigh. "Yes, a vehicle is waiting."

"Of course you planned ahead. You are Beckett Steele." She didn't mean to sound bitter, so she held up three fingers. "Three minutes," she promised.

Beckett removed his jacket. He handed it to her and left the room. He returned shortly with thread and a needle. The thread color didn't match the jacket, but beggars could not be choosers. She knew how to hide stitches.

Gwendolyn set to work mending the jacket while he went off to see to other matters. This was something he would let her do, and it seemed insignificant considering what he faced. As she sewed, she thought of the things she should tell him. For one, Dara would be furious if she returned without a proper chaperone.

Then again, both of her sisters would be thankful to know that he was removing Gwendolyn from a dangerous situation.

Beckett appeared in the doorway just as she'd finished. She offered his jacket. He put it on. "Well done," he said.

She nodded. His praise would have mattered more if he wasn't sending her away. She looked up at him. "I'd still feel better if I was there to protect you."

Beckett's smile was gentle, his gaze full of love. "I know. Now come, Gwendolyn."

She glanced around the room that for a heartbeat of time had been heaven. She gave him her hand.

In the kitchen, old Charles was busy at work. However, he had prepared bread and ham wrapped in a clean rag along with a jug of sweet cider for her trip.

There was a group of women in the main room gossiping around a table as she and Beckett left. Mr. Stimson called out his farewell.

The day was remarkably clear after last night's rain. Gwendolyn was charmed at how quaint the village was. The cottages were small but the gardens very tidy. They had been fortunate in stumbling into it last night.

A ramshackle post chaise stood waiting for her. The horse was not slick or particularly well fed. The postillion appeared to be a farmer's lad.

"I'm sorry. This is the best I could manage," Beckett said.

"It's fine," Gwendolyn said. She ran a hand over the repair seam at one shoulder of his jacket. His neckcloth had disappeared at some point during their adventure. "Please—" She paused, almost overcome. She forced herself to finish. "Take care."

"I will." He caught her gloveless hand and gave it a kiss. "This will be over soon. I will come as soon as I'm able to your sister's house."

"I'll be waiting."

He gathered her in his arms and swept her into a deep, promising kiss. And she didn't care who saw them.

Beckett helped her into the vehicle. "Have faith, Gwendolyn."

She nodded, and then, because protracted goodbyes would only make her seem needy and burdensome, she sat back on the hard, cracked leather bench of the coach.

The postillion hopped on the horse. "Keep the shades down," Beckett warned her.

"There won't be any dust after last night's rain," she argued. Besides, this vehicle didn't have anything as fine as shades. Instead, the windows were covered with an unrolled flap of leather. It would make the inside of the coach as dark as Hades . . . something that might fit her mood.

He shook his head, but he was smiling. She waved an assurance, and she and the driver left.

They were only three hours from London. Perhaps four. The trip with Lady Orpington had seemed forever because they'd had to stop for Magpie. Gwendolyn didn't wish to stop. She wanted to curl into a ball and let time speed by until Beckett came for her.

She ate the sandwich. She was actually very hungry. She even drank most of the cider.

To her frustration, with a single horse drawing the vehicle, they did not travel fast, and the driver was not in a hurry.

At some point, she dozed. She'd agreed to keep the flaps drawn as Beckett had asked, and so she did. However, not having open windows meant the post chaise was a touch too warm. Between the closeness and not having much sleep, a nap was an easy choice.

She came awake to find the vehicle had stopped moving. She heard male voices. She had thought she was dreaming them.

Gwendolyn wasn't.

She peeked out around the leather shade. Two armed riders had stopped her carriage. One was giving the driver a coin while another moved toward her door.

And Gwendolyn knew she was about to be kidnapped again. She reached for the door on the opposite side of the post chaise. It jerked open on its own.

Standing there in riding clothes was the Middlebury butler. She had to think to remember his name. Nathaniel.

"Please come with us, Miss Lanscarr," he said.

CHAPTER NINETEEN

$\mathcal{B}$eckett had watched Gwendolyn leave with both relief and regret.

Sending her back to her family was the right thing to do. He'd made a grave error in judgment when he'd enlisted her help. She had met Lady Orpington's needs—a card sharp with the air and grace to fit in with the Colemore's other guests. However, he had not anticipated his enemies would lash out at her. Or that he would learn of hidden memories and a murder.

His letter to Lady Middlebury had asked her to meet him that night at ten o'clock at the cottage by the river. It turned out Colemore was only an hour or so cross-country from where he was now.

He looked forward to clearing the air. He had questions; she had answers. He wished to secure her promise that Gwendolyn would always be safe. In return, he would tell her he had no designs on the title or the estate.

Then there was the question of justice. He believed he had avenged his mother's death when he'd killed Winstead. But what of the one who had ordered the henchman to commit the deed?

Beck wasn't certain what road he wished to take. He trusted his instincts and the belief he would make the right decision once he understood the full scope of what had happened that afternoon years ago.

The message he had sent to Jem Wagner had instructed him to be armed and in hiding close to the cottage. He didn't trust the marchioness.

IT WAS A clear night. By the light of a waning moon, Beck quietly left the cart path, moving into the woods' shadows. He'd left the hired horse in St. Albion's cemetery, hobbling it to graze among the stones.

Beck had arrived early for the meeting. He wove his way through the trees, following the line of the river, until he reached the cottage. He didn't worry about where Wagner was. Jem was an excellent marksman and would put himself where he needed to be.

The windows of the building were dark. The thought teased him that Lady Middlebury might ignore his summons. He didn't believe she would. After all, she had believed he was on his way to Australia.

He crouched by the riverbank and watched the cabin. Darkness had fallen. The hour was around nine. He waited.

The time passed slowly. However, waiting was part of battle. His thoughts drifted to Gwendolyn. She should be at her sister's house by now.

She had not been happy with his decision, but he could live with that as long as she was safe.

He'd never loved anyone the way he did her—

Light moved through the trees from the bridle path and caught his attention. They were on foot. Beck lay flat against the earth. The marchioness held a lantern. She was early, and she had not come alone. Several other people were with her.

Interesting.

One was a man—the marquess, he decided. Another man must be a guard. No, it was the butler. He carried a lantern and a musket. Beck smiled. That was an odd weapon of choice.

The marchioness wore a hooded cloak. Her arm was around another woman in the same sort of hooded garment. The second woman was taller—*Gwendolyn*.

Beck knew without seeing her face. They had Gwendolyn. Had she defied him and turned back to be captured?

It didn't matter. She was in danger now.

He watched as the group entered the cottage.

The lamp lit the main room. The marquess shoved Gwendolyn into one of the chairs. She sat awkwardly as if her hands were bound. Lady Middlebury took the chair next to her. The marquess prowled around the room. They all appeared to watch the front door. The hood over Gwendolyn's head fell back. A scarf was tied around her mouth as a gag. She appeared pale, but determined. He had to grin. He knew what she was thinking—that he should have kept her with him. Lady Middlebury tied her to the chair.

The butler stood on the front step. He did not appear comfortable holding the gun.

Beck wondered if they had servants hidden in the woods around the cottage as well, so he waited.

Five minutes after the Middlebury party had arrived, he heard the soft "oompf" and knew Wagner had taken his man.

He wasn't the only one who heard the sound. The butler came off the step and started walking the perimeter of the cottage. He'd left the lantern behind, the better to hold the musket. He didn't call out to anyone, because he expected someone to be there.

As the minutes passed, the butler became more confident. After all, he had a musket. He widened the circle he followed, moving a bit past the light. He moved ever closer to where Beck had secreted himself.

When he was close enough and looking in another direction, Beck rose behind him. He tapped the servant on the shoulder. The butler turned, and one hard strike against the side of the man's head cause him to drop like a stone. Beck half carried the unconscious servant down the bank, made a quick gag with a piece of the man's own neckcloth, and bound his hands with the rest. Beck left the musket on the ground in the trees where the butler had dropped it.

Two were down. If there were others, Beck would leave them to Wagner. He was lucky the Middleburys had not spotted his movements out the cottage windows.

Since they were all waiting for him, he decided not to disappoint them.

Beck edged along the bank so that he could emerge from the forest in a different place. He paused a moment before coming into view. Gwendolyn's life might depend on his getting this right.

He marched out of the woods, whistling as if he didn't have a care in the world. He wanted them to know he was coming. He wanted them to believe they had the best of him.

As long as they held Gwendolyn, they did.

He was certain the marquess was armed. However, nothing was going to stop him from saving Gwendolyn. They should never have involved her in this.

Beck went up the step. He did not wait for an invitation to enter. He opened the door and stepped inside.

Lady Middlebury came to her feet. Gwendolyn, tied to her chair, was between them. She looked up at him as if pleased he was here.

"We shall be out of this shortly," he assured her.

"Unfortunately you will not be," the marquess said in his wavery voice. Beck caught the silver gleam of a dueling pistol in his hand. The gun was cocked. His finger was on the trigger. The weapon shook slightly.

"This is it, then?" Beck said, holding his arms out to show he had no tricks to play.

"Yes, it is," the marquess answered.

Lady Middlebury's expression appeared strained in the lamplight, her brow furrowed. "Walter—"

"*Quiet*," her husband barked. He didn't sound befuddled at all.

"How did you know who I was?" Beck said, assuming that his disguise as Curran was no longer useful.

"Lady Orpington should be kinder to her companion," the marquess said.

Beck released a sound of frustration. "Mrs. Newsome. I liked her," he admitted readily. "I believed her loyal to her mistress."

"You were wrong," Lady Middlebury said. "Sooner or later, everyone tires of Ellen Orpington. And that dog of hers. I received a message from her a few days ago not to trust Ellen. Or Mr. Curran. I will say I was hurt. Ellen would betray me over cards—" Her voice broke off.

"And what did Mrs. Newsome receive from your generosity?" Beck had to ask.

Lord Middlebury spoke up. "A cottage of her own at Colemore and the promise that she'll never have to see her cousin's damned dog ever again."

"Well, that makes sense," Beck conceded.

"I'm glad you approve."

"So, now," Beck pushed, "you are going to do your own handiwork. It never was just Lady Middlebury, was it?"

"My wife?" The marquess looked to the marchioness, who appeared miserable and anxious. "She knew nothing of my plans. Of course, if Winstead had killed you years ago as I had instructed, we wouldn't be in this fuss."

"But he didn't," Lady Middlebury told her husband, speaking as if this was a long-standing argument between them. "And then, when I learned the child was alive—to murder an innocent is not right."

"You were never ruthless, dear," he answered.

"Apparently neither was Winstead," she responded.

"True. However, you were as happy as I that Catalina was dead. Don't deny it, Franny."

"But I didn't plot to *kill* her," Lady Middlebury lashed back.

"What started it?" Beck wanted to know.

"*Her,*" Lady Middlebury said. "She started it. She was unreasonable. She made me angry." Her voice grew louder with each accusation. "She threatened to cut us off. She didn't want us at Colemore, even though we had a right to live here. More so than she did. We had been here longer."

"Why did she wish you to leave?"

"She believed herself superior to us. And all because I had run up some expenses—"

"Gambling debts," her husband corrected her.

The marchioness glared at him. Her jaw hardened.

"Whist," the marquess said to Beck as if that explained everything. "Her downfall. Always her downfall."

His wife straightened her shoulders and admitted, "Very well, I had run up rather serious debts. I understood"—she paused to shoot her husband a look—"that it was not wise of me. However, they were debts of honor. They had to be paid. Your mother refused."

His mother. Lady Middlebury had used the words.

Beck was Robert Chaytor.

Not that he needed her confirmation. And he doubted they would stand in a court and admit their wrongdoing.

"Catalina laughed at me when I told her I was desperate," Lady Middlebury said tightly, but then her manner changed. The anger left her. She seemed to collapse a bit. "I didn't expect my husband to do what he did."

Beck tilted his head toward the marquess. "You sent Winstead."

"I did. I had it all plotted out, too. I decided that both you and Catalina needed to go."

"But Winstead couldn't kill you," Lady Middlebury said. She smiled at Beck. "You adored him when you were little. You used to trail after him, asking questions and behaving as if he was a hero because he was strong. You were a lively lad. A favorite of all of us. Well, except my husband. Then one day, after we all thought you dead, Winstead, out of guilt, confided in me what he'd done."

"Which was?" Beck prodded.

"The murder," she answered. "He told me he couldn't kill you. So he'd handed you over to his sister. She was a ne'er-do-well but on her way to London. He'd told her he didn't care what happened as long as you didn't return to Colemore. Back then, he'd told Middlebury you died."

"I was disappointed to hear you were alive," the marquess confirmed.

"More than disappointed," his wife murmured. "You were furious. But I insisted it was a good thing you were alive. One doesn't want that on one's conscience."

"I would have managed," her husband assured her.

"Is that why you visit this place," she countered, "and why you come here at night to listen to Catalina sing?"

"It is nothing—"

"It is your conscience. Ever since you had her murdered, you haven't known peace. Neither of us has."

Beck spoke up, addressing Lady Middlebury. "Was it you who took me from the brothel and sent me to school?" He had moved several small, unnoticeable steps toward the marquess. He needed to be closer. Gwendolyn watched. He knew she waited for some signal from him.

Dear God, he loved her.

The marchioness nodded. "It was the least I could do," she said, without humor. "Our family has royal blood in our veins. It seemed a sin to leave you in such a horrid place. I wanted to give you a chance to have a good life."

"But then something changed," Beck surmised. "Who sent Winstead last year?"

"I did," Lord Middlebury volunteered. "I finally learned that you were alive. It was a complete shock to me that my wife and most trusted servant would dare to disobey my command." He sent a pointed look at his wife. "I thought you were dead, Steele, until Winstead's sister reported to him that a man was going around brothels and asking questions about a boy who'd been taken away years ago. She's still a whore. She likes the life. She heard you were looking for your mother and she isn't a stupid woman. She feared what would happen if anyone learned the truth . . . unlike my wife—"

"Walter, I've apologized."

"You have, dear . . . and I have forgiven you— for *years* of deception. But now we have to do all of this"—he waved the pistol in the air to encompass the room, Beck, and Gwendolyn—"because my wishes were not carried out when he was small enough to be easily dispatched."

"You sent Winstead after me to clean up the mess," Beck said.

The corners of the marquess's mouth tightened. "Yes," he answered curtly.

"And being a recluse . . . ?" Beck wondered. "Is that a ruse, too?"

"I don't like London. Or people, for that matter. I do have research. This estate means more to me than my country." Lord Middlebury's hand holding the pistol was shaking harder now. He had to brace it with his other hand. He was not a well man. That part, at least, was true.

"Colemore even means more to you than your family," Beck suggested, hoping to goad the man into more revelations.

The marquess grinned agreement. "It *is* my birthright. Franny is the one who worried because you are related to us. *I* didn't have any pangs of conscience. However, she is not being completely honest. She was happy to know our sons would inherit. But what I find of interest is that, if Catalina had agreed to pay my wife's gambling debts, you and I would not be having this conversation. If Franny had let me kill you the way I wished, we'd not be having this conversation either. Fortunately, she will not stop me now. However, I want you to know, I enjoyed our few moments together the other night. You have some habits that remind me of my brother. Rather liked my brother. And now, I have one question for you. What happened to Winstead?" His voice hitched on the name. "He never returned. I assumed he had done the job and then had been forced to flee . . . however, here you are. Is he dead?"

The question surprised Beck. He thought the answer obvious. "Yes. He's dead." He even took satisfaction in saying those words.

An unholy light came to the marquess's eyes. "Do you think I haven't noticed you creeping closer while we talked?" He lifted the pistol higher—

At the same moment, Gwendolyn threw her body weight in the chair toward the marquess. Both she and the chair fell at his feet, almost knocking the frail man over.

His pistol fired harmlessly into the air.

Beck was on him immediately. The man was not in good health, but he fought back, his thin arms and legs actually quite strong. The heel of his hand hit Beck's chin. Beck rolled him over, placing a knee on his back. The marquess's flailing fist struck the lamp. It fell onto its side. Hot wax hit the floor and spread, a line of flames feeding off it.

The flame caught Gwendolyn's hair. Beck released the marquess as he reached over and slapped the fire out with his bare hands.

That didn't stop other flames from continuing

to spread. The marquess started shouting for his butler, "*Nathaniel.* Come, Nathaniel." He clambered to his feet. "*Shoot them.*"

Lady Middlebury had already run out the door.

Beck scooped up Gwendolyn, chair and all. He ran for the door. They met Wagner, who had come out of hiding and was already half up the steps. He helped Beck carry Gwendolyn to the lawn as a coughing Lord Middlebury stumbled out of the cottage.

The fire was climbing the inside walls. Soon the place would be engulfed.

"Jem, your knife," Beck said. He took it and cut Gwendolyn free of her bonds. She threw her arms around him, and he held her just as tight.

"You did need me," she said.

He did. *Always.*

The marchioness had fallen to her knees not far from them. She was openly sobbing.

Meanwhile, Lord Middlebury erupted in a red-faced rage. He didn't have a pistol, but he pointed his finger at Beck. "You will not escape me this time, Steele. I own Colemore. I'll have you flogged—"

He went rigid as if struck by pain. He grabbed his chest. His eyes widened. He whirled toward his wife and reached out.

"My lord?" she cried and started to scramble to her feet just as he crumpled to the ground.

Lady Middlebury crawled over to her husband's still form. Beck rose and walked over to join her, leaving Gwendolyn with Jem. The man's eyes were open in death, his mouth wide as if he was still shouting his ugly threats. Beck knelt and felt for a pulse. There was none.

He looked to the marchioness. "I'm sorry, he's no longer with us."

Her response was a keening wail. It mingled with the crackle and whooshing crash of the fire consuming the cottage. She tugged on his arm as if she could wake him up, as if she feared for him.

Gwendolyn came to her side. "My lady," she said softly. Lady Middlebury shook her off.

Shouts could be heard. People in the main house had seen the fire. They were now rushing to the cottage to help or gawk.

Beck looked to Wagner. "Get Gwendolyn out of here. I'll meet you at the stables."

"Wait, what of you?" Gwendolyn demanded.

"I will join you. But right now, you must leave."

Jem took her arm. "You do what the major says," he assured her.

She didn't go quickly. "Beckett—"

"Gwendolyn, I will come. But first, you need to be removed from this night. The gossip will overtake your family."

The shouts and voices were coming closer. In minutes, this area would be filled with people asking questions.

"Come, miss," Wagner said. "The major will manage this."

Gwendolyn shot Beck a last look, and then she turned and went with Jem.

Beck looked down at the man he had once believed to be his father. Almost reverently, he closed the man's lids. He put a hand under a sobbing Lady Middlebury's arm. "They will be here soon."

She didn't want to move.

"This is over between us," he said.

She stopped her wail and looked to him. "What do you mean?"

"We are done. I shall not tell anyone of what happened here."

"Or what we did . . . ?"

"I wanted the truth," Beck said. "I have the truth. It is not of importance to anyone else. Besides, would you support me if I tell it?"

"*No.*"

"Then it is your word against mine. And the world believes I am dead."

"You can accept that?"

He thought of Gwendolyn, who would be waiting for him. He thought of Ellisfield, who had been raised for this life. Colemore was not Beck's home. It never would be. But the time had come to find a place to call home. He knew that would be with Gwendolyn. "I accept it."

"What do we say then?" she asked. She didn't seem to think it strange that she would expect him to make up the story.

"You and your lord wished to go for a walk. Will the butler support your story? He and another fellow are tied up waiting for me to release them."

"They both will."

"Then there you have it. You saw the fire. Middlebury collapsed."

Another gasp of grief escaped her. "He was a good man."

Beck didn't agree, but he was done with it all.

Ellisfield and his trio of companions burst from the woods. They were followed by servants with buckets. Ellisfield saw his mother standing next to Beck . . . and his father on the ground.

His step slowed. He approached them. "What happened?" he demanded.

Beck helped Lady Middlebury stand. She wobbled a moment but regained mastery over her emotions. "He had a fit," she said, nodding to her husband on the ground. "We came down here to look at the cottage."

"At night?"

"It was a lovely night," she murmured. "You know how your father enjoyed exploring the grounds."

Ellisfield knelt beside his father. He placed a hand on his father's chest. He was silent a moment but then came to his feet, his expression troubled. "And you, Curran? We heard you and Miss Lanscarr had eloped."

There were close to sixty guests at the house party. Who would know what other guests were doing at any given moment? "Obviously not," he said to Ellisfield. "I have no idea where Miss Lanscarr is. Up at the house, I suppose."

"And you were here because?"

Beck smiled to himself. His cousin was no fool. Someday he might learn the truth, but not this night. "I was riding back from the village."

Ellisfield's brother joined them. The sons turned their attention to their father. Their mother joined them, and there was weeping. Beck watched a moment, and then he walked away.

True to his word, he freed the butler and the other servant. He warned them to keep their mouths shut about the goings on this night. They were not fools.

Then, Beck made his way to the main house. For a moment, he stood in the grand entry hall, drinking in the feel of the place.

This could never have been a haven for him. It had also not been one for his mother. She would not have built the cottage if it were.

He took the stairs two at a time. Lady Orpington met him at the third floor, where the library was located. She held Magpie in her arms. Mrs. Newsome stood close behind her.

In a whisper of indignation, Lady Orpington said, "Mr. Steele, what do you have to say for yourself? Where is my coach? And what have you done with the woman who was supposed to be my whist partner?"

"I don't know where your coach is, but Mrs. Newsome may have an idea."

The companion had the good sense to shrink back at the knowledge that he knew of her duplicity. Magpie gave a growl.

"As for your whist partner," he continued, "I am returning her to London for her own safety."

"Safety? What is going on?" Lady Orpington demanded, the ribbons on her lace cap bouncing with her curiosity. "They say there is a fire. They all ran to see it."

She wasn't a bad sort. She had served a purpose. He took her hand in his. "It's just a cottage on the property. And thank you for your help, Lady Orpington."

Her brows lifted. "Did you solve the mystery? Did you find answers?"

"Yes, and I am at peace."

She gave him a motherly smile, then abruptly turned, shifting her dog in her arms. "Well, Vera, what is he talking about? What do you know about my missing coach?"

Beck didn't wait to listen. There was no porter at his post on the landing. Beck imagined every available male servant was needed at the cottage. Soon everyone would know that the marquess had died. Collapsed, they would repeat. Probably overcome by smoke from the fire . . . or whatever gossip would be concocted. They might even make him sound heroic. But that would be their tale, not his.

Beck wanted nothing from the Chaytors save for two things.

He walked into the library. The room was dark. He looked out the window, but he couldn't see the fire.

He was not a sentimental man. He prided himself on being practical. So he took what truly belonged to him. He lifted the portrait of his mother from its place on the wall. Then he went downstairs to the larger library and removed the portrait of his family. He tucked the two paintings under his arm, and he left Colemore, never to return again.

By the time he reached the stables, Jem had

the horses ready. Gwendolyn was still wearing the hooded cape Lord and Lady Middlebury had used to disguise her.

She noticed the portraits and smiled. "To London?" she asked.

"Most definitely," he replied.

CHAPTER TWENTY

Beckett, Gwendolyn, and Mr. Wagner rode through the night.

On the ride, Mr. Wagner proved to be a colorful character who kept them all awake by telling stories of his and Beckett's adventures on the Peninsula.

"No better officer to be found," he informed Gwendolyn. He leaned toward her to confide, "Major doesn't like hearing me say that, but we lads all loved him. He never asked anything of us that he wouldn't do himself. Stood beside us, he did. Even Wellington respected him. Saved the battle for us at Nive."

"And earned a bullet to my head," Beckett replied dryly. He had tried to stop Mr. Wagner's stories several times. The compliments seemed to embarrass him. He was not one to shout his own praise, another quality about him that Gwendolyn admired. She was much the same.

"Aye, a shot that started the dreams," Mr. Wagner noted soberly. "Did you find your answers, sir? Is it an end to the dreams?"

"Did you overhear anything that was said this past night?" Beckett countered.

"Nothing I would repeat, sir."

Beckett smiled. "You are a good and loyal friend, Jem. Thank you for your help."

"'Tis my honor, sir."

They parted company with Mr. Wagner around Charlton.

After that, they silently made their way to Dara and Michael's home. Mr. Wagner's conversation had been entertaining, but she and Beckett didn't need words to fill the silence. His presence alone was enough for her, and he seemed to feel the same. They rode in perfect accord.

They arrived at Dara and Michael's home in time for breakfast. To Gwendolyn's surprise, her whole family—Dara, Michael, and Tweedie, along with Elise and her duke, Winderton, who had apparently recently returned from Ireland—were gathered around the table. She knew she looked a mess. She still wore the gown from two days earlier. After being trussed up several times and kidnapped, there had been no time to change. She held Beckett's hand and greeted her sisters, daring them to say something.

They all rose to their feet. There was a long, stunned pause, and then Dara asked, "He liked the new riding habit, did he?"

Gwendolyn thought that so funny, she almost choked on her laughter. Beckett joined her, and then her sisters and Tweedie, and finally a confused Michael and Winderton, were all practically rolling on the floor with good humor.

"It is a long story," Gwendolyn told her family. And then she turned to Beckett, and without preamble said, "We are going to marry." She didn't ask permission or offer any of the niceties.

If she thought this would shock her family, she had been wrong.

"Of course you are," Dara said. "Mr. Steele is the only one for you." She turned to him. Opening her hands in welcome, she said, "It will be nice to know where you are from now on, Mr. Steele. Or are you going to expect my sister to live above that tavern by the docks with you?"

"Please call me Beckett," he answered, before tucking a wild curl of Gwendolyn's wind-tousled hair behind her ear. "And no, I have a home in mind that I believe will please us both. There will be no tavern involved."

"Good," Dara said. "Please, sit and join us."

"Should I be asking brotherly questions right now?" Michael queried.

Winderton nodded. "I wondered the same thing. However, I know my wife."

"As I know mine," Michael agreed. "Steele, prepare for the questions. Winderton and I will enjoy watching."

Elise waved them off, dismissing them as "The two of you," before turning her attention to Beckett, who was now seated by Gwendolyn at the table. Herald offered them both plates with fresh bread, butter, and a bit of sirloin. It smelled delicious because they were both famished. "I have only one question," Elise continued. "Do you care for her?"

"I love her," Beckett replied without hesitation.

Gwendolyn smiled up at him, her love bringing tears to her eyes.

Elise turned to their sister. "I think, Dara, they managed that kiss we prevented in Dublin."

"Oh, by the looks of them, they managed more than a kiss," Tweedie assured them, and everyone laughed, especially when Gwendolyn confirmed their suspicions by blushing. Even Beckett had a bit of red in his cheeks.

"See what I tolerate?" she told Beckett.

"A family," he acknowledged, and then he smiled. "It is not a bad bargain."

News began arriving from Colemore. The most important piece of information was that the Marquess of Middlebury had died. They said he'd collapsed, just as his brother had years ago.

Gwendolyn saw the notice in the paper about his death. Ellisfield would soon be even more eligible than before. Beckett had liked him. She had thought him a decent man and hoped he was truly not like his parents.

There were other rumors. Three days after Gwendolyn's return, Dara came home from a meeting of the ladies' church guild to report, "It is said you eloped to Scotland, Gwendolyn."

"That can't be true. I'm right here." She stood on a stool while Elise, the best hemmer in the family, sewed a flounced hem to the pale yellow muslin gown Gwendolyn would wear for her wedding. Beckett had acquired a special license, and they would be sharing their vows on the coming Tuesday.

"Which was exactly what I told them," Dara replied. "I know how rumors start. And I know how to put an end to them."

"With the truth?" Gwendolyn suggested, and Dara smiled her agreement.

"Although," Elise said, taking the straight pins from her mouth, "the idea of a Lanscarr doing something so scandalous might delight some people."

"Not if they knew who she was truly marrying," Dara responded.

For a moment, Gwendolyn's heart gave a start. Could Dara have learned about Beckett being the true marquess?

Then Dara declared gleefully, "The mysterious Mr. Steele." She sounded delighted that such a dubious figure would soon be in the family.

"Then you approve of him?" Gwendolyn asked.

Dara's expression softened. "I can be overly protective," she admitted. "I just want what is best for you. However, he has come up to scratch, and the more I know of him, the more I'm convinced he will make a very fine husband."

That evening at dinner, Michael mentioned that Beckett had asked him to stand with him for the vows.

"He also asked Winderton," Elise said.

Gwendolyn looked to the duke, who had just put a spoonful of soup in his mouth. He shrugged and nodded.

"Who will stand with you?" Dara said, giving Gwendolyn a pointed look and holding out her hands to say she was willing.

"I imagine that you and Elise should?" Gwendolyn hadn't thought of any of the details yet other than the dress. She was marrying Mr. Steele. What more mattered?

"We'd be delighted," Elise said.

"I might have to mull over the matter," Dara replied teasingly.

"Then I shall stand in your place," Tweedie assured them.

"You will not. It's mine," Dara declared. "Speaking of Beckett, why couldn't he join us this evening?"

"He said he has a surprise he is preparing for me," Gwendolyn answered.

"Have you discussed where you shall live?" Tweedie wondered.

"They can stay with us," Dara answered.

"Or us," Elise chimed in. "Winderton and I barely use a third of the London house."

"I think living quarters are the surprise he is planning," Gwendolyn answered.

"And you don't wish an opinion on such a large decision?" Dara asked.

Gwendolyn smiled. "No. I would happily live in a hovel with him."

"Hopefully you won't have to do that," Elise said, making a face. "I mean, he can afford a wife, can't he?" She looked around the table for confirmation.

"As a matter of fact," Michael said, "I asked him that same question today."

"And what did he say?" Winderton asked.

"You will all be happy to know Gwendolyn will not be living on love alone. Beckett Steele is a wealthy man."

This was news to Gwendolyn. "How?" she asked.

Dara made a frustrated sound. "I'm glad you have family to look after you or you *would* be living in a hovel."

Gwendolyn gave her a laughing shush. "Did *you* question Michael's circumstances?"

Her sister's expression softened as she looked at her husband. "Oh, no, he was my one and only."

"As you are mine," Elise said, reaching for her duke's hand.

"I knew that," he answered her. "I couldn't have looked more poor than when we met."

"And yet here we are now," Elise whispered happily.

There was a moment where everyone seemed lost in their happiness until Tweedie piped up. "Yes, yes, this is all well and good. You girls are in love. However, I want to know how Beckett built a fortune. He was in the military, but does one grow rich there?"

"He said he didn't spend money," Michael answered. "He was an officer, he was frugal, and he made investments. He gave me the name of his banker. Fielding is well-known and highly reputable. You shall have a nice life, Gwennie," he finished, using a pet name her sisters used on occasion. Gwendolyn liked to hear him say it.

She had much love for both of her brothers-in-marriage.

So IT WAS that on the twenty-third day of September 1817, Gwendolyn married the only man she could ever love.

Beckett arrived at the church in an elegantly cut black double-breasted tailcoat over a white brocade vest and cashmere pantaloons. He appeared every inch a marquess, even if he didn't wish to be.

The ceremony was simple, the vows heartfelt.

Afterward, they enjoyed a wedding breakfast at the Duke of Winderton's London home. The event was prestigious enough that a small crowd had gathered outside to admire the guests and would certainly show up as a morsel of gossip beyond the announcement in the papers. That should lay to rest any nonsense about an elopement.

When the breakfast was finished, Beckett informed Gwendolyn he had a surprise. She knew something was up. He had been evasive when she'd asked about where they would spend their wedding night. She also sensed that her sisters were a party to his secrets. She'd caught some whisperings . . .

Beckett led her to the front hall. He opened the door. Two carriages drawn by teams of matching grays waited at the front step.

"Where are we going?" Gwendolyn asked.

"To see my wedding present to you."

"Beckett, I didn't expect—"

He hushed her with a kiss. "Are you curious as to where we will live?"

"Yes, but—"

"Then let's find out, Mrs. Steele."

Mrs. Steele. No title could be finer. And he had a gleam in his eye as if he was certain he was going to surprise her. She sat back against the seat.

Her curiosity grew when they began driving to the docks along the Thames. She thought of Dara's fear that he would expect her to live above the tavern where he'd had his quarters. She glanced back at her sisters in the following carriage and saw by Dara's expression she was thinking the same thing. The wind had picked up a bit. She held her bonnet to keep it from misbehaving on her head.

The carriage pulled to a stop by the wharf, and a line of ships docked there.

She and Beckett and her family climbed out of the vehicles. Men shouted as they rolled barrels and heaved crates, loading the ships. Gulls circled in the air over their heads. The air smelled of salt and a hint of the exotic.

One of the ships was sleeker and newer than the others. Beckett took her hand and led her to it. The masthead was of a dark-haired siren with a gold coin in her mouth.

"What do you think?" Beckett asked.

"It is a fine ship," she said, slightly confused.

And then Dara called out, "Look at the name." She was pointing at the stern of the ship.

Gwendolyn went over, conscious that the ship's company were now lining up along the gunwales. She looked at the gold lettering over the captain's quarters.

The Gambler's Daughter

"You own this ship?" she said, turning to Beckett.

"*We* own this ship," he answered, his smile letting her know he was inordinately pleased with himself. He had been busy the past couple of days. "It even has a small library."

"And we will live on it?" She couldn't keep the excitement from her voice.

"If you wish." He watched her closely, she realized. He wasn't certain if she would like his plan.

"I *do* wish, Mr. Steele. This will be a wonderful adventure."

His grin broadened, and his shoulders relaxed.

"When do we sail? Where shall we go first?" she wondered.

He had an answer for that as well. "I thought perhaps Spain. I've a desire to see if my mother has relatives there. I'd like to meet them."

"That is a good idea."

"And then Barbados?" he suggested.

"*Yes*," she said. "I'll see if my memories hold true. And after that?"

"After that, we travel wherever your heart desires."

Gwendolyn threw her arms around him. "You understand everything about me."

"Because I wish you to be happy. I always want *us* to be happy."

She turned to her sisters. "You knew." They

didn't deny it. "Did you know when you were going on about where I would live over dinner the other night?" she asked Dara.

"Yes," Dara said.

"He asked our permission first," Elise added. "We don't wish to see you go."

"But after all those books you've read about faraway places," Dara said, "we knew you would adore this idea."

"And we expect letters," Elise instructed. "Many, many letters."

"I will send them." Tears of gratitude filled Gwendolyn's eyes. "I love you all so very much."

The next hour was spent with her family going over the ship. There wasn't a nook they didn't explore or a crew member, including Captain MacDonald, they didn't badger with questions. Even Michael and Winderton were engaged in the venture. Winderton actually climbed the rigging in his formal dress. They met the cook, a man by the name of Block who assured them he cooked well enough for the king's table.

Everyone was impressed with the quarters Gwendolyn and Beckett would share. It was a small apartment at the stern of the ship with mullioned windows overlooking the water. She was certain it was usually the captain's quarters, but Captain MacDonald assured her he was quite satisfied with his cabin elsewhere on the ship.

And Gwendolyn was touched by another gift from Beckett—the three volumes of Maria Edgeworth's *Belinda* stored on a shelf for when she could read them.

At last, Winderton asked, "When will you sail out?" He looked to Beckett.

"Now, if Gwendolyn is ready."

"I need to pack—" Gwendolyn started, but Dara cut her off.

"You are packed," Dara said. "I had Molly do it during the ceremony and bring everything over. Your clothing is stored in the cupboard of your cabin. I checked while we were touring the ship."

Gwendolyn looked to her sisters, to Tweedie. They understood her. They might have always known she longed for a life different than theirs. And, now, they were giving her their blessing.

She gave them hard hugs, afraid to speak lest she be overcome by tears.

It was Elise who said, "Go, Gwendolyn. We'll always be here. We know you won't forget us."

The sisters gathered in a tight circle, their arms around each other, and Gwendolyn remembered they had done just this sort of thing when Gram had died and life had seemed so fraught with peril.

She loved her family. She loved her husband.

And she wouldn't trade any of them for all the titles and all the money in the kingdom.

Soon she and Beckett waved goodbye as her family walked down the gangway back to the waiting coaches. She waved until they were out of sight.

Beckett took her to their quarters. Hanging in this cozy room were the portraits of Beckett's mother and his family. "Have you dreamed of her since we left Colemore?" she asked.

"Actually, I haven't had the dream since I met

you. It is almost as if she set me on the journey to find you." He drew her to him. "We leave at high tide, but that is hours from now." She nodded up at him, liking the way his hand at her hip pulled her tighter to him. "Cook has a special meal planned, but that won't be ready until evening."

"It seems, Mr. Steele," she said, going up on tiptoe to place her arms around his neck, "we will have to do something to while away the time."

His response was to sweep her up in his arms and carry her to the bed. "That we will, Mrs. Steele. That we will."

More from
CATHY MAXWELL

The Gambler's
—Daughters—

The Logical Man's Guide
— to Dangerous Women —

—— The Spinster Heiresses ——

—————— Marrying the Duke ——————

—The Brides of Wishmore—

—— The Chattan Curse ——

—— The Scandals and Seductions Novels ——

The Cameron Sisters

The Marriage Novels